Born in Hertfordshire, Danielle Shaw initially studied fashion and design and worked at the Royal Opera House before moving to Geneva to work in a nursery school. Returning to England, she achieved her long-held ambition to become a full-time author. Her other titles include *Cinnabar Summer* and *Sunflower Morning*. She now lives in Northampton-shire with her Swedish husband.

A FABRIC OF DREAMS

Working in the costume department at the Alexandra Theatre, the lives of Anna, Madge, Beattie, Gavin and Fudge are woven and fashioned together like a richly embroidered tapestry. Unfortunately, however, while their friendship and support for each other remains intact, their fabric of dreams is torn to shreds when they learn the theatre is to close. As a result their lives, loves and aspirations are thrown to the wind like gossamer threads, leaving them to go their separate ways . . .

Books by Danielle Shaw
Published by The House of Ulverscroft:

MARRIED TO SINCLAIR
CRAVEN'S BRIDE
CINNABAR SUMMER
SUNFLOWER MORNING

DANIELLE SHAW

A FABRIC
OF DREAMS

Complete and Unabridged

ULVERSCROFT
Leicester

First published in Great Britain in 2008 by
Robert Hale Limited
London

First Large Print Edition
published 2009
by arrangement with
Robert Hale Limited
London

British Library CIP Data

Shaw, Danielle
  A fabric of dreams.—Large print ed.—
  Ulverscroft large print series: general fiction
  1. Theaters—Employees—Fiction
  2. Large type books
  I. Title
  823.9'14 [F]

  ISBN 978–1–84782–520–9

Published by
F. A. Thorpe (Publishing)
Anstey, Leicestershire

Set by Words & Graphics Ltd.
Anstey, Leicestershire
Printed and bound in Great Britain by
T. J. International Ltd., Padstow, Cornwall

This book is printed on acid-free paper

In remembrance of
Göran Gustav Olof Lindberg.
Deeply missed,
but many happy memories remain.

1

SILK —

London, early 1970s

'*Overture and beginners please.*'

The concentrated silence in the cramped and dismal workroom was shattered by the abrupt, crackling summons. Three anxious faces turned in Anna Mason's direction where, conscious of her audience, she held the last ruby gemstone in place. Securing it with a flourish of scarlet thread, the needle darting in and out like a snake's tongue, Anna wound the remaining thread around her finger and pulled sharply. Severing contact with needle and fabric, she shook out the costume, held it at arm's length and announced, 'That's it! All finished. Gian-Carlo here we come.'

'I only hope he's satisfied this time,' Beattie Norman muttered from her chair in the far corner of the workroom, 'All this constant messing about and changing his mind.'

Beattie's fingers twitched as she drummed them against the table. Working through both her coffee and lunch break, she was practically gasping for a cigarette.

'I'm sure they'll be fine,' Anna replied, checking the array of brightly coloured costumes suspended on the rail.

'Here, let me help you into the lift and over to rehearsal with those,' a voice called from Beattie's side. Leaping to his feet, Gavin Turner gave a hefty shove and manoeuvred the cumbersome rail through the narrow doorway. He knew from experience the rails always became stuck there. Years of constant traffic meant the workroom floor had sunk steadily lower than the corridor outside, causing the crumbling linoleum to form a jagged, shark's-tooth edge. It was almost as if the dingy workroom, that had spawned such beautiful creations, was reluctant to let them go.

Anna fixed him with a grateful smile. 'Thanks, Gavin, but I thought I'd take Fudge with me today. It will be her first chance to see a full dress-rehearsal. Besides, you were on duty at last night's performance and must be exhausted. Why not stay here and relax instead? You can also make sure Beattie doesn't set fire to these salubrious surroundings.'

The gentle irony in Anna's voice inferred that the moment she and Fudge left the room, Beattie would fling open the window, place a lighted cigarette between her bright scarlet lips and try in vain to fan away the evidence. Even now her matching scarlet talons were already scratching for the comforting feel of a familiar gold packet.

Following Anna to the lift, Fudge struggled with the ancient wrought-iron gates until both the rail and its precious cargo were securely wedged inside. Her eyes shone in anticipation, thoughts of the ghostly lift shaft forced to the back of her mind. As the lift jerked and shuddered into action, she clung to the rail and began nervously, 'Anna . . . I feel so embarrassed that you had to finish my costume. Goodness knows what Mr Player thought — seeing you sewing and me doing nothing at all.'

Fudge coloured at the memory. Julian Player (head of the costume department at the Alexandra Theatre), simply terrified her. Usually when Julian came into the room, Fudge busied herself with her handwork or else moved to one of the two sewing-machines, where she felt infinitely safer. Even there, she still felt his dark, penetrating gaze, boring into her from behind thick, horn-rimmed spectacles.

'You mustn't worry about Julian,' Anna reassured, 'he's really quite harmless. The person we have to worry about is Gian-Carlo Andretti. Something's already telling me we're in for an *Andretti Afternoon.*'

Exiting from the still groaning lift, Anna braced herself and pushed the unwieldy dress rail to where hordes of people scurried back and forth. Bustling along the narrow, winding corridors of the theatre, they reminded her of some half-crazed mice she'd seen on a TV documentary. All part of a so-called behavioural experiment, the presenter had said at the time. She shuddered, recalling Gian-Carlo's behaviour of recent weeks. How was it that he always managed to upset the entire company?

As usual, Andretti's entourage — dressed in camel coats regardless of the weather — sallied forth from every direction of the stage. Clipboards in hand, and full of self-importance, they issued instructions in broken English to all and sundry. The result was not that of the required order and co-operation but one of complete and utter chaos.

'Dresser!' A voice shrieked from an open doorway and a matronly figure, wearing a fearsome wig and make-up, emerged demanding her shoes. Fudge froze in her tracks before moving even closer to Anna's side.

'Fudge dear, run and look in the other

dressing-rooms for Madame Alicia's shoes.'

'H-how will I know what they look like?' In a state of panic, Fudge stared about her. She'd wanted desperately to see life backstage and couldn't believe her ears when Anna had refused Gavin's offer of help. Now she wasn't so sure, even to the extent of wishing she was back in the dingy workroom with its frosted glass windows, peeling paintwork and shabby, brown linoleum floor.

Spying Madame Alicia silhouetted in the light from her dressing-room, rendering her appearance even more horrifying, Anna whispered, 'It shouldn't be too difficult. She's got the most enormous feet. None of the *corps de ballet* have feet that size.'

With a nervous smile, Fudge set off on her search. Three doors down she found the missing scarlet and black footwear and, resisting the urge to try it on, hurried back to Madame who received her shoes graciously. Anna meanwhile, deep in conversation with Madge, the wardrobe mistress, noted the surge of relief on Fudge's face.

'Found them? Good. Now, if you to want to watch rehearsals for a bit, just tuck yourself at the back of the theatre. Don't stay too long because it's pay day, remember, and they'll soon be bringing round the wages. And Fudge . . . when you do return to the

5

workroom, please thank Beattie and Gavin for all their hard work. Tell them to have a nice weekend and I'll see you all on Monday.'

'Seems like a nice kid,' Madge said. 'What did you call her?'

'Fudge. It's a nickname by all accounts. Something to do with her mother making it — or else the vast quantity she ate as a child.'

'How weird. Doesn't she mind being called that?'

'Apparently not, and as she loathes her Christian name, she's told everyone to call her Fudge. Joining us straight from college, something tells me she'd far rather be wearing our costumes than sitting in my workroom making them.'

Nodding in understanding, Madge was about to comment on Fudge's ungainly size when movement in the stalls caught every-one's attention. Julian Player was leading Gian-Carlo Andretti to his seat. 'Anyone would think he was bloody royalty,' she hissed.

'Maybe that's because only royalty can afford to watch his productions,' Anna murmured in reply.

When Madge made as if to continue, Anna put a finger to her lips, nodded in Julian's direction and found her own seat in the stalls. Following on behind, Madge emitted a low, drawn-out sigh and sat down beside her. She was desperate to talk to Anna, but now was not the time, she concluded sadly. It would simply have to wait.

Sometime later, running upstairs to the workroom now heavy with the smell of Youth Dew perfume and cigarettes, Fudge narrowly missed colliding with a familiar figure exiting from the ladies' cloakroom.

'Blimey! You nearly knocked me flying,' Beattie said, teetering on her mock crocodile stilletos. 'Why on earth didn't you use the lift?'

'I'm — er — trying to lose weight,' Fudge lied, not wanting to admit her fear of lifts. 'Don't they say climbing stairs is a good form of exercise?'

'Hmph! You'll never find Beattie Norman using stairs, not while there's a lift about. Climbing stairs plays havoc with my chest,' and, as if on cue, a dreadful coughing spasm burst forth from Beattie's throat. Fudge stared in wide-eyed disbelief. How could anyone as thin as this, produce such a booming noise?

'She's like a stick insect on stilts,' she'd told her parents following her first day at the theatre. 'A stick insect with red hair, red nails and scarlet lips.'

Fudge's parents had listened, spellbound,

to their daughter's description of her fellow workmates: gentle Anna, with her mane of sleek, dark hair and equally dark eyes, who was in charge of the theatre workroom; the strangely effeminate Gavin with his high-lighted hair worn in a pony-tail and last but not least, the ever colourful Beattie.

'So ... how's it going at rehearsals?' Beattie enquired, breaking into Fudge's chain of thought. 'We've already heard Andretti on the Tannoy, screaming at everyone and getting his knickers in a twist. He's worse than my old mother-in-law.'

Fudge was too polite to ask which mother-in-law. In her very first week at the Alexandra, she'd been horrified to learn that Beattie had been married three times. The outrageous tales, pouring forth from scarlet lips, had caused her to blush on more than one occasion. Now gradually coming to terms with Beattie's unconventional lifestyle, Fudge listened again to a highly vivid description of mother-in-law number one.

Gavin, meanwhile, painstakingly disentan-gling pins from the brightly coloured threads and slithers of fabric on the workroom floor, looked up at their approach.

'How's the finger?' he asked, his gaze alighting on the pad of white lint and bandage on Fudge's index finger.

'Much better, thank you. At least I can move it again. Look.'

'Good. So that's your little initiation ceremony over with.'

'That's right,' Beattie joined in, giving her familiar throaty laugh. 'They say you're never fully qualified until you machine right through your finger.' Seeing Gavin shudder, she continued with a grin, 'Even I have to admit I didn't know who to deal with first. What with Fudge going as white as a sheet, and you turning such a horrible shade of green. Thank goodness I always carry a bottle of smelling salts in my handbag.'

Fudge suppressed a smile, reminded of Beattie delving into her enormous trademark handbag in search of the aforementioned smelling salts, initially offering them to herself, while Anna dressed the sore and wounded finger, and later to the whey-faced Gavin. it was this unfortunate, though not serious, accident which had left Fudge unable to finish the sixth and last ballet costume, thus necessitating that Anna step in and help.

With their wages duly distributed and signed for, Fudge, Gavin and Beattie prepared to leave the workroom for the weekend.

'I still feel awful about Anna having to finish that beading. Do you think she's angry with me?'

'Don't be silly, Fudge. It was an accident,' Gavin assured. 'Why would Anna be angry? She's one of the gentlest, calmest people I know.'

At that precise moment, Anna was anything but. Gian-Carlo Andretti had complained about everything: the lighting was wrong; the scenery not altered to his specifications; the prima ballerina's dress kept catching on her partner's costume (the result of too many jewels on his shoulder pads) and then there were the six exquisitely bejewelled princesses. In abject horror, Anna watched an intricate piece of scenery topple over at the very same moment that her six princesses arrived on stage!

'It's all wrong! The colour is all wrong!' screamed Andretti. 'Why does no one listen? It is all too yellow.'

Julian Player fidgeted nervously by Andretti's side. 'Too yellow?'

'*Sí*, too *giallo*. Didn't you hear me the first time?'

The sudden brief mix of Italian and English was enough to warn Julian there was an almighty storm brewing. Leaving his seat, Andretti beckoned to *the camel coats* to assist him on to the stage. There, he thrust the offending piece of scenery to one side, grabbed one of the princesses roughly by the arm and frogmarched her forwards.

'You see this? Three layers — *uno*, *due*, *tre*,' he called to Julian, deliberately fingering each layer of soft, yellow silk chiffon as he lifted them into the air, all the while exposing the slim legs and thighs of the young ballerina. Even from where they were sitting in the stalls, Anna and Madge could see the poor girl was trembling with fear.

Andretti dropped the layers of fabric in disgust and peered into the footlights. 'Anna! Are you there?'

Dreading what was coming next, Anna stood up, becoming more anxious when Gian-Carlo's tone softened obsequiously.

'Anna, *mia cara*. Don't you see? The middle layer . . . it is simply too yellow. You will take it away, won't you?'

While Anna remained speechless, it was a brave Julian Player who broke the stunned and awkward silence. 'Ahem, here at the Alexandra Theatre, we always use three layers of silk chiffon for such costumes. They hang so much better that way.'

'*Hang*? Julian, my dear, you of all people should know that Gian-Carlo Andretti does *not* do what everyone else does. That is why I was chosen for this production. I do not want my princesses to look as if their clothes *hang*! I want them to look as if

'. . . as if they are floating on clouds of — '

'Jewels?' Madge broke in sarcastically, giving Anna a gentle dig in the ribs, reminding her of the previous dress rehearsal when Gian-Carlo had insisted the costumes were to be *simply smothered in jewels.*

Andretti turned, his face beaming. '*Exactly*! I can see you at least understand me, Madge. Perhaps you can explain to Anna?' With that he clapped his hands impatiently, thus dismissing the six subdued and terrified princesses from the stage.

In a daze, Anna collected the offending costumes and hung them carefully on the rail. 'I don't believe it. I simply don't believe it,' she cried, her voice filled with anger and despair. 'Please Madge, tell me this is all a bad dream.'

'Afraid not, ducky. That's what the man said, and you know he always gets his own way. Mind you — if I had my way — I'd give him bloody jewels! First I'd stick some up his arse, then I'd smother every last inch of fabric with jewels. I can just see the critics review now: *A sparkling new production from Gian-Carlo Andretti.*'

Anna gave a feeble smile. 'I'd find that almost amusing if I didn't feel quite so desperate. When I think how hard everyone's worked on these costumes. What on earth am

12

I going to tell them?'

'That Andretti's a right bastard for a start,' Madge suggested, her voice as sharp as her features. She lifted a tell-tale layer of yellow silk chiffon. 'Anyway, it's no use thinking about it now, it's Friday night.'

'All the more reason for me to be thinking about it. By now everyone in the workroom will have gone home.'

'I know. Sorry, Anna. I didn't mean to sound so glib. It's just that you look all in and I was hoping I could persuade you to join me for a drink — before I meet Frank. He says he wants to discuss something important . . . and I'm trying not to get too excited.'

'Mmm. That sounds promising. Do you think he's finally asked Pamela for a divorce?'

'I hope so, ducky. I certainly hope so.' Madge's face shone with an air of renewed expectancy. She and Frank, the chief electrician, had been having an affair for the past ten years. Almost the same length of time Frank had been promising to ask his wife for a divorce. Last weekend, Madge had delivered her final ultimatum and Frank had been given one week in which to decide where their future lay.

With her thoughts on Madge and the immenseness of the task ahead of putting the costumes to rights, Anna failed to notice the tall, remote figure coming towards her. Pushing the rail along the dimly lit corridor, she suddenly struck an obstacle.

'Hey!' someone exclaimed from the shadows.

'Oh! I'm dreadfully sorry. I'm afraid I didn't see you.'

'I am not surprised. Are they saving the electricity?'

'Quite possibly. The whole place is falling apart — or hadn't you noticed?'

'Not exactly. I am not long enough here to find out.'

Hearing Andretti's renewed yelling at the far end of the corridor, Anna soon forgot the figure in the semi-gloom. Instead, she gave an almighty shove, followed by a whispered curse of despair when the rail engaged yet another stubborn obstacle.

'I can be of help?'

'Not unless you can sew,' she snapped into the darkness, extricating one of the dresses now caught on the corner of a costume basket. Hearing the softly spoken stranger respond with something unintelligible, Anna proceeded on her way. I shall assume that was very rude, she told herself. However, as I wasn't exactly pleasant myself, what can I expect?

Five minutes later, and once more alone with her thoughts, Anna slammed shut the creaking lift gate, pushed the rail back in the direction of the deserted workroom and wept.

2

In the George and Dragon, those of the theatre crew not heading for home immediatelty, or required for that evening's performance, all sipped at their drinks in subdued silence.

'I still think it's a bloody disgrace!' Madge said eventually, never afraid to air her views. 'Julian should have put his foot down for once and told Andretti where to go.'

Frank Webster pushed his glass to one side. 'C'mon, Madge, you know it's more than Julian's job's worth to do that. Andretti might be a bit of a so-and-so but opera or ballet, he always produces a damned good show. It's what the public want and pay to see.'

'And you think we should just sit back and take it, Frank? All that bloody hard work in vain!' Madge threw Frank a withering look, then paused thoughtfully. It hadn't been her intention to discuss Gian-Carlo Andretti. She'd far rather be discussing her future with Frank instead. She was still waiting to hear of his impending divorce.

'No, Madge, I do not think we should sit back and take it. In fact, I've already tried to step in and help. Jerry and I even told

Andretti that if we altered the lighting a fraction, we could quite easily achieve the softer effect he was looking for.'

Madge gazed longingly at her lover of ten years, genuinely surprised that he should have spoken up for Anna. 'And?'

'And he wasn't having any of it,' Frank replied, rubbing at his droopy moustache.

'Can anyone join in this discussion, or is it a closed shop?' Beattie stood at the far end of the table, dressed in black satin skirt and gold lurex top, the red hair, scarlet mouth and nails duly tended for her regular Friday night visit to her local.

Frank raised his eyebrows in disbelief. 'Good heavens, Beattie! I thought you'd be at home getting some beauty sleep, especially as you could be working twenty-four hours a day until next week's final dress rehearsal. Didn't Anna tell you Andretti wants the costumes altered?'

'He what?' Beattie studied Frank's chubby face for the merest glimmer of a smile. 'I take it you are kidding, Frank?' she wheezed, tearing away the cellophane wrapper from yet another packet of cigarettes.

'Sorry, ducky, not this time,' Madge interrupted, outlining the disastrous sequence of events at rehearsals.

'The dirty rotten bastard! So . . . where's

Anna? Is she here?'

Pausing to light her cigarette, Beattie narrowed her eyes to scan the hazy, smoke-filled bar. She recognized many faces. Sadly, Anna's was not among them.

Madge reached for her jacket, hanging on a nearby chair. 'I think Anna's gone back to the workroom and Frank and I are just going for a meal. I suppose I could call in on her later . . . to see how she's getting on.'

Inhaling deeply, Beattie sat down and reached towards an ashtray. 'Always the gentleman eh, Frank?' she said, watching him help Madge with her jacket.

'You know me, Beattie. Always trying to do my best.'

'Yes, I do,' she muttered moments later, seeing the couple disappear from view. 'Only too well in fact and it's that which bothers me.'

★   ★   ★

Anna sat slumped at the workroom table, her tears long-since dry. It was no good, she must make a start on something. With heavy heart she walked to the rail of costumes and studied one of the sleeves, hanging rigid from the weight of so much beading. Completely out of character she shook the rail so violently that the sleeves, sparkling in the harsh neon light, all appeared to be waving at her. 'Damn you! Damn you! Damn you!' she cried, kicking angrily at the wheels, firmly embedded in the linoleum.

'You will have sore feets, I think.'

Anna gasped, looking in the direction of the open doorway. There, to her amazement was the young man she'd quite literally bumped into — or should that be run over?

'I am sorry if I startle you. My name is Bjorn Carlson. I am here to see the theatre and visit my cousin, Erik Carlson. He is making with the scenery using my father's trees and — '

Wide-eyed, Anna brushed her hair from her face. First Andretti's distinctly unpleasant outburst and now this softly spoken stranger with the curious accent, talking about feets and trees.

'I am thinking my English is not yet good, but my father grows the trees and Erik uses them for scenery. He says Swedish trees are best for the theatre.'

With a curious smile, Anna regarded the tall, blond figure filling the doorway, his clear blue eyes fixed intently on her own bewildered brown ones. Quickly averting her gaze, she caught sight of his beige suede ankle boots. On one of them was an ugly black mark, no doubt evidence of the rail she had pushed so angrily. 'I'm — er — sorry about your shoe. Is it ruined?'

'I think not. But I see your shoes are hurt too. Your feets must also be black.'

'Yes. I think they are and my feet perhaps a little bruised,' Anna replied, touched by his somewhat unusual turn of phrase.

Moving swiftly to Anna's side, Bjorn helped her to push the rail into a better position. 'You are very angry and upset. Erik tells me of the bad afternoon. Would you like to go for a drink and talk about it? I have good ears.'

'I'm sure you have,' Anna acknowledged, a flicker of a smile playing at the corner of her eyes. 'Unfortunately, I have to work. The costumes — '

'You cannot work without food. I will find you a coffee and something to eat.'

Before she had a chance to protest, Anna watched Bjorn turn on his heels and walk away leaving her to ponder the delights of freshly brewed coffee. Doubting very much if he'd find any, she picked up a pair of sharply pointed scissors and set to work. So much for being single and unattached, she thought grimly, placing the first of the costumes upon the table, particularly as she was in for an awfully long and lonely weekend.

Perhaps not quite so lonely, Anna concluded moments later, hurrying over to the stage door. If she left a message for Gavin who was still on duty as a dresser, she might have the bonus of one extra pair of hands tomorrow. As for Beattie, she would have to try her again in the morning. There'd been no reply when she'd rung from the public phone box in the corridor. Reminding herself that it was completely pointless even thinking of Fudge, Anna began cutting savagely into the scarlet thread. Not only was there Fudge's wounded finger to consider, but also the fact that she lived miles away in the suburbs and her parents didn't even possess a phone.

Hearing lift gates open and close, followed by footsteps along the corridor, Anna looked up expectantly. Surely Bjorn couldn't have organized coffee and something to eat quite so quickly? Besides, his shoes had made no sound at all. To her complete and utter surprise it was Beattie who stood in the doorway, dressed in satin and lurex and perched on high, black patent leather stiletto heels.

'Beattie! What on earth are you doing here?'

'Come to help, haven't I,' came the abrupt reply.

Anna studied the clothes more suited to

pubbing than sewing. 'Isn't Friday night your big night out?'

'Usually it is, but as I've been to the pub and they're all down in the dumps due to our dear friend G-C Andretti, not to mention the fact that I don't fancy going home just yet, in case I bump into my landlord again — '

'You've got problems with your landlord? You never said anything earlier.'

'Not exactly problems, but it does look as if Ariadne is in the family way again. I was going to say old Stavros will have kittens when he finds out,' Beattie chuckled. 'Still, I suppose that's exactly what he will have, seeing as our friendly neighbourhood tom's been up to his old tricks again.'

★   ★   ★

Tucked into the corner of a cosily lit bistro, Frank and Madge gazed into each other's eyes. Disregarding cost, Frank had ordered the most expensive bottle of wine on the menu and even toasted their future together. Madge's hopes were running high. She'd waited ten whole years for this. Ten years of watching Frank exist in a stale, loveless marriage while his wife constantly threatened suicide if he ever left.

In the early days Frank had pleaded with

Madge to be patient. It would be far easier when the children were older, he'd said. But as the children got older and Frank made no attempt to leave — how could he when the girls were taking exams? — Madge had become more and more depressed. Tonight, however, her spirits soared. In September the youngest of Frank's daughters had left to go to university and with the eldest already living away from home, there was no conceivable need for further delay.

Madge sighed contentedly, savouring the delights of such an excellent meal. What a simply perfect evening they'd spent together. Unlike poor Anna, who was no doubt still slaving away all alone in that dismal workroom of hers.

'I take it Pamela has at last agreed to a divorce,' she whispered, reaching for Frank's hand. 'That is what we're celebrating, isn't it?'

'Um — not exactly. You see . . . I need more time, Madge. Time to discuss it properly with Pamela.'

'Time?' Madge cried, letting go of his hand. 'You've already had ten years.'

'Please Madge . . . you don't understand. It's not that easy — '

'Not that easy! It bloody well is from where I'm sitting!' Ignoring Frank's pleading grey eyes, Madge paused only momentarily when the waiter brought their coffee and brandy. 'Well, I'm waiting,' she exclaimed, watching Frank stir his coffee in silence. 'Why isn't it easy, Frank?'

'I simply can't do it, Madge. I can't leave Pamela . . . not now the girls have left home. She misses them, you see. And what with me working most nights at the Alexandra, she gets lonely. It . . . it wouldn't be fair.'

'Lonely? Fair?' Madge's voice reached a crescendo, causing other diners to look in her direction. 'Christ, Frank! You can't even begin to know the meaning of the words.'

'Madge, *please*. People can hear you.'

'I don't give a shit if the whole damned world can hear me. In fact I want them to. Don't you dare lecture me about being lonely or fair. Do you have any idea what I've been through all these years while I've been waiting for you?'

Frank shook his head, convinced Madge was about to tell him — once she'd finished her brandy.

'Ten years,' Madge continued, banging her empty glass upon the table. 'Ten long, lonely years when all I ever wanted was for us to be together. Ten years of listening to you saying you wanted us to get married, so we could have a child of our own. And now all you can do is throw me on the scrap heap.'

Scrap heap? Frank looked up mortified. He'd never do a thing like that. Wanting to say so much all that came out was a feeble, 'You've got it all wrong, Madge. It's not like that at all. You don't understand.'

'Too damned right I don't! I don't understand how all these years I could have been so bloody stupid. When I think how I've been completely taken in by all your pathetic, feeble excuses.'

'But I love you, Madge. I'll always love you. You know — '

'Oh, shut up, Frank! I already know enough. I know that I'm forty-four and you've already had the best years of my life. If you think I'm going to sit at home and wait for you till I'm an old woman — just like Beattie and her bloody cats — then you're very much mistaken.'

With that Madge flew to her feet, plucked an almost-full bottle of brandy from a nearby drinks trolley and strode towards the exit.

'*Signora!* The brandy?'

Acknowledging the anxious waiter with a grunt, Madge called acidly in reply 'The *signor* will pay!' and, nodding in Frank's direction, disappeared into the night. Too distraught to head for home and still clutching the brandy bottle to her chest, she traced Beattie's footsteps to the theatre lift and workroom.

25

'That must be Bjorn,' Anna said, turning to Beattie. 'I expect he got lost if he's new to the area. Goodness knows I could certainly do with a coffee and some . . .'

The words died on her lips. It was not Bjorn but Madge, standing in the open doorway. Madge with her fingers clasped grimly around a bottle, while tears flowed freely down her mascara-streaked cheeks.

'Bloody Frank! Bloody, bloody men!' she sobbed over and over again.

Eventually returning with coffee and sandwiches, Bjorn discovered the lift wasn't working. Someone, on one of the upper floors, had presumably forgotten to close the gates. No matter, he told himself and, clutching the flimsy cardboard tray to his chest, climbed the stairs slowly, surprised to hear female voices in the distance. The first he recognized as Anna's and there was also someone with a dreadful cough. Bjorn stopped and listened. Were there now two people with Anna, and if so, who was crying? For it was clear someone was sobbing uncontrollably. Recalling Anna's earlier distress, he hoped that he wouldn't find her in tears again.

'I am sorry, I intrude?' he began apologetically, taking in the scene before him where a middle-aged woman with dyed red hair sat in a corner, a cigarette wedged between her scarlet-stained lips. From time to time she blew smoke in the direction of an open window. Bjorn watched transfixed as talon-like fingernails plucked savagely at the beading on the costumes until it lay like jewelled confetti, scattered across the table.

Shifting his gaze from Beattie, he then turned his attention to the opposite corner. There Anna was attempting to console Madge, whilst at the same time trying to wrestle a half-empty brandy bottle from her tenuous gasp.

'I am sorry,' he said again. 'I have only two coffees and I see you are three. Shall I fetch one more?'

'Bugger off!' Madge snapped, looking up through a drunken haze. 'We don't need your bloody coffee. In fact, we don't need men at all.'

In response to Bjorn's puzzled expression, Anna motioned him towards the corridor and followed him outside. 'I'm so sorry about my friend,' she whispered, leading him to the open lift gate. 'She's very sad and upset. Please don't take it personally. Just like me, Madge has had a very bad day.'

'It is also very sad that I cannot help you, Anna. You see I am unable to sew.'

Anna coloured at the reminder of her earlier caustic remark. 'Actually, there is one way you can help. The sandwiches and coffee . . . that's if you don't want both cups?'

Bjorn's face brightened, he'd completely forgotten the coffee. 'Yes, of course. With my pleasure. You must have everything.'

'What about yourself?' Anna said, finding the tray and all its contents thrust in her direction.

Bjorn shook his golden head and gave a lopsided smile. 'No problems. I will eat from Erik and Jane's fridge when I get back. I think perhaps the lady with red hair would also like a coffee?'

'Beattie? I doubt it. She survives mainly on nicotine and whisky. But I'm sure Madge will soon change her mind about the coffee.'

'And will you change your mind about coming out with me one day?'

Anna hesitated, watching Bjorn step into the lift. 'That depends on how long you are staying in London. For the moment I have all the costumes to finish and — '

'Oh, I shall be here for some times,' he replied with a shy grin, closing the wrought-iron gates behind him.

Waiting until he'd finally disappeared from

view, Anna felt an unfamiliar stirring in her stomach which quite unnerved her. Convincing herself it was merely a result of sheer exhaustion and lack of food, she was also reminded of Madge's drunken ramblings about Frank and men in general. 'Pull yourself together, Anna,' she scolded, checking to see no one was listening. Nevertheless, preparing to rejoin Madge and Beattie in the workroom, she knew it wasn't going to be easy to dispel from her mind the vision of a tall, blue-eyed blond, making his way into the cold October night.

As the hours ticked slowly away, Anna yawned sleepily and laid down her scissors. 'I don't know about you, but I've certainly had enough of dismembering costumes for one night. I think it's about time I ordered us a taxi. Beattie, I can't begin to thank you enough for all your help. As for what we're going to do about Madge . . . From the state of her, I suppose the best thing is to take her back to my place.'

'Rather you than me. I wouldn't mind betting she's going to feel absolutely lousy in the morning.'

Fifteen minutes later, struggling to help Anna push Madge's crumpled form into the waiting taxi, Beattie was heard to mutter, 'Did you manage to get out of her what happened? I thought Frank was supposed to be asking Pamela for a divorce.'

'It seems he couldn't go through with it after all, because of Pamela.'

'Hmph! Luckily, I never had that trouble with any of my husbands. In fact I couldn't wait to see the back of them. Best stick to cats, I say,' Beattie snorted, contemplating her landlord's reaction when he discovered yet another litter of unwelcome kittens in the boiler-room.

'*Pets are not allowed, Mrs Beattie,*' he would say for the umpteenth time, but just as before, she would take absolutely no notice whatsoever.

'It's lucky old Stavros is Greek and not Chinese,' Beattie explained, following Anna into the taxi. 'Because if he was, he'd probably eat them!'

Sitting patiently in his cab, the taxi driver studied each of his female passengers in his rear-view mirror. He'd already smelt brandy on Madge's breath and was also faintly amused by Beattie's appearance, not to mention her infectious, throaty laugh. As for Anna, a pretty girl he concluded, with long dark hair and heart-shaped face, she simply sat quietly between the two older women, barely able to keep her eyes open.

'Well, ladies,' came the chirpy retort, 'it

certainly looks as if you've all had a jolly good evening.'

'Oh, yes. Absolutely wonderful,' Anna said drily, 'and I expect we shall have an even better one tomorrow.'

3

When Gavin arrived early on Saturday morning, Anna and Beattie were already hard at work. He frowned, seeing the dark circles under their eyes.

'Don't tell me you two have been here all night.'

'Not exactly,' replied Anna, 'though it certainly feels like it. Thanks for coming to the rescue, Gavin. I hope I haven't ruined your weekend.'

'No. It's OK. I'm on theatre duty again this evening, dressing Felix. He was at his most difficult and demanding last night. To be honest I'm almost relieved to be in the company of quieter and less temperamental folk.'

Beattie looked up through a cloud of yellow silk chiffon. 'You wouldn't have said that if you'd been here with us last night.'

'Why? What happened?'

Anna nodded to the piles of scattered beads, brandy bottle, discarded coffee cups and plastic sandwich wrappers. 'As you can see we had quite a night.'

'Looks like I missed out on a great party.

Who came off worst?'

'Madge. She and Frank have finally split.'

Gavin raised a bemused eyebrow and unbuttoned his leather jacket. 'You honestly don't expect me to believe that, Anna? Their relationship's been blowing hot and cold for the past ten years and will probably continue in the same vein for another ten.'

'I very much doubt it this time. When I left Madge this morning, not only was she nursing an extremely sore head but also her language was far from polite. As far as Frank is concerned, she never wants to speak to him again.'

Cupping his hands together, Gavin scooped some of the beads into an empty cardboard box. 'That's going to be virtually impossible working here.'

'And I can't see how they ever got together in the first place,' Beattie joined in, pushing more beads in his direction. 'Those two are like chalk and cheese.'

'And opposites attract,' Anna ventured.

'That's as maybe, but Frank's far too soft and Madge could do with watching her tongue sometimes. My old Mum would have made her wash her mouth out with soap and water. Look how rude she was to that young man.'

Gavin's eyes widened in interest. 'What young man?'

'The one who brought Anna the coffee and sandwiches.'

'Really. Am I to understand that he's an admirer?'

Feeling a flush of colour flood her throat, Anna decided this conversation had gone on for long enough. 'Admirer is hardly the word I'd use. I merely ran over his foot when I stormed out of rehearsals yesterday. Later, he — er — offered to fetch me a coffee.'

Gavin winked in Beattie's direction. 'That's certainly a novel way of getting to know someone, running over their foot. Who was he, anyone I know?'

When Anna wasn't forthcoming it was Beattie who replied. 'I gather he's Erik Carison's cousin.'

'Ah, the Swedish chap, with the long blond hair who's always saying hey.'

'Idiot!' Beattie chortled, dispensing with yet more beading. 'He's not saying hey! He's saying *hej*, H-E-J- that's Swedish for hello.'

'You seem to be very knowledgeable on the subject, Beattie. How come?'

'Well, I once knew a very nice Swedish sailor who — '

'Who what?' Gavin teased, leaning over to clasp her hand. 'C'mon, Beattie, you've started so you'll have to finish *and* you've gone all misty eyed.'

Anna coughed pointedly. 'Gavin, while I greatly appreciate you giving up your Saturday — and much as I enjoy hearing about Beattie's past love life — don't you think you should make a start? The costumes?'

Sensing both urgency and concern in her voice, Gavin reached for one of the costumes, suddenly grateful for a welcome splash of colour in the otherwise dreary and depressing workroom. Anna and Beattie, he noticed, were both wearing black today. Beattie, a figure-hugging knitted jersey two-piece, and Anna a black woollen pinafore dress, with a black and tan patterned blouse beneath. Studying first the two women and then the depressing view, he likened the whole scenario to that of an Ibsen play. About to share his observations, he heard Anna emit a weary sigh. She, too, was looking towards the window, no doubt also wondering, as they were three floors up and looking out onto a disused warehouse, why the windows were made of frosted glass?

An hour later and deeply engrossed in his work, Gavin asked himself what mattered if the surroundings were grim and cheerless? At least working with Anna and Beattie was sheer delight. Only last night he'd told Felix le Sage, the leading opera singer whom he'd been dressing for the past three years, that it was like working with his mum and his gran. Felix could see the connection with Beattie, as for Anna . . .

'My dear boy!' Felix had said, frowning. 'How can Anna be like your mother, when she's only a few years older than yourself? What an insult to the dear, sweet creature. What is she twenty-five, twenty-six?'

Duly corrected, Gavin had changed the word mum to sister which was, they both agreed, a far better description. On reflection, Anna certainly understood him far better than his mum ever could.

For the rest of the morning the atmosphere in the gloomy workroom was extremely tense with little time for idle chatter. As lunchtime approached, Anna left only briefly to telephone Madge and also fetch welcome supplies of sandwiches and coffee.

'How is she?' Beattie enquired, stretching her arms and flexing her long, thin fingers. 'Is she feeling any better?'

'Very subdued and extremely apologetic. She also asked if she could spend the rest of the weekend with me. There was no mention of Frank.'

Beattie sipped at her coffee. 'I expect she's

hoping to forget all about him.'

Once more pointing out that it was highly unlikely in the circumstances, Gavin wondered what would happen on Monday, when Madge and Frank came face to face.

To everyone's surprise the confrontation, when it arrived, was one of an anti-climax. Braced for a typical Madge-style verbal onslaught, they were almost disappointed when it never materialized. Frank, in particular, was highly relieved. The embarrassing scene in the restaurant had been bad enough; he had no desire for another in front of the people whom he knew. Concluding Madge would need at least a couple of days to calm down, Frank assured himself that by the weekend, they would no doubt carry on as before. This time he was clearly wrong. Madge had already told Anna on more than one occasion that *enough was enough*. This time she was sticking to her word.

Arriving for work herself, Fudge stared at the scene of devastation with shock and incredulity. She was even more surprised to find her colleagues already busily installed and layers of discarded yellow silk chiffon, strewn haphazardly across the floor.

'Whatever's happened? Am I late?'

Fudge listened as Anna broke the awful news. She was devastated. The dresses had been so very beautiful. As for all the time and effort involved. 'Why didn't you phone me?' she pleaded. 'You could have rung the neighbour and left a message with Mrs Fincham. I would have come in. All that work, Anna. I simply can't believe it.'

Fudge looked so hurt and distressed that Anna thought she was going to cry. 'It's very sweet of you, Fudge, but you live so far away. It didn't seem right to expect you to come in.'

'But they're my costumes too. I should have been here to help you. It's only fair.'

'Don't worry, love, there's still plenty to do,' Beattie consoled, pointing to the remaining costumes. 'You can still do your bit.'

Hugely relieved, Fudge removed a costume from its hanger and joined Beattie at the work table. 'I'll also stay and help you this evening. I don't mind working late.'

The problem was Anna did, or, more to the point, she didn't like the thought of Fudge travelling home alone across London late at night. Fudge however, was adamant.

Listening in on their conversation, Gavin put forward an alternative suggestion.

'Why doesn't Fudge stay the night at my place? There's plenty of room.'

Fudge looked round horrified. Stay the night with Gavin? Her mother would never agree to that, regardless of the fact that she would be perfectly safe in his company. Mary Freeman was still trying to come to terms with flower power, the hippy explosion and her son's recent obsession with *Woodstock the Movie*? Not to mention his *Make Love Not War, Mum*, every time she criticized the state of his bedroom.

Acutely aware of Fudge's unease, it was Anna who came to the rescue.

'If you're really sure about working late, you could always stay with me. Madge was using the put-u-up at the weekend but she plans to go home this evening. Why not ring your mother and see what she says? I'll speak to her, too, if you like.'

$\star$ $\star$ $\star$

Going back with Anna on the tube later that night, Fudge could hardly contain her excitement. Until now her life had been extremely sheltered and here she was, spending her first night in the capital. What mattered that her back ached from working a twelve-hour day, and the 'initiated' finger still throbbed from the constant stitching. As far as Fudge was concerned, she was in heaven.

Few would have regarded the box room in Anna's ground-floor flat as heaven, but to

Fudge, still clutching the toiletries Anna had insisted on buying from the all-night chemist's on the corner, this could be the Ritz. Unlike the theatre workroom it was light and airy with the walls and floors in the latest shades of muted desert colours, all cleverly complimented with open weave curtains and Berber rugs. Spying an array of eye-catching postcards from cities she had never even heard of, Fudge looked on in awe.

'Have you really been to all those places?'

'Most of them,' Anna replied. 'My father was in the diplomatic service and we travelled all over the world, until I was sent to boarding-school.'

Boarding-school. Fudge had never met anyone who'd been to boarding-school.

'What was it like — all that travelling? And didn't you mind being sent away?'

'Not really. In fact it was quite exciting for a while. Although, Granny was always accusing my father of dragging us around the world like gypsies.'

Fudge studied Anna carefully. With her smooth olive skin, mane of shoulder-length dark hair and deep, soulful eyes, she could just imagine Anna in a gaily coloured skirt and bodice, sitting in an old-fashioned horse-drawn gypsy caravan. Her gaze drifted to one of the many nearby photos. 'And you even had the horse.'

Fudge's vivid imagination was momentarily lost on Anna until she pointed to the teak-framed photo of a fine chestnut mare.

'You mean Trudi. Yes, she was one of the reasons why I didn't mind boarding-school. But then I only had to board during the week. At weekends and holidays, I was allowed to stay with Granny, where Trudi was stabled, leaving my parents to continue with their travels.'

'Where are they all now?'

Anna looked suddenly melancholy. 'Trudi is no longer with us, I'm afraid, but at least Granny is still alive and my parents have retired to Spain.'

'Wouldn't you like to live in Spain too?'

'Goodness no! I find sun and sand boring. I much prefer to live here. Galleries, concerts and theatres are more my scene, with the occasional quenching draught of our beautiful English countryside.'

Sudden mention of the theatre reminded Anna of the chaos they had left behind in the workroom and the subsequent decision for bringing Fudge home. It was already extremely late and they both needed a decent night's sleep before rising early to tackle the remaining costumes. 'This really won't do at all,' she said kindly, glancing at her watch.

'With only two more days before the final dress rehearsal, I suggest no more chatting. We need sleep. How about a hot drink before you go to bed?'

Marvelling at the ingenuity of the put-u-up, Fudge sat with her hands clasped around a mug of comforting hot chocolate while studying assorted photos on the wall: Anna as a child with her parents and grandmother, Anna in the netball and hockey teams as a happy smiling schoolgirl, and Anna at gymkhanas and ballet displays. In each and every photo she looked quietly confident and content. How different to her own childhood, Fudge mused, especially with her dad working in the local aircraft factory and her mum working part time in the local tea-rooms. As for schooling at the local comprehensive, which she'd hated so much because of the constant teasing about her weight . . .

'*Fatty Freeman*,' Fudge whispered to herself, reminded of the cruel taunts she'd constantly had to suffer. Small wonder then that she'd raised no objection to being called Fudge. As far as animals and after-school activities were concerned, there she'd taken solace in a small black and white pet rabbit from one of the many litters bred in her father's garden shed, and Mrs Grainger's dancing classes, held in the village institute on Monday afternoons, after school.

* * *

Clutching her own precious bundle of black and white fur, Beattie caressed the newly pregnant Ariadne, who nuzzled against her and purred contentedly.

'Well, puss,' she sighed, easing off her shoes. 'What a day! To think it's only Monday and I'm already wishing it was the weekend. Although, perhaps I should rephrase that. Wishing it was the weekend but certainly not looking forward to it.'

Beattie's gaze alighted on the invitation propped against the mantelpiece. Since its arrival three weeks ago, she was still undecided how to reply. Should she ring her brother and accept, or else stay at home and . . . ? 'And what, puss . . . sulk? Because, what I'd really like to know is why Tom didn't invite me to the wedding in the first place instead of getting his father to arrange a party to meet the bride, three weeks after the event.'

Ariadne flicked her tail and half opened an eyelid before resuming her slumbers. If cats could speak she would have said she was already quite fed up with Tom Hudson, her mistress's only nephew. Beattie had talked of little else ever since receiving the shock invitation. Tom, or to give him his full name: Thomas Roy Hudson, was the son Beattie had always longed for but somehow never had. Her brother's only son and youngest child, was a handsome, madcap, fun-loving rogue and, in short, Beattie absolutely adored him.

'At least I used to adore him,' she said, reaching for her cigarettes. 'That was when he used to join me for a drink *and* before he became involved with the local rep. Now he's gallivanting all over the place.'

'You mustn't be too hard on him,' Thomas Hudson senior told his sister, ten minutes later on the phone. 'For a start you're only young once, and as Tom's finally landed his first plum television role, I thought you'd be pleased for him, Beattie.'

'I am,' she conceded, 'but if his acting career's just beginning to take off, shouldn't he have waited before tying himself down?'

'Lucy's a nice girl. You'll like her,' Thomas said, good naturedly, despite being called at such a late hour. 'Anyway, are you sure you're not simply cross with him because he didn't let you know about the wedding?'

Beattie didn't reply. In a way her brother was right. She'd felt distinctly hurt and left out when told of Tom's wedding, despite it being only a simple register office affair: bride and groom and only two witnesses. Deep down, however, what really irked Beattie the most was that since she'd joined the Alexandra, she'd been hoping to engineer a meeting between her handsome rogue of a nephew and the delightfully pretty Anna. Now that was totally out of the question, she reflected sadly. Her nephew Tom was a married man. As for Anna, she puzzled, studying the lengthening ash on her cigarette, surely such a pretty, caring and hard-working girl like Anna, deserved someone special. Deep in thought, Beattie stroked the soft, gentle curve of Ariadne's tummy.

'I wonder ... What was it my Swedish sailor friend used to say about Sweden?'

Casting her mind back to last Friday evening, when Bjorn Carlson had suddenly appeared in the open doorway, and Anna had looked up from where she was ministering to the very drunken Madge, Beattie's face broke into a slow, satisfied smile. Perhaps she could cope with the rest of the week *and* Tom's belated wedding celebrations after all.

4

A week after the much talked about *Andretti Afternoon*, Anna left the final dress rehearsal and returned to face the anxious occupants of the workroom. Exhausted, she fixed them with a satisfied smile.

'Yes! We've finally got Gian-Carlo's approval. Everything is *bellisima*!'

'Thank God for that,' huffed Beattie, reaching for the handbag at her feet.

Anna smiled indulgently. 'It's all right, Beattie. Go ahead and smoke if you want to, as long as you sit by the window. After all I did let you get away with it last Friday evening. Believe it or not, as the costumes have now been duly despatched to Madge for safekeeping, Julian's even said we can go home early.'

Beattie prepared to wedge a cigarette between her lips. 'Not without my wages, I'm not. We've got some overtime due to us, don't forget.'

'How do you suggest we celebrate?' Gavin called back, making his way to the open doorway to look for Sally with the wages tray. 'Anyone fancy a slap-up meal together?

46

Perhaps Eric and Frank would like to join us too? There's that new Italian place on the corner. What do you think, Anna?'

'In principle, I think it's a great idea. Aren't you forgetting something, however?'

'You mean Madge and Frank?'

'Not exactly, but you do have a point. I was thinking more along the lines that we all work different hours. We work days — '

'Apart from when Andretti's around,' Beattie quipped.

'And you work days *and* evenings, when you're dressing Felix le Sage,' Anna continued. 'As for Madge, Frank and Eric . . . '

Gavin gave a disgruntled sigh, knowing only too well that because of matinees, Saturday lunchtimes were also out of the question. He looked at Fudge, who as yet had said nothing. To her the thought of them all going out for a meal sounded absolutely wonderful. Unfortunately, just like working late, there was still the problem of the last train home.

'OK, so why not make it a Sunday?' he said at length. 'And don't start giving me excuses, because I'll have a lunch party at my place *and* make sure it doesn't finish late. That way we'll all be bright eyed and bushy-tailed, ready for work on Monday morning.'

'Speak for yourself,' Beattie groaned,

inhaling deeply on her cigarette. 'I'm never bright eyed and bushy-tailed on a Monday morning. Besides, what about — '

'In case you were going to ask about Fudge travelling on her own, that's simple: I'll invite her brother as well.'

'But you don't know my brother.'

'That doesn't matter. We know you. The more the merrier as far as I'm concerned and you'll have someone to travel home with.'

Any further dialogue came to an abrupt halt when Sally appeared in the workroom to distribute the wages and collect their union dues. Her task completed, she wished them all a good weekend and made her way along the corridor to the tailoring department.

Moments later, Beattie looked up from where she'd been checking her salary slip.

'Gavin . . . when you mentioned having your party on a Sunday, you didn't mean this coming Sunday did you?'

'Lord no! You know me Beattie, I like to plan these things properly. I thought in a couple of weeks. Give everyone time to check their diaries and that sort of thing.'

Fudge smiled to herself. The only diaries to appear in her house were those given to her mum by travelling salesmen who called at the tea-rooms after Christmas. Tossed into the kitchen drawer, they usually only saw light of day when they needed a scrap of paper to leave a note for the milkman.

Stubbing out her cigarette and carefully disposing of the evidence, Beattie stood up. 'That's a relief, cos I'm already going to a party this weekend.'

Intrigued, Gavin rose and helped Beattie into her pearlized green raincoat. 'You haven't said anything about a party before. You usually tell us what you're up to.'

'Maybe that's because I'm not in a party mood.'

Studying the look of intense sadness in Beattie's eyes, Anna gestured to Gavin to refrain from further questioning. It was only when the two women were alone together in the ladies' cloakroom, she decided to broach the subject further.

'Beattie, it's probably none of my business. This party . . . is there a problem?'

Emitting a deep, languid sigh, Beattie met Anna's gaze in the less than flattering cloakroom mirror. 'No, not really a problem. It's simply that I feel so hurt and let down.'

'Hurt? In what way? Can I help?'

'Not unless you're prepared to tell me I'm a stupid old woman who's behaving completely irrationally,' Beattie replied, scrabbling in the depths of her handbag for lipstick, tissues and a comb.

Anna shook her head. 'No. I'm certainly not prepared to do that, because I'm sure you're neither stupid nor irrational.'

'That's kind of you to say so, Anna. Nevertheless, you're entitled to change your mind when I tell you why I've been so worried of late. It's Tom you see . . . '

'Tom, your favourite nephew? Isn't he in rep or something?'

'My one and only nephew in fact. Who, according to my brother, has landed himself his first plum television role.'

'Shouldn't you be happy for him, or don't you approve of acting as a profession?'

'Oh, I approve all right. What I don't approve of is the fact that just as his career's taking off, he's gone and got himself married.'

'You never told us you'd been to Tom's wedding.'

'Exactly. That's because he never invited me. When I think how close we've always been . . . '

Anna placed a comforting arm about Beattie's shoulder. 'I see. I think I'm beginning to understand now. You feel hurt because you weren't told about the wedding. I expect Tom and his — er — wife had their reasons.'

'So my brother keeps telling me,' Beattie

said grimly, raking a comb through her fine, wavy hair. 'By all accounts it was just a simple register office do, and the reason for the party on Sunday is to get to know the bride.'

'Then I expect she'll be lovely and you'll have a fantastic time. From what little I know of your nephew, I'm sure Tom wouldn't have settled for anything less than the perfect wife.'

Beattie gave a begrudging snort, wishing she shared Anna's optimism. Something in her bones told her that Lucy *wouldn't* be the perfect wife, least not as perfect as Anna. If only Tom had waited a little while longer until she'd had the opportunity to introduce them both. 'Well, this won't do,' she muttered, pressing her lips against a tissue to seal a fresh coat of Flamenco-glow lipstick. 'I don't know about you Anna but before I go home, I intend to spend part of my hard-earned wages on something special. I need to cheer myself up in preparation for Sunday.'

'Sounds like a jolly good idea,' Anna called, watching her depart. 'Have a nice weekend, Beattie, and don't worry too much about Tom.'

Combing her own hair and freshening her make-up, Anna cast her mind back to the previous Friday, when she'd bumped into Bjorn Carlson. She had seen him only once during the week and that was discussing scenery with his cousin Eric. Looking up he'd smiled at her, fixing her with steady blue eyes the colour of a clear summer sky.

Mmm, summer, she thought, reaching for her coat and making her way into the cold October night, bracing herself for the usual chilly wind that gusted in from the alley behind the theatre. Summer was such a long way away. There was winter and spring to get through first. Perhaps her parents had the right idea after all, choosing to live in Spain. 'Sunny Spain,' she murmured out loud.

'Who's going to Spain?' queried the stage doorman.

'Oh, hello, Sam. You've caught me talking to myself again. I was simply thinking how cold it's been lately and how nice it would be to see some sunshine for a change.'

Sam nodded and shook his head ruefully, launching into one of his favourite topics — the long-term weather forecast. 'And the Met Office never seem to get it right,' he grumbled. 'Mind you, we mustn't complain,' he said, his gaze drifting over Anna's shoulder. 'It's a great deal colder where he comes from. Isn't that right, Bjorn?'

Surprised, Anna turned to find Bjorn moving almost immediately to her side.

'I was just telling Anna about Sweden,' Sam explained. 'All that snow and long, dark, winter days when you see hardly any daylight.'

'That's only in the north of Sweden, surely?' Anna said, anxious to avoid a repeat performance of trampling on Bjorn's feet. 'Don't forget in the summer they have endless hours of daylight, when the sun never sets at all.'

Bjorn nodded thoughtfully. 'You have been to Sweden?'

'No. But my great aunt went there many years ago. She described it as a truly beautiful country and was always promising to take me to see the midnight sun.'

'Then you must remind her to do so.'

Fixing Bjorn with a sad smile, Ann replied softly, 'I'm afraid that won't be possible. She died several years ago.'

'Then perhaps I can show you?'

Completely taken aback, Anna turned sharply. Had Sam overheard Bjorn's whispered invitation? Relief flooded her face when she saw he was dealing with an enquiry from a would-be autograph hunter. Acknowledging her farewell with a quick nod of the head, Sam continued with his duties.

'I hope I did not offend,' said Bjorn. 'Of course you must get to know me first, that is if you want to? We could perhaps start with a drink? You had to work last Friday evening, remember?'

Last Friday evening! Anna blushed, recalling how she'd first looked up to find Bjorn standing in the doorway, not to mention Madge's little outburst.

'How is your friend?' Bjorn asked, breaking into her chain of thought. 'Is she suitably recovered from her distress?'

'If you mean Madge, I wouldn't go so far as saying suitably recovered.'

'Then she and Frank are still not friends?'

'Oh, you know all about that?'

'I think not all,' Bjorn grinned, sidestepping a puddle. 'But Erik tells me there has been much talk of Frank and Madge during the week. He also said the Italian restaurant on the corner is very good. Perhaps tomorrow lunchtime we could . . . '

'I'm very sorry, I can't,' Anna said, her voice tinged with regret. 'I've arranged to see Madge before the matinee. She's finding it so very difficult to cope at the moment. However, I am free tomorrow night.'

'And I'm afraid I am not.'

Which is hardly surprising, Anna thought, almost regretting her earlier promise to Madge. The thought of this gorgeous blue-eyed Swede, spending a Saturday night on his own, was extremely unlikely.

54

'Like you offering to help your friend, Madge, I have offered to help my cousin Erik. What about Sunday?'

Sheer relief coursed through Anna's veins. 'Sunday would be perfect.'

'I am sure it will,' Bjorn smiled in reply, before noting down her telephone number and walking with her as far as Leicester Square underground. There he said a quick goodbye and hurriedly retraced his footsteps to the theatre.

★   ★   ★

Stepping from the taxi outside her brother's imposing West Hampstead residence, a perfect Sunday was the last thing Beattie had envisaged.

'Aunt Bea, you old rogue,' came a voice. 'And there was me thinking you weren't coming, especially as Dad told me I'd offended you.'

'Not so much of the old rogue, if you don't mind!' Beattie said tersely, trying to extricate herself from her nephew's firm but fond embrace.

Tom watched as his aunt's face filled with tears. 'Aunt Bea? Dad said you were really upset. Why? It was only a small Register office do: Me, Lucy and two witnesses we grabbed from the street. I didn't think you'd be interested if it wasn't a full blown, top hat and tails affair.'

'You honestly thought that, after all the years you've known me?'

Tom shifted uneasily. 'Well — er — it's just that I always remember you and Mum forever planning and talking about the big weddings you wanted for me and Sarah.'

'At least your sister did things properly,' Beattie sniffed. 'Sarah and James didn't just sneak off and get married without telling anyone. I couldn't understand it at all when your dad told me.'

'Couldn't you, Aunt Bea?' Tom said sadly, cupping his aunt's distraught face in his hands. 'Couldn't you really?'

Reaching into her pocket for a handkerchief, Beattie looked up to meet her nephew's questioning gaze. 'You don't mean . . . she . . . Lucy is pregnant?'

'Afraid so.'

'I thought most young women were on the pill these days.'

'So did I, at least that's what Lucy told me when we — um — you know.'

Beattie dabbed at her eyes. 'Are you saying she lied to you? That she tricked you into getting married?'

Tom gave a laconic smile. 'I don't know

about tricked. I do love Lucy you know. It's simply that — '

'You hadn't planned on a wife and a baby quite so soon, especially with your career suddenly taking off?'

Tom nodded, sometimes he thought his aunt Bea understood him better than he did himself. 'Got it in one,' he said, giving her a hug and leading her towards the house.

'I see, so what are you planning to do now?'

'Do? Try and make a go of things, I suppose. I'm frequently being told I've got what it takes to be a serious actor. Only time will tell if I've got what it takes to be a good husband and father.'

'I'm sure you have,' Beattie replied, attempting reassurance. She refrained from adding, *as long as you've married the right woman.*

Following Tom inside to the warm, Beattie choked back fresh tears. She'd often thought of the right woman for Tom and it was most definitely *not* a Lucy!

'Ah! This must be Aunt Bea,' a thin voice echoed, from a blaze of brightly coloured swathes of silk. 'I'm so pleased to meet you. Tom's told me all about you.'

Coming face to face with Lucy, Beattie froze visibly. No one, apart from her nephew,

57

was allowed to call her Bea! Sensing his aunt's abject disapproval, Tom leaned forward and kissed his wife.

'Lesson number one, Lucy,' he grinned, trying to make light of the matter. 'Only I'm allowed to call her Aunt Bea. That's because she once wore a startling yellow and black striped dress and I said she — '

'Looked like a bee?' Lucy broke in, giggling.

'That's right,' Beattie said with a thin smile, stooping to kiss the petite, flaxen-haired girl on the cheek. 'So . . . welcome to the hive, Lucy.'

With that initial hurdle over, Tom allowed himself to relax. At least some attempt had been made to welcome his new bride. Though, he sensed only too well that as far as his Aunt Bea was concerned, Lucy would never be accepted in this particular hive.

Hearing the opening strains of 'When a Man Loves a Woman', Lucy reached for her husband's hand and led him to the middle of the room to join the other happy couples, already dancing.

'Now that you've had a chance to meet her, what do you think of Lucy?' Beattie's brother questioned, offering her a glass of champagne.

'She seems like a nice girl.'

'But not his type eh, Beattie?'

'I didn't say that.'

'Perhaps not, but it is what you're thinking. You're my sister, don't forget. I know you only too well.'

'And I suppose you're also going to say that as yet I don't know Lucy very well?' Beattie responded coolly, raising her glass to her lips.

Looking towards his aunt at that particular moment, Tom acknowledged her raised glass, grinned broadly and winked at her.

'I'll admit she looks paler and thinner than most of Tom's previous girlfriends,' Tom Hudson senior announced, 'but I expect in a few years she'll soon fill out a bit.'

Beattie almost choked on her champagne. From her brother's comment, it was painfully obvious that he and the rest of the family had absolutely no idea that Lucy was pregnant. 'Oh, I'm sure she will,' she muttered as an aside, watching her brother leave to fetch another bottle of champagne. 'And it won't take a few years, either.'

Several glasses later and feeling suitably mellowed, Beattie gazed adoringly at her nephew. Lean and strong with tawny-coloured wavy hair, amber lights glinting in his eyes and a handsomely rugged face, Tom had somehow always reminded her of a lion.

Yes, she reflected, deep in thought. You're a

real king of the jungle, Tom. Who knows . . . perhaps you will be happy with that dainty little humming bird flapping its wings by your side after all. For if I'm to be perfectly honest, I'd hate to see you pounce on my precious *gazelle* only to have you tear her to pieces and scatter her discarded remains to waiting jackals. Unbeknown to Beattie at that particular moment, the gazelle in question, namely Anna, was enjoying a delightful day with Bjorn.

'Cheer up, Aunt Beattie. It will probably never happen.' Tom's sister, Sarah stood by her side, offering her aunt a tray of assorted canapés.

'You're quite right, Sarah,' came the sad response. 'Despite all my long held hopes and prayers, I don't think it ever will now.'

5

Up with the lark on Monday morning, or at least the first London sparrows and pigeons, Gavin waited eagerly for Beattie's arrival in the workroom.

'All the young what?' she asked, listening to him singing the opening strains of his favourite pop song.

' 'All the Young Dudes'. It's by Mott the Hoople.'

'Mott the . . . ? No. Don't even bother to tell me, Gavin. Forget I ever asked. I'm obviously getting old. Whatever happened to Dickie Valentine and Jimmy Young?'

'I think he's on the radio in the mornings,' Fudge broke in. 'My Mum listens to him all the time. She's even tried some of his recipes.'

Gavin raised a surprised eyebrow. 'Recipes? I thought he was a crooner.'

Listening to Fudge explain that as far as she knew Jimmy Young wasn't singing on the radio in the mornings but hosting a consumer and music programme instead, Gavin thought that somehow or other he couldn't exactly imagine the lead singer of Mott the Hoople doing that in later life.

'OK, Beattie,' he teased, 'if you don't rate 'All The Young Dudes', listen to this one instead. Perhaps it's more appropriate in the circumstances.'

'He's attempting to sing 'It's a Family Affair',' Fudge replied, in response to Beattie's blank expression.

'Well done, Fudge. Got it in one,' Gavin grinned. 'Give the young lady a coconut. So, how did it go, Beattie? Your family affair? The party?'

Not exactly in the mood for Gavin's chirpiness, Beattie gave an exasperated snort.

'Sometimes, Gavin, there are moments when you completely exhaust me. I only wish I was as bright as you first thing on a Monday morning.

'Now then, don't evade the issue. You can tell Fudge and me all about the party before Anna comes. As you can see we haven't got much work to do this week.'

Looking around the almost empty work-room, Beattie heard dainty footsteps approaching and a quiet voice proclaim, 'Who says you haven't got much work? And what was Beattie going to tell you before I arrived?'

'Anna! How long have you been here?'

'Long enough to hear your excrutiating rendition of 'A Family Affair'. I've been talking to Julian about the next production.'

Horrified that Julian Player was in such close proximity, Fudge shifted uneasily. If he was to come into the workroom now, he would see nothing but empty tables.

'It's all right,' Anna reassured. 'There's no need to panic. Julian's on his way to a meeting to discuss the future of the touring company.'

Reminded of the quiet whisperings of late, Beattie's face registered concern. 'That sounds ominous. I know we can't ever compete with The Royal Opera House but The Alexandra has always had its own touring company.'

'I'm sure there's nothing to worry about: it's purely speculation and rumour. Let's just concentrate on the job in hand, shall we? Madge is already on her way. I gather some of the costumes for the Christmas pantomime need repairing or replacing.'

Greeted by a chorus of deep, mournful groans from Gavin and Beattie, Madge suddenly appeared pushing a rail of assorted costumes. She grinned wickedly. 'Nice to see you too, folks. At least this little lot should keep you going for a bit. By the way Anna, how was your date with the Swede?'

Already forgetting the ghastly costume repairs, Gavin looked expectantly in Anna's direction. 'You've been on a date with Bjorn?

Wow! That's fabulous news. What's he like and where did he take you?'

'For the moment that's none of your business, Gavin,' Anna demurred, throwing Madge a black look. 'There's work to be done — or had you forgotten?'

'Oops! Me and my big mouth,' Madge hissed. 'This is where I exit stage left, I think. You'd better tell me before I go, should I slit my throat now or later?'

'Now,' Anna glowered, depositing a jester's costume, with ripped and worn sleeves, on the table in front of Gavin. 'That way I won't have to entertain you at Christmas, as you requested. Remember?'

Mention of Christmas soon wiped the smile from Madge's face. Previous years as Frank's mistress were bad enough — waiting to spend the odd snatched moment together — but the prospect of a Christmas without any sign of him at all, was something she was reluctantly coming to terms with. Hence her request when she and Anna had lunched together last Saturday.

Sensing a sudden frosty chill in the atmosphere, Fudge, Gavin and Beattie mumbled farewells in Madge's direction, carried on with the tasks in hand and worked away for most of the morning in silence.

Later in the day, when the tension had

eased, Beattie produced a photograph wallet from her handbag and placed it on the table in front of her. 'I thought perhaps you might like to see these. They were taken yesterday at Tom and Lucy's party.'

Fudge pounced eagerly on the first of the photos. 'Yesterday. How did you manage to get them developed so quickly?'

'My brother's got one of those special Polaroid cameras. You simply take the photo, wait a couple of minutes and Bob's your uncle.'

'Or in this case, Tom's your nephew,' Gavin chuckled, hearing Fudge sigh as he peered over her shoulder.

'Oh, Beattie. Isn't he handsome?' Fudge gasped, flicking through the photos, hoping to find more of Tom on his own. 'And is that his wife?'

'Mmm,' Beattie acknowledged begrudgingly, casting a wistful look in Anna's direction, where she too was studying the photos and hoping to offer a shred of comfort.

'Lucy's very pretty, Beattie. They make a very attractive couple.'

'I don't know about couple. They'll very soon be three.'

'You mean she's pregnant?' Reminded of their conversation in the ladies' cloakroom on

Friday afternoon, Anna patted Beattie's hand. 'I can see why Lucy couldn't resist him,' she whispered. 'He's exceptionally good-looking. And I love the suit he's wearing. He's obviously got good taste in clothes too.'

Mention of clothes prompted Gavin to take a closer look at Tom's suit. He gave a low whistle of approval. He was far more interested in the latest male fashions than the pale-faced blonde clinging on to Tom's arm in virtually every photo.

'I only wish I approved of his taste in women,' Beattie huffed and, pushing aside the assorted photos of Tom and Lucy, fumbled in her bag for a lace-trimmed hankie.

'Well, I certainly approve of this one,' Anna said, tactfully picking out the only photo of aunt and nephew, arm in arm together.

Beattie blew her nose. 'Yes, that's my favourite too. I intend to treasure that one. Perhaps even get it enlarged.'

'Just as I intend to treasure these,' Anna replied shyly, reaching into her own handbag and placing a strip of passport-sized photos on to the table. 'I know they're only those dreadful things taken in photo booths, but the bottom one isn't too bad, is it?'

Blinking back tears, Beattie studied the four simple black and white photos of Bjorn and Anna, huddled together in the confined space of the photo booth. 'Looks like you had a good day together,' she sniffed.

'Yes, we did. However, I still can't believe I actually agreed to having those taken. Bjorn insisted. He said they'd be a special reminder of our first day together.'

Something in the tone of Anna's voice prompted Gavin to look at her photos without further teasing. Acknowledging Beattie's warning glance with a gentle squeeze of her shoulder, he began discussing plans for his forthcoming party instead.

⋆ ⋆ ⋆

'Sorry I put my foot in it,' Madge said, when she and Anna were alone. 'Me and my big mouth. Frank's always telling me . . . Oh, shit! Why do I still keep talking about that rotten bastard?'

'Quite possibly because you still love him?'

' 'Course I do. You know I bloody do! I only wish I didn't that's all.'

'After ten years it's not going to be that easy, Madge. And, at risk of sounding like Marje Proops, dare I suggest one day at a time?'

'As long as you don't add Sweet Jesus at the end, just like that bloody song Erik's been singing in the theatre all day. Because if you do, I'll go and jump in the Thames.'

'You wouldn't do a thing like that?'

'No. Too right I wouldn't, Anna. Much as I still love Frank, I've no intention of topping myself. But . . . I do have a little something lined up my sleeve for him. Like you being all coy and secretive about Bjorn, I don't intend to tell you what it is, either.'

'I wasn't being all coy and secretive. I simply didn't want to discuss it in front of the others — that's all. You know what Gavin's like. He can be a real old woman at times.'

'Yeah, and he also makes a wonderful Black Forest Gateau don't forget. He's even promised to make one for his party the week after next.'

'You're going to Gavin's party? What about Frank? Won't he be there too?'

'Don't worry, Anna. I expect I shall be speaking to Frank again by then — just. Anyway, I must dash. I need to get to the chemists for some Tampax. I've got the most awful stomach ache, which probably explains why I've been so foul-tempered just lately.'

Watching her go, Anna felt a brief surge of disappointment. For some reason she'd been hoping to tell Madge about the wonderful Sunday morning she had spent in Bjorn's company; catching the tube together and walking hand in hand on Hampstead Heath. Later, there had been a trip to the Everyman cinema and even later still, the amusing episode in the confined space of the photo booth, where they had talked and giggled like teenagers.

'I think you are very special, Anna,' Bjorn had whispered, holding her close, when they reached her front door. 'I like you very much and would like to know you better. Do you think that will be possible?'

With a murmured. 'Yes, I hope so,' Anna had lifted her face to be kissed.

6

Following rave reviews for their latest production, life at the Alexandra soon settled down once more. Frank and Madge appeared coolly polite towards each other; the wardrobe staff busied themselves making costumes for the Christmas pantomime; Bjorn and Erik were involved with an intricate scenery project and Gavin was bursting with plans for his forthcoming party.

'We're all going to have a fabulous time,' he said, reeling off the list of food he was preparing and music he intended to play. 'I've catered for everyone, even the oldies.' Here he winked slyly at Anna and Fudge, fully anticipating Beattie's subsequent reaction.

'If you mean me, I'll have you know I'm not quite ready for my bus pass.'

'You, Beattie? Why should you think that? Actually, I was thinking of Felix.'

'You've invited Felix le Sage?'

'No. He invited himself.'

'And is he coming?'

' 'Wouldn't miss it for the world, dear boy',' Gavin repeated, mimicking Felix's distinctive, sonorous voice.

Fudge frowned, deeply apprehensive. She and her brother were going to this party. How on earth would they fit in? Her mother's words echoed once more in her head. '*I don't know what to make of it all. You two going to London to mix with them there theatre folk.*'

'We're not exactly country bumpkins, Mum,' Steve, had remonstrated. 'For a start we don't go around saying ooh-argh, me old pal me old beauty, like Walter Gabriel from the 'Archers'. For your information, they're only rabbits in Dad's shed at the bottom of the garden, not a herd of Jersey cows.'

Nevertheless, Fudge still found herself full of nervous apprehension when she and Steve set off for London on Sunday morning.

'I don't know why you're looking so worried,' Steve said kindly. 'You know all these people. Apart from you, I won't know a soul.'

'I don't know about all. I know Anna and Beattie and, of course, Gavin, who's holding the party, but it's Julian Player and Felix le Sage I'm worried about. And if Anna's friend Madge and her — er — boyfriend, Frank start arguing, it might be awful.'

'Then again it might not,' Steve suggested, giving her arm a reassuring tap. 'From what you've said in the past, Anna, Beattie and Gavin all sound extremely nice. I'm sure I'll be able to cope with them. As for Julian and Felix, they sound just like those two characters from 'Round the Horne'. So . . . by process of elimination, I reckon it's going to be Madge and her boyfriend I'll have to worry about.'

'Why is that?'

'Because if this woman Madge goes on at wotsisname, like our Mum goes on at Dad, I only hope Gavin's got a garden shed, where we can seek refuge.'

Suitably cheered by her brother's approach to the party, Fudge determined to enjoy herself at all costs. On arrival at the tiny, rented Victorian house, a furtive glance to the bottom of Gavin's neat and well-tended garden, told her that he did indeed possess a garden shed. To her surprise and immediate relief, however, she discovered it wouldn't be necessary. Frank and Madge were already standing arm in arm in animated conversation with Anna and Bjorn.

The initial introductions over, Gavin took Fudge and Steve to one side with a whispered, 'Thank heavens for that, we can all relax for the day. Apparently Frank's wife and daughters have gone to visit his mother-in-law in hospital. As she lives in Coventry, they decided to leave yesterday and won't be back until late tonight.'

'Then Madge and Frank are friends again?' Fudge ventured.

'That's not quite how I'd put it,' Gavin said, with a sly grin in Steve's direction. 'Let's just say that according to Anna, Frank was able to spend last night at Madge's place without fear of the Prickly Pamela having a touch of the vapours.'

'He seems like a pretty decent sort of bloke,' Steve said, watching Gavin walk away to greet some new arrivals, 'and who's the distinguished-looking chap, with the silver hair and goatee beard, just coming in through the door?'

'Oh no! That's Felix le Sage and behind him in the thick horn-rimmed glasses is my boss, Julian Player. Julian simply terrifies me, but Anna says he's absolutely charming when you get to know him. Personally, I think he's got a soft spot for Anna.'

'You don't mean Julian fancies her? But he's ancient. He must be at least fifty.'

'No. I don't mean that at all. More like father and daughter I suppose, and before you say anything else, watch what you say about age in front of Beattie. She's extremely sensitive about growing old.'

Turning to see Beattie scrabbling for the ubiquitous gold packet, Steve reached into his pocket for a lighter. Hurrying to Beattie's side, he left his sister to respond to Gavin's plea for an extra pair of hands in the kitchen.

Fudge stared in amazement at the selection of food covering every available inch of work surface. Quiches, assorted cold meats and salads of every description, filled one side of the kitchen, while Gavin peered into two enormous casserole dishes, bubbling away on the stove.

'Gosh, that smells delicious. What is it?'

'*Coq au vin*,' Gavin replied, tasting the rich reddish-brown sauce before turning to lift the lid on another steaming saucepan. 'And the rice is in there, although there's also a heap of jacket potatoes for those who want them. Could you pass that dish please?'

With the speed of a practised chef, Gavin deftly tipped the rice into the serving dish, before summoning his guests to lunch. 'Hot if you want and cold if you don't,' he announced, pointing to the stripped-pine kitchen table, heavily laden with food.

'My boy! You're an absolute wonder,' Felix said, appreciatively, eyeing the mouth-watering feast. 'Now I know why I can't manage without you.'

'Yeah. He'd make someone a good wife, wouldn't you, Gavin?'

Gavin grinned, acknowledging the cheeky stagehand in the far corner. 'As a matter of fact I think I would. And any more rude comments about my *coq au vin*, Brian, and you can do the washing up.'

Ignoring the ribald comments and exchange of banter taking place in the kitchen, Bjorn led Anna to the relative quiet of the sitting-room. 'Gavin is a very good cook,' he said, sampling his first mouthful of chicken.

Anna nodded in agreement. 'He certainly appears to excel at everything he does. He's also incredibly neat and tidy. Have you noticed?'

'Then he's not like me. My mother tells me I'm very untidy. As for my cooking . . . '

'Ah, but Erik tells me you are very clever with your hands. I understand you've designed and made some wonderful furniture.'

Laying down his fork and meeting Anna's gaze, Bjorn said softly, 'I like to think so. Although I work mostly for the theatre in Stockholm, I have also made some individual pieces of furniture. One day I hope to have my own studio and workshop.'

'You mean back in Sweden?'

'That depends on you, because I'd like to know what you think of my country.'

Anna paused, mildly curious, a forkful of rice midway between her lips.

'I'm sorry, Anna. I have not yet made

myself clear. I was wondering if you would care to spend Christmas in Sweden with my family?'

Avoiding the full implication of Bjorn's suggestion, or at least her own interpretation of it, Anna said quickly, 'I've — um — invited Madge for Christmas. Or at least she invited herself, when she and Frank had that terrible row.'

Bjorn looked to where Frank was feeding Madge a morsel of chicken. 'They are happy again now,' he reasoned.

'That's as may be, but come Christmas, Pamela won't let Frank out of her sight.'

'So . . . if you can't manage Christmas, when will you come, Anna? I must return to Sweden eventually, because of my work permit.'

Panic coursed through Anna's veins. In some ways she felt as if she'd only just met Bjorn, yet here he was already talking of returning to Sweden.

Pushing his plate to one side, Bjorn went to great lengths detailing his ambitions for his studio. Wasn't it worth serious consideration? Anna prevaricated, not knowing how to respond. Where did she fit into Bjorn's plans? Because, unless she'd read the signs all wrong, he certainly intended for her to fit in somewhere. There was little chance to discuss the matter further, however, Gavin suddenly appeared with slices of his celebrated Black Forest gateau and issued instructions for the furniture to be pushed back, ready for when people wanted to dance.

'Dance!' Felix exclaimed, wiping chocolate and cream from his beard, 'We've only just eaten. I shan't be able to move for at least two hours.'

'Great. 'Cos that's my problem solved, Felix. You will be the perfect disc jockey.'

Leading the bemused Felix to the record player in the far corner of the room, Gavin produced an assorted pile of LPs. 'As you can see they're already in chronological order,' he explained, with a wink in Beattie's direction. 'Chosen to cater for all ages and all tastes. Just to get things going, this one's for you, Beattie.' In his hand Gavin held up a compilation LP of hits from the fifties. 'It's amazing what you can find in Oxfam,' he told an intrigued audience, reading from the record sleeve. 'Jimmy Young, Dickie Valentine and someone called Edmund Hockridge.'

'Ooh, I remember him,' Felix exclaimed proudly. 'Isn't he Canadian? He used to sing that lovely song 'Young and Foolish'.'

Listening to the strains of 'Young and Foolish', Beattie found herself thinking of her nephew Tom. He'd certainly been both young and foolish in allowing himself to be tricked into marrying Lucy. Because, the more Beattie thought about it — and she'd thought about it a great deal lately — the more convinced she became that Lucy had chosen deliberately to become pregnant. 'I only hope you two don't do anything quite so foolish,' she whispered out of earshot, regarding Anna and Bjorn side by side on the sofa. 'At least wait until you're both married.'

★   ★   ★

'What makes you so convinced Bjorn and I are going to get married?' Anna replied, several weeks later in response to Beattie's leading question. 'Don't forget I haven't known him very long.'

'You don't have to know someone long to know that he's right for you. I take it you do think he is right for you?'

'Yes. I suppose I do in a way. But he hasn't exactly asked me to marry him.'

'And I certainly hope he hasn't asked you to live with him. I don't approve of all this hippy lifestyle thing. What with free love and living in communes.'

'Beattie, Bjorn comes from a highly respectable family. Rest assured, he hasn't asked me to live in a commune, nor have we

78

— er — slept together. In fact the only thing he has asked me, is if I'd like to go to Sweden to visit his parents.'

Anna blushed, surprised to find herself discussing the intimacies of her relationship with Bjorn. She hadn't even divulged those to Madge. Though, come to think of it, she hadn't seen much of Madge since Gavin's party. With the run up to Christmas things were once again reaching fever pitch in the theatre.

Sensing her embarrassment, Beattie murmured approval. 'I'm relieved to hear it, Anna. Far better to have your babies when you've a wedding ring on your finger.'

★　★　★

'Can you believe that?' Anna called, to where Madge was packing costumes into a basket. 'There's Beattie already talking about me having babies and Bjorn and I aren't even engaged.'

'And do you think you will?'

'Um — he has sort of suggested it.'

Madge dropped the lid of the costume basket with a dull thud. 'What? Why the hell didn't you tell me before?'

'Because you've been so wrapped up with Frank for the past few weeks and exactly like

I said, he's only sort of asked.'

'Sweet Jesus! And what is that supposed to mean?'

Explaining the conversation she'd had with Bjorn and later the discussion with Beattie, Anna combed her fingers through her fringe. 'Do you think that sounds as if Bjorn's really interested? I've only known him a little while, remember?'

'Hmph! And I've known Frank for ten long years and look where it's got me. Still, I suppose things are looking up at the moment.'

'Is that why you're acting so smug?'

Madge tapped the side of her nose. 'Perhaps it is, perhaps it isn't? Either way I'm saying nothing at the moment. It's a big surprise and I am saving it for Christmas.'

7

On a cold winter's day, Alexandra's Rag Time Band, as they'd recently taken to calling themselves, sat by a blazing log fire at The George and Dragon. Their main topic of conversation was Christmas, who was going where and with whom: Gavin, Madge and Frank would be working in the theatre; Beattie was going to join her brother's family, and Fudge was expecting a visit from her loveable and extremely lively, Aunt Dolly.

As usual at this time of year the strains of Bing Crosby's 'I'm Dreaming of a White Christmas' crackled from an ancient Bakelite speaker, decorated with yellowing tinsel and dusty paper chains. When Bing Crosby eventually gave way to the opening verse of 'Hallelujah Freedom' sung by Junior Campbell, Beattie gave a cynical smile.

'And it's freedom I'm looking forward to. At least getting away from this dump.'

Gavin sipped thoughtfully at his drink and put down his glass. 'The George and Dragon's your local, Beattie. I've never heard you complain about it before.'

'That's when I enjoyed coming here. Now

everyone's a picture of abject misery.'

'You can hardly blame them,' Anna joined in.

'You mean the rumours you told us not to worry about,' Beattie said, looking in her direction.

'I know, and I'm sorry I led you to think otherwise. I truly believed it was only rumour. Still, nothing's definite and we know the current programme goes right through until next July. Shouldn't we try and concentrate on enjoying Christmas instead?'

''Course we should,' Gavin agreed, his arm curled protectively about her shoulder. 'At least it's not like last year when most of the service industries were on strike.'

Standing up with an empty glass in his hand, Gavin hunched one of his shoulders, gave an almost perfect and combined rendering of Laurence Olivier's Richard III and Hamlet, beginning with, '*That was the winter of our discontent, alas I remember it well*,' and concluded by announcing, 'The next round's on me.'

Greeted with loud applause, Gavin made his way to the bar, leaving Beattie to shake her head in mock despair. 'I give up, Anna. I simply can't win with you two. Why are you and Gavin always so cheerful and optimistic?'

'Thank God someone is,' Madge replied.

'The atmosphere backstage has been decidedly tense of late. From the carpenter's shop
to the paint shop and even as far as the green
room, rumours have been flying thick and
fast. Only this morning, Erik was saying he
might look for work when he visits his family
at Christmas. His contract's coming to an
end anyway.'

'If Erik's wife is English,' a voice broke in,
'he doesn't necessarily have to go back to
Sweden to find work, does he?'

Anna didn't catch all of Madge's reply, but
she certainly noted the words, '*Yes, I know.
But doesn't the wife usually follow the
husband, not the other way round?*'

Deeply pensive, Anna considered this off
the cuff remark. Would Jane want to go and
live in Sweden? More to the point, what
about herself? Having travelled extensively
with her parents, how would *she* actually feel
about living in Scandinavia? Dismissing the
likelihood of this ever happening — as yet
Bjorn still hadn't mentioned the all important
word *marriage* — Anna pondered the myriad
thoughts racing through her head.

'Penny for them,' said a voice at her elbow,
where Gavin stood with a tray of drinks.

'Oh, I was miles away, thinking about
Christmas,' she lied.

'What will you be doing, Anna? I already

know what most of the others are up to and I'd love to meet Fudge's Aunt Dolly. She sounds an absolute scream.'

'For the most part staying at home trying to keep Madge cheerful. She's spending what's left of Christmas with me, once she's finished wardrobe duties at the theatre.'

'Does she need cheering, when she's been unusually perky of late? There was me thinking after that last major bust-up, it was going to be a case of pistols at dawn.'

Spying Frank and Madge huddled closely together, Anna wondered if her services were indeed going to be required, to the extent she was not only beginning to regret turning down her parents' offer of Christmas in Spain, but also Bjorn's invitation to join him in Sweden.

'Christmas in Sweden is like a fairy-tale,' he'd said in his soft, lilting voice. 'Of course, we have already missed the *Lucia Fest* — the festival of light — but in Mora, where my grandparents live, they go to church on Christmas morning in a horse-drawn sleigh.'

Anna stifled a sigh, it had sounded simply magical. Regrettably, because Madge had talked ceaselessly of their forthcoming Christmas together, she'd therefore found herself declining both a Christmas in the sunshine and one in the frozen north.

★　★　★

'So, I guess it's just you, me and that grotesque-looking creature,' Madge grinned on Christmas morning, watching Anna stuff the turkey's gaping crop with sausage meat.

'Afraid so, but I did warn you that Christmas *chez Mason* would probably be rather quiet. And by the way, please don't tell me, now that I've gone to all this trouble to prepare you a traditional Christmas dinner, that you've suddenly become vegetarian.'

'Me a veggie?' Madge replied, 'You've got to be joking. Do I look like the lentil and sandals brigade? That bird might look truly disgusting, trussed up like that with its arse in the air, but I can assure you once it's cooked to perfection, with all the trimmings, I'll soon forget about its pre-oven appearance.'

With a grateful smile Anna filled the aforementioned cavity with raw apples, carrots and onions, laced the turkey breast with streaky bacon, covered the whole with butter, seasoning and foil and placed it in the oven. 'Speaking of appearances,' she remarked cautiously, closing the oven door, 'and not wanting to dampen your Christmas spirit in any way, I don't suppose Frank will be putting in an appearance today?'

Anna interpreted Madge's shake of the

head as a no and assumed Frank would be spending Christmas (as he always did) with his wife, Pamela, two headstrong daughters and a particularly vitriolic mother-in-law. 'If you don't mind my saying so, you don't seem unduly bothered about it.'

'Why should I? I'll be seeing him at tomorrow's matinée. Besides, I've already had my Christmas present from Frank.'

Anna's face registered bewilderment. This morning when they'd both sat by the Christmas tree with their presents, Madge hadn't opened anything from Frank. 'I don't recall seeing you with a — '

'You wouldn't, because it's not that sort of present.'

Not wishing to pry, Anna turned her attention to the box of assorted vegetables waiting to be chopped, peeled or sliced.

Deep in thought, Madge watched her reach for a swede. 'Did you know they use those for sound effects in radio plays and horror stories? When they want to create the sound of chopping off someone's head, they simply wallop a swede with an axe or something. It makes a wonderful noise. Terribly realistic, or so I'm told.'

'Madge! Do you have to? It's Christmas. Not Tales from the Black Museum.'

'Sorry. I was forgetting. I suppose you'd far

rather be thinking of a different Swede, like one beginning with 'B' for instance?'

'At least thinking of Bjorn is a great deal more pleasurable than thinking of someone being decapitated.'

'Especially as you've already lost your head and your heart, eh, Anna?'

'Perhaps. Though quite what the future holds for us, I hardly dare think.'

Clearing away the vegetable peelings, Anna listened to Madge reeling off a list of reasons why the future didn't really matter at all. Surely, what happened now was of more importance? Or at least what would happen once Bjorn returned from Sweden in the New Year. Not wishing to contemplate how she'd feel if Bjorn didn't come back, Anna conceded that Madge was right. Deciding to remain Beattie's eternal optimist, she gave a nonchalant shrug, opened the oven door to baste the turkey and concentrated on Christmas dinner instead.

★   ★   ★

'Anna, that was absolutely delicious. I couldn't eat another thing,' Madge groaned, pushing away her empty pudding plate. 'And, as you prepared that wonderful feast, I insist you put your feet up. I'll see to the washing up.'

'No way! I wouldn't dream of it. Why don't we do it together? Between us we'll soon have it done in no time at all. Then we can both put our feet up.'

Reaching for a brillo pad to attack a stubborn vegetable dish, Anna was faintly surprised when Madge again made another oblique reference to her Christmas present from Frank. 'Either you're being utterly polite by not asking what it is,' Madge said, with a sideways glance, 'or else you've already guessed.'

'To be honest I didn't like to pry, particularly when you didn't elaborate on it this morning . . . unless Pamela's finally agreed to a divorce?' Anna looked expectantly in Madge's direction, only to see her friend shake her head and give a self-satisfied smile.

'Nope. Something far better than that. At least I think it is. Though, whether or not Frank agrees with me still remains to be seen.'

Now completely baffled, Anna ignored the contents of the washing-up bowl for a moment. 'How can Frank give you a Christmas present and not know about it?'

'Take those rubber gloves off for a moment and I'll show you.'

Reaching for one of Anna's Marigold-free hands, Madge placed it firmly on the gentle curve of her stomach, her face glowing with excitement. 'There!' she beamed. 'Contrary to what you might be thinking, especially after the enormous meal I've just put away, that little bulge isn't all roast turkey and Christmas pudding.'

'What? You can't mean you're — '

'Can and do, ducky. I'm *pregnant*! Your friend Madge decided to have a few extra trimmings of her own this Christmas and you're the first to know. You are going to be an aunty. Not the proper sort, of course — because we're not related — but as I don't have any sisters.'

Anna stood open mouthed. 'What about Frank? Are you saying he doesn't know? He didn't plan for this to happen?'

'Yes, to all your questions,' Madge replied, matter-of-factly. 'Frank might not have planned it, but I damn well did. As for letting him know, I'll tell him before curtain up at tomorrow's matinée.'

'Y-you deliberately got yourself pregnant?'

Finally registering the shock in Anna's voice, Madge was momentarily taken aback. She'd been expecting Anna to be as thrilled as she was with the news. 'It depends what you mean by deliberately?'

With her hands now resting firmly on her own lap, Anna sat down at the kitchen stool. 'I suppose what I'm really asking is . . . did you get yourself pregnant in the hope that Frank would marry you?'

'Definitely not! Though, I suppose once news of this happy event gets out, that's what everyone's bound to think. Don't look so guilty, Anna. I honestly don't blame you for thinking like that. I'd be a bloody liar if I said the idea had never occurred to me in the past. In fact there were times when I frequently toyed with the idea, in the vain hope Frank would leave Pamela. As the years progressed however, I realized otherwise.'

'Even when you gave Frank that ultimatum last October?'

'Especially then,' Madge whispered sadly, 'and after a few days I got to thinking if I couldn't have Frank all to myself, what would be the next best thing?'

'His child?' Anna ventured.

'Got it in one. And so did I by the looks of it,' Madge chuckled, patting her stomach, 'because it all worked out so beautifully. Don't you remember — the weekend of Gavin's party? Pamela went to Coventry to visit her sick mother and I invited Frank back to my place, having first flushed what remained of my contraceptive pills down the loo.'

Ignoring what remained of the washing-up, Anna led Madge through to the sitting-room and regarded her gravely. 'I insist you sit down. I'm not taking no for an answer.'

'Me, sit down? I think you should, more like. If only you could see your face.'

Anna forced a weak smile. 'I take it you are pleased? You fully intend to go through with this?'

'You bet! I'm convinced it's going to be the best thing that's ever happened to me. I'm not getting any younger, am I? Having this baby will give me something to look forward to, not to mention company in my old age. I also realize that it means giving up work — eventually. As we both know the future of the Alexandra is already in jeopardy.'

Nodding in agreement, Anna had to admit that Madge was right on that count. The future of the theatre hung precariously in the balance.

'And, as I've got my own place, I can always take in sewing,' Madge said blithely. 'I know Boston Gardens isn't exactly Buckingham Palace but when Mum died, at least I was able to pay off the mortgage.'

'So . . . when is the happy event? When am I going to become an aunty?'

'Some time in late July, I think,' Madge

replied, delighted with the sudden change in Anna's tone.

★ ★ ★

Frank stood alone in the wings, his face etched with concentration. After yet another tense and cheerless Christmas Day spent in Pamela's company, he was glad to be back at work. With his mother-in-law sufficiently recovered to travel from Coventry to London, yesterday had followed the same inimitable pattern as before. Not wishing to dwell on his usual presents of record tokens and socks, followed by the ever familiar kitchen drama when Pamela managed to ruin everything from the turkey to the sprouts, Frank turned his thoughts to the fun-loving Madge.

'I must be mad staying with Pamela, when I could be with you,' he muttered, spying her hurrying towards him, a naval costume in her arms. Briefly reminded of the angry and embarrassing scene in the restaurant, closely followed by that wonderful weekend of Gavin's party, Frank reached into his pocket for a tiny blue box. 'Madge,' he hissed as she drew nearer. 'Quick, I've got your Christmas present.'

Without stopping, Madge breezed past, blew him a kiss and called softly, 'Thanks,

Frank, but there's no need. I've already had it. I'm pregnant.'

'You're what?' he croaked, watching her disappearing figure and clasping his hands to his head, turned to check no one else was within earshot.

'*Infanticipating*,' came the chirpy reply, before Madge darted into a nearby dressing-room and hurriedly closed the door.

For the forty-eight-year-old Frank Webster, that particular Boxing Day matinée was one of the longest he'd ever experienced. Surely he'd imagined it? Madge was merely teasing, wasn't she? Simply getting her own back. It was probably her idea of a joke. Only if it was a joke, he concluded angrily, it was a very bad one and as humourless as the jokes in the crackers they'd pulled on Christmas Day. Frank groaned, how many more curtain calls and cries of encore, before he could go and look for Madge?

'I take it you are pulling my leg?' he said stiffly, when he eventually caught up with her. 'That little display was purely your own idea of a pantomime?'

'Pantomime? I don't quite follow,' Madge replied, feigning innocence.

'When you said you were — er — pregnant.'

'Oh, I'm pregnant all right, Frank. And in

93

answer to your next question, yes again. You are the daddy. You can't blame this one on Father Christmas or the immaculate conception. The weekend of Gavin's party . . . '

Casting his mind back, Frank remembered only too well Gavin's party. Numbed and at a complete loss for words, he directed his eyes to Madge's stomach.

'Don't worry. It won't be that obvious for quite a while. As I told Anna — '

'You've told Anna! Christ, Madge! Was that necessary? Particularly, as you surely don't intend to keep it?'

Frank stopped abruptly when shock and anger filled Madge's face. 'Of course, you won't have to worry. I'll pay for an abortion,' he added hurriedly. 'One of the lads in the paint shop got his girlfriend in the family way a while back. I'll ask him. He'll know what to do.'

'So will I!' Madge snapped, a devastating hurt flooding her features, 'because like it or not, Frank, I intend to have this child. Nothing you can say or do will ever make me change my mind.'

'What about Pamela? What if she finds out?'

'Pamela? Pamela! Is that all you bloody well care about?'

'No, but . . . '

94

Grabbing at the naval costume, Madge bundled it onto a hanger and, fighting back tears, faced Frank head on, her tone icy. 'Oh, you don't have to worry, Frank. Your precious Pamela will never know. As for your bloody money — you can keep it. I've suddenly come to my senses at long last. From now on you no longer exist. And . . . just in case you were wondering, I shall also be leaving the Alexandra. Quite clearly from the look on your face, the sooner I go, the better.'

'Leaving? But Madge, how can you leave the . . . ?'

One frosty, withering look, told Frank he'd outstayed his welcome. For a brief moment he appeared to hesitate, took a faltering step in Madge's direction and swiftly changed his mind.

Slamming the dressing-room door behind him, Madge turned and sobbed uncontrollably into the naval officer's uniform, her heart twisted and cold like the ornate gold braid and brass buttons decorating the sleeves, shoulders and lapels. 'You bastard, Frank Webster. You absolute bastard! If only I didn't love you so much.'

8

Bjorn's eyes were wide and incredulous. 'Madge is pregnant. Is that . . . ?' He shrugged his shoulders, unsure whether to say good or bad. 'Are Madge and Frank happy about it?'

'It depends who you're speaking to at the time,' Anna said, telling him of Frank's subsequent reaction to Madge's shock announcement.

'And will Frank leave his wife?'

'I doubt it. Anyway, it no longer matters. Madge doesn't care one way or the other. Not since Frank suggested the abortion. Her mind's quite made up. She's leaving the Alexandra and has already handed in her notice.'

'Can she afford to do that if she's expecting a baby?'

Pushing her empty coffee cup to one side, Anna stood up ready to leave. 'Just about. She's convinced herself she can quite easily work from home.'

'Then I only hope she knows what she's doing,' Bjorn replied, helping Anna with her coat, before leaving the comforting warmth of the restaurant.

Out in the cold January air, Anna snuggled close against his side, linking her arm in his. 'I like to think she does.'

'Do you also know what you're doing, Anna? Will you come with me to meet my parents? I've told them so much about you. Mother suggested May, as they plan to go to our summer house, but I would rather you met them before I do my National Service.'

'National Service? I thought Sweden was neutral.'

'Like Switzerland we are an armed neutrality, but everyone has to do their duty.'

Anna felt her throat go quite dry. 'H-how long?'

Stepping into a shop doorway, Bjorn studied her anxious face. 'How long before I go — or how long will I be away?'

'Both,' she whispered. 'I had no idea call up still existed in Sweden. It finished in England years ago. I confess I know so little of Sweden, other than what my great aunt told me, and also that Stockholm is the capital.'

'Here is your chance to find out, at least to discover Stockholm.'

'You said you have to go away. The army . . . '

'I know. However, it is not as bad as you think. I've already completed my National Service, what happens next are *repetitions övningar.* It's a sort of refresher course. Two weeks in the classroom and two weeks on military exercises.'

Anna did a quick calculation. 'That's only a month. I thought you'd be away for ages.'

'Would it bother you if I was?'

Tears of relief welled in Anna's eyes. In those few brief moments all manner of wild imaginings had galloped through her head, initially thinking of him going away for months on end and then not knowing where. From the moment they'd first met she had known herself to be in love with Bjorn. Until five minutes ago however, she hadn't realized quite how much.

Cupping her face in his hands, Bjorn brushed away a single tear from her cheek with his thumb. 'Then, will you come to Sweden before my *repetitions*?'

★   ★   ★

'Remind me, when exactly are you going to meet Bjorn's parents?' Beattie puffed, heaving a heavy velvet costume from the rail.

'The second weekend in February.'

'How romantic,' Fudge said, moving out of Beattie's way as she passed. 'Valentine's Day in Sweden. Will you see any reindeer?'

'I doubt it, not in Stockholm. I think

98

they're usually to be found in the north of the country. Although, Bjorn says it's not unusual to find moose on the roads outside some of the larger towns. Oh, and as far as I know, they don't celebrate Valentine's Day.'

'Rather you than me with the moose. They're enormous great beasts,' Beattie remarked. 'I'll stick to the chocolate kind. And before you say anything, Gavin, I do know that's a different spelling.'

Gavin didn't reply. He was far too busy fixing tiny slivers of fur on to his eyelids, to give the impression of enormous eyelashes. 'There, girls. How do I look?'

'Completely daft,' Beattie muttered, tugging at the hem of the velvet gown she was struggling to spread across the work table.

'Ooh, I think they're wonderful,' Fudge giggled. 'You look like that Fenella woman from the television. The one with enormous false eyelashes and kinky boots. Can I try? I've always wanted false eyelashes, but Mum would never approve.'

Looking about him, Gavin spotted another half-inch remnant of fur trimming from the velvet dresses. This he cut deftly in two and passed what looked like two furry caterpillars across the table to Fudge, who promptly fixed them to her own eyelids.

'If only you could see yourselves,' Beattie

tutted, securing a band of fur in place. 'You look like a pair of Jersey cows.'

'And very nice Jersey cows you are, too,' Anna said with a broad smile, glad of some light relief on a dismal January day.

'Speaking of which, will you please remind me to ring Tom at coffee break?'

Gavin fluttered his lashes in Beattie's direction. 'What's your nephew got to do with Jersey cows? Has Tom decided to give up on the acting profession and take up farming instead?'

'No. He hasn't, more's the pity. If he had, perhaps, he would never have met Lucy. And in case you were all wondering, she was the cow I had in mind.'

Anna laid down the piece of tailor's chalk she was holding and looked up. 'I thought you were warming to Lucy? What's made you change your mind again?'

'Oh, I don't know, Anna. She's pleasant enough, I suppose. Deep down I've always had this feeling she simply isn't right for Tom — that's all.'

'She's probably right as well,' Gavin whispered, watching the tall spindly figure disappear in the direction of the public phone booth in the outer corridor. 'Our Beattie's normally a pretty good judge of character. At least you're OK, Anna. She certainly approves of Bjorn. So come on . . . while we're having coffee, tell us some more about your forthcoming trip to Sweden.'

★ ★ ★

With trepidation, Anna followed Bjorn down the steps of the aircraft at Arlanda Airport. She shivered and reached for his hand.

'Cold?' he asked.

'Cold and also extremely nervous.'

Bjorn gave her a reassuring hug. 'There's no need to feel nervous. You have my word there will be no welcoming party at the airport. I insisted my parents wait at home. Mother's preparing a special meal for tomorrow.'

'Like ham and custard?'

'Especially ham and custard,' Bjorn said, in response to the playful glint in her eyes, suddenly reminded of his description of a typical Swedish Christmas, when he'd confused mustard with custard.

Still smiling at his mistake, Anna linked her arm in Bjorn's as they hurried across the concourse to the car hire office. 'Arlanda is minute, compared to Heathrow,' she said, glancing behind her. 'With so few people about it's far less daunting and bewildering.'

'That's probably because many years ago

Sweden was largely a farming community. Even now there are perhaps only eleven people to the acre.'

Shaking her head in disbelief, Anna turned her attention back to Bjorn's parents and the journey ahead, discovering it would take them only about forty minutes to reach Djursholm on the outskirts of Stockholm.

'Is it really minus fifteen?' she said at length, watching an illuminated sign at a petrol station, flashing both the time and air temperature.

'I expect so. It could even drop as low as minus twenty after midnight. My father told me, when I rang, that it's been snowing hard all week.'

'Yet the roads are so clear.'

'They have to be, otherwise the country couldn't function. That is why we Swedes are perhaps better equipped at dealing with snow. We have so much of it.'

Peering across the wide expanse of clear motorway, Anna discerned tall mounds of snow, piled neatly on either side. 'I think you're probably right. In England, if it snows for more than a couple of hours, the whole country grinds to a halt.'

'Then I hope it snows in England while we're away and I shall be able to keep you here for longer than just a weekend.'

Digesting his remark, Anna scanned each road sign for the approach to Djursholm, while at the same time trying desperately to remember a few simple, yet all important phrases of greeting and thanks.

'You're very quiet,' Bjorn's voice murmured in the darkness. 'Still nervous?'

'Not exactly. Besides, it's too late now. The last road sign said eight kilometres to Djursholm. Isn't that about five miles? Actually, I've been wondering why — despite the cold — no one appears to have drawn their curtains. I'm fascinated by the vast assortment of lamps and candles, shining in every window. They look like something from a fairy-tale.'

'That's because in most Swedish homes there's very effective central heating and double glazing. Light is also very important to us. Our winters are extremely cold and dark.'

Reminding Anna of the December *Lucia Fest* Bjorn also explained the ancient tradition of keeping lamps shining in the windows. 'To welcome weary travellers and keep the dark at bay,' he told his own weary traveller, who by this time was thinking of her flat in London.

On the ground floor, with its single glazed and badly fitted window frames, there was no way Anna could dispense with curtains at any time of year. And, if she was to put even the smallest of lamps in her windows, she concluded with a wry smile, she'd probably find travellers of the most unwelcome variety calling at her door!

Moments later, Bjorn's voice broke into her chain of thought. 'Welcome to Djursholm and my parents' house,' he said, driving through impressive double gates.

Anna gasped, enchanted. On either side of the driveway leading to the front door were rows of candle flares, all flickering brightly in the darkness. 'Another tradition?' she enquired, her dark eyes reflecting the welcoming flames. Bjorn nodded and heard her whisper, 'How simply lovely,' before helping her from the car.

In no time at all a huge rectangle of light flooded the front porch and cries of *'Wilcommen, Anna! Wilcommen til Djursholm,'* greeted her ears as she was engulfed in Karen Carlson's fond embrace, and Bjorn's father, Henrik, stepped forward and shook her hand warmly.

'You are ve-ry wel-come, Anna,' he said in slow, precise English. 'My wife and I are most pleased you are now come to see us with Bjorn.'

Nodding in reply, Anna responded with a shy *tak* and with Henrik leading her into the house, left Karen and Bjorn to chatter away in Swedish, behind her.

'You will excuse Bjorn and his mother for a moment,' Henrik said kindly. 'Karen wishes to make sure you will be com-fortable during your stay.'

Suppressing a yawn and trying hard to concentrate on the alien language, Anna had discerned only two words: *Kafe* and *sovrum-met*.

Coffee would be wonderful she thought — they'd already eaten on the plane — and as for bed . . . An inexorable feeling of panic filled Anna with alarm. When Karen Carlson was talking to her son about *sovrummets*, exactly which bedroom and what sleeping arrangements did Karen, or more to the point, Bjorn, have in mind?

'My mother thinks you are very tired from the journey. Perhaps after coffee you would prefer to go to bed? As we are only here for the weekend, it might be better to have an early start in the morning?'

Watching Henrik disappear with the suitcases while Karen made the coffee, Bjorn whispered in Anna's ear, 'It's OK. Separate rooms. That's what you wanted, wasn't it?'

'Yes,' came the faltered response. 'I'm afraid I don't feel quite ready for . . . '

'I know,' Bjorn smiled, his face full of

understanding. 'And certainly not under the same roof as my parents. Perhaps later in the year, when we can have the summer house to ourselves?'

Bjorn's question remained unanswered. Henrik was bringing in the coffee, followed by Karen with a *Prinsesstårta*: a wonderful combination of feather-light sponge and cream, completely enrobed in pale green, wafer-thin marzipan.

9

During the next forty-eight hours, Anna found herself introduced to the delights of Stockholm in winter. If the temperature outside was well below freezing, inside was quite the reverse. There it was warm and welcoming. Warm and welcoming were the same words she would later choose to describe Karen and Henrik Carlson, who despite the language difficulties, treated Anna as if she was already part of the family.

'Weren't you overwhelmed by it all?' Gavin enquired on Monday morning when they stopped for coffee break and Anna produced a *Prinsesstårta*, purchased frozen before leaving for the airport.

'I was at first, but Bjorn's parents made me so very welcome. As for the language, fortunately most of their friends knew some English and even I managed to pick up a few Swedish phrases. In the end we found ourselves using what Henrik laughingly described as *Swenglish*.'

Fudge looked up from where she was studying the Swedish newspaper, used for wrapping the now defrosted *Prinsesstårta*.

'Goodness. It all looks like double Dutch to me. All these funny letters with dots and circles on. Whatever do they mean?'

Cutting into the cake Anna explained the three extra letters in the Swedish alphabet. 'They make an *aw*, *air* and *ur* sound. At least I think they do. It's still very confusing. Also confusing was being introduced as *Bjorn's flicka*. At the time I could only think of Flicker the horse, from children's television, until I discovered *flicka* meant girlfriend.'

'Not for much longer, I think,' Beattie mused with a wry smile. 'What's Swedish for bride, Anna?'

Anna blushed, passing her a slice of marzipan-covered cake. 'I don't know.'

'Then I suggest we try and find out. We can ask Bjorn when we see him.'

'Don't you dare, Gavin, or I'll — '

'Um — it could be something connected to a *Brollops Dag*,' Fudge suggested, peering again at the newspaper, coincidentally opened at a page of numerous wedding announcements and photographs.

Seemingly ignoring the wedding feature, Gavin took an appreciative mouthful of cake. 'Wow! This is heavenly and, of course, terribly fattening for all you ladies watching your figures. What did you say it's called?'

'*Prinsesstårta*,' Anna said, hoping to divert Gavin's attention.

'How very apt,' he replied, popping a stray morsel of green marzipan into his mouth. 'A princess cake for Bjorn's princess. Come on, Anna, when are you and Bjorn going to get married? He wouldn't take you to meet his parents if he wasn't serious.'

'Well, he hasn't exactly got down on one knee and asked.'

'Maybe they don't do that in Sweden?'

Gavin fixed Fudge with a glare of mock irritation for interrupting. 'OK, if he didn't get down on one knee, what did he do instead?'

'I suppose he sort of suggested we get married — that's all.'

'That's all!' Beattie snorted. 'And what did you reply?'

'Um . . . I sort of went along with the idea.'

'Anna!' Three excited voices chorused in unison.

Stepping forward to hug her, Gavin plonked a kiss on both cheeks. 'How can you be so damned calm about all this?'

'Am I being calm? I certainly don't feel as if I am. My tummy's still full of butterflies. It was such a magical weekend and Stockholm is so very beautiful. With the Baltic frozen over and the city bathed in wintry sunlight, it

109

was as if everywhere was covered in pink sugar frosting. I still keep pinching myself, wondering if it was real.'

'Oh, it was real all right,' Beattie sniffed, retrieving her handkerchief from the sleeve of her jersey dress and blowing her nose hard. 'Haven't we got this delicious, fairy-tale cake to prove it? You know, Anna, this marzipan's such a pretty shade of green. The perfect colour for bridesmaids' dresses, I shouldn't wonder.'

★   ★   ★

Later that evening, delivering cake to one of the dressing-rooms, Anna gave an exasperated sigh. 'Not you as well, Madge. If it wasn't bad enough with Beattie and co. giving me the third degree. I only went to Sweden for the weekend.'

'And I only said — '

'No, you didn't. You practically asked me when we'd be sending out wedding invitations. I've already had Beattie suggesting a colour for the bridesmaids' dresses.'

'Really. What did she suggest?'

'The same colour as that marzipan, which if you don't hurry up and eat, is about to fall all over that velvet costume.'

Relieved to see her friend eating — at least

it meant she was quiet — Anna sat down on a dilapidated bentwood chair, her eyes drifting in the direction of Madge's swollen stomach. She was anxious to know the outcome of her recent visit to the doctor.

'Well?' she enquired, watching Madge finish the remains of sponge, marzipan and cream.

'Well, what?'

'Aha. Now who's being evasive? You know perfectly well what I'm getting at. Your appointment with the doctor. How did it go?'

Madge shrugged her shoulders, brushed a crumb of marzipan from her sweater and replied, 'All right, I suppose. And before you start nagging me, I only said that because I've never been pregnant before. I therefore haven't a clue what should be happening to me or what to expect. According to the doctor everything seems to be OK, although, there could be certain risks involved because of my age.'

'And have you discussed it with Frank?'

'Not bloody likely! He'd probably still suggest I had an abortion, like he did before. I told him what I thought of him at Christmas, remember? I want nothing more to do with that miserable bastard.'

Anna placed a comforting arm about Madge's shoulders. 'You don't really mean that. I'm sure Frank didn't mean it, either. It came as such a shock, that's all. How can you give up on ten years of a relationship, Madge? You know how much you mean to Frank.'

'Too right I do. Don't forget he also made that abundantly clear.'

Anna passed Madge a box of tissues. 'I know, but believe me, he didn't really mean what he said about the abortion. He told me it was simply his reaction to the way you chose to announce it. Even you must admit five minutes before curtain up wasn't exactly perfect timing.'

'Perhaps not,' Madge conceded, dabbing at her eyes. 'Nevertheless, nothing or no one's going to stop me from having this baby.'

'And I'm sure no one will,' Anna whispered, offering up a silent prayer.

★   ★   ★

As the weeks progressed, concern for Madge's welfare, coupled with disturbing rumours about the future of the Alexandra, made it infinitely easier for Anna to cope with Bjorn's absence.

Madge yawned sleepily and rubbed at her tired eyes. 'I'm fine, ducky. Simply fine. I'm weary that's all. Do stop worrying. By the end of next week I'll be back to my usual bouncing self.'

'Why? What's happening next week?'

'Pining away for Bjorn you've obviously forgotten: it's when I leave that dump of a place they call a theatre.'

Anna turned to look at the calendar, her face registering acute delight. 'That means Bjorn's already been away for a whole fortnight!'

'So he has,' Madge replied, placing a nourishing bowl of homemade minestrone on the table in front of her, 'so better make sure you finish this and then try some of the lasagne I've made, or there'll be nothing left of you by the time he returns.' Madge patted her bulging tummy. 'Unlike me, Anna Mason, you need fattening up. We can't have you wasting away.'

'I'm not wasting away and though I confess I've missed Bjorn dreadfully, what's upsetting me most at the moment is the threatened closure of the Alexandra. Fudge keeps bursting into tears; Gavin's in a permanent state of panic; as for Beattie — '

'What about Beattie? Come to think of it, I haven't seen her since she asked me to have the last of Ariadne's kittens.'

Finishing her soup, Anna gave a knowing smile. 'Not so much a kitten, more a miniature tiger by now. Very soon it will be almost as big as its mother. Stavros, Beattie's landlord, is tearing his hair out, at least what's left of it. Beattie says the poor old chap will be bald by next Christmas if Ariadne and the neighbouring tom keep on at this rate.'

'Poor Ariadne, I say. Why doesn't Beattie have her neutered?'

'She doesn't like the idea of taking away what's only natural.'

'Hmph! Not like someone *I* could mention.'

'Madge. That was uncalled for. Frank never suggested anything of the sort and well you know it.'

'Perhaps not,' Madge acknowledged begrudgingly, stacking the empty soup bowls together and making her way towards the kitchen. 'Mind you, I still have to say that as far as Frank and old Stavros are concerned, I'm highly relieved I'm not a cat.'

Determined to change the subject, Anna called through to where Madge was taking a bubbling lasagne from the oven. 'Have you heard about Gavin's latest madcap idea? He's suggesting Alexandra's Ragtime Band have a final fling together. Hire a cottage or something for the Easter weekend. How do you feel about that?'

114

Madge gave a cynical smile and patted her bump. 'Not me, ducky. I think my flinging days are well and truly over, don't you?'

Hurrying to Madge's assistance, insisting that she carry in the heavy Le Creuset dish, Anna continued, 'I doubt we'll be doing anything too energetic. The idea's also to make it within reasonable driving distance.'

'You're not going abroad then?'

Anna shook her head. 'I don't think anyone can afford abroad. Fudge was proposing Dorset. Her Aunt Dolly, who lives there, suggested — '

'That you all go and stay with her?'

'Good heavens, no! Can you imagine poor Aunt Dolly coping with the likes of us? Gavin, Beattie, Fudge and her brother, not to mention Felix. Even Frank said he'd go.'

'Then you can definitely count me out.'

Anna took a deep breath. For days Frank had been begging her to put in a good word for him. Maybe even suggest to Madge that she joined them on Gavin's proposed excursion. 'Madge, you've got to speak to Frank eventually. Perhaps a weekend break will help you both sort out your differences?'

'And what about the Prickly Pamela? Or does he intend to take her along too?'

'Of course he doesn't. Besides, he's already told Pamela he intends to have a weekend away — without her.'

'Big deal,' came the muffled retort through a mouthful of lasagne.

Reaching for her glass of wine, Anna took a deep gulp before adding, 'Oh well, cheers anyway, and here's to absent friends. At least you can't blame me for trying.'

Sipping at the half glass of wine that she'd allowed herself, Madge appeared lost in thought. 'What's that? Yes, Anna Mason, I'd say sometimes you can be *particularly* bloody trying. However, you're still one of the best friends I've ever had. Now, are you going to eat that lasagne or not?'

10

Early on Good Friday morning, Anna picked up her hold-all and made her way to the front door. Her initial plan had been to wait outside for Frank and the mini bus. He however, had thought otherwise.

'Best wait indoors instead,' he'd advised, when they were checking their final travel arrangements. 'I've no idea how long it will take me to fetch the others. I might get caught up in traffic. And you never know, Madge might change her mind and decide to come with us after all. If you wait outside you won't hear the phone ring.'

Poor Frank, thought Anna, studying the silent telephone. She knew only too well that despite all their pleadings, Madge had refused point blank to join them.

'Like I said, ducky, I'm staying put. Off you go and have a wonderful time in Dorset. I promise I won't even expect a postcard. Just make sure you ring me the moment you're back. I shall want to know each and every detail.'

Contemplating this recent, brief conversation, Anna failed to notice the ancient mini

117

bus, drawing to a halt outside. Startled by the sudden tooting of a horn she ran to open her front door.

'All ready and waiting,' Frank said, bending to pick up her solitary travel bag, trying to disguise his disappointment at finding her alone. 'Is this all you're taking?'

'We're only going for a couple of days. We won't need much in the way of clothes, apart from jeans and sweaters.'

'Try telling that to Felix and Gavin,' Frank chortled. 'You'd think they were doing the Grand Tour. Travelling chests, hampers, the lot.'

Amused by such a prospect, Anna glanced towards the mini bus. There was no sign of Felix or Gavin anywhere. Frank answered her unspoken question.

'Would you believe, Felix took one look at the mini bus, announced there was no way he was going to travel '*like a herd of cattle, dear boy*' and despatched Gavin to fetch the Bentley. They intend to journey to Dorset in style.'

'To be honest, I'm not surprised. I'm still reeling from the shock that Felix actually wanted to come on this trip in the first place.'

Picking up her keys, Anna was in the process of locking her front door when Frank called out, 'Don't forget your guitar.'

'Why should I take my guitar?'

'Strict instructions from Gavin, not to mention Felix, who remembered hearing you sing at Gavin's party. Felix was talking about evening entertainment while we're away, and Gavin mentioned you used to sing at a folk club.'

'It's been simply ages since I've played in public.'

'No buts,' Frank grinned, stroking his moustache. 'Orders are orders and must be obeyed, *dear girl*.'

Flashing him a smile, Anna disappeared to fetch her guitar. Dusting off the worn, black carrying case, she locked the flat and made her way to join the others.

Beattie yawned sleepily, covering her mouth with scarlet fingernails before raking them through her mass of fine wavy hair. 'I can't believe I'm doing this,' she groaned. 'I hate getting up this early in the morning. It's not fair, I'm still missing my hour.'

'She means the hour she lost when we put the clocks forward to British Summer Time,' Anna explained to her fellow, bleary eyed and bewildered travelling companions.

Eric Carlson nodded in understanding and motioned in the direction of his dozing wife. 'I think Jane would agree with you, Beattie. She always complains about losing an hour's sleep at this time of year, but look at the glorious early morning sunshine. At home in Sweden the mornings will still be very dark.'

Beattie grunted and felt for the comforting gold carton in her pocket. Prior to Anna's arrival, Frank and the others had already decreed no smoking in the bus. Deciding she didn't want to upset them so early in the morning, she made a mental note to leave the mini bus at Victoria where they were to meet up with Fudge and Steve, and have a quick ciggie. Muttering something about brother and sister travelling up on the milk train, Beattie burrowed deep into the magenta cowl collar of her sweater and closed her heavy-lidded eyes.

Meeting Frank's gaze in the rear-view mirror, Anna fixed him with a sympathetic smile. 'I've somehow come to the conclusion that we're all far more used to dealing with late nights than we are early mornings.'

'You can say that again,' he replied, pulling away from the kerb. 'Let's hope we all liven up by nightfall.'

'Anyone would think we were vampires,' Beattie mumbled from beneath the warmth of her collar. Opening first one eye and then the other, she prepared to make her exit from the bus the moment Frank pulled up outside Victoria. She'd already concluded there wouldn't be time for a whole cigarette but a few welcome puffs would certainly help her on her way.

Ten minutes later, exhaling a comforting cloud of white smoke, she watched Frank load Fudge and Steve's luggage into the van. Fudge, she noticed had already climbed in and was sitting beside Anna. Steve meanwhile, sprang jauntily in to the front passenger seat.

'Time's up, Beattie,' he called back to her. 'Blimey. You're surrounded by so much smoke out there, I mistook you for one of those old-fashioned steam trains.'

'Don't you be so cheeky,' she grinned, reluctantly grinding the heel of her shoe into what remained of the cigarette. 'Have a bit of respect for your elders.'

To Anna's acute relief the same light-hearted banter continued for most of the journey to Dorset; a sure sign that failing any unforeseen disasters, they were in for a pleasant weekend. Getting on with people was half the battle, she reflected. Luckily, none of Alexandra's Ragtime Band were really foul tempered or miserable. Temperamental perhaps, but in most instances that was usually perfectly justified. They all worked to such impossible deadlines issued by equally impossible people. Anna frowned as one such person came to mind. Gian-Carlo Andretti!

Brilliant! Dazzling! A Masterpiece! The headlines had proclaimed. What they had failed to mention, however, was that the cost of producing such epic performances had not only crippled the theatre but also was partly responsible for its current demise.

'I thought you always play to packed audiences and the productions are a sell out,' Anna's mother had insisted over the phone, when she'd been told the grave news.

'That's as maybe,' Anna had replied at the time. 'But extravagant sets and costumes have to be paid for, and parts of the theatre are literally crumbling to pieces. If you could see some of the working conditions.'

Thoughts of her own dingy working conditions, prompted Anna to think of last October, when Bjorn had discovered her alone and crying. Looking back on it now it was almost surreal: Beattie, dressed in satin and lurex had appeared out of nowhere like a fairy godmother, while Madge, sobbing her heart out and clutching a bottle of brandy, had suddenly materialized through a haze of yellow silk chiffon and scattered beading. Six months on and everything had changed. Save for a miracle, which was highly unlikely, the curtain would soon come down at the

122

Alexandra for the very last time. Beattie's nephew Tom was about to become a father; Madge was pregnant, Bjorn had . . .

'Penny for them?' a voice called softly. 'You look miles away. Thinking about Bjorn, I expect?'

Anna nodded in Beattie's direction, deciding it was far wiser to keep her thoughts to herself. Mention of either Madge or Tom at this stage of the journey seemed totally inappropriate. Their brief and very welcome mini-break had only just begun.

'Yes. You're quite right. I was thinking about Bjorn. I suppose it must have been Erik's comment about Sweden's long, dark winters. I was also wondering what he'll do once he's finished his *repetitions.*'

'His what? I thought you said he was doing his National Service?'

'He is. That's what they call it in Sweden. Ask Erik. I expect he does them too.'

Beattie shrugged her shoulders in bewilderment. As far as she was concerned the only repetitions she was familiar with were those requiring a large dose of liver salts, following an evening of over-indulgence at The George and Dragon.

★   ★   ★

Eventually passing through what she discerned to be familiar scenery, Fudge cried out, 'Ooh, we must be nearly there. That was Tolpuddle.'

Frank glanced quickly into his rear-view mirror. 'You mean Tolpuddle of Tolpuddle Martyrs fame?'

'That's right,' Steve replied, anxious to impress. 'Did you know those poor devils were sentenced to seven years' transportation, just because they formed a union branch and swore one simple oath.'

'What was so wrong with that? We have a union in the theatre.'

Jane Carlson stirred sleepily by her husband's side. 'That's because way back in 1834 it was illegal.'

While Erik pondered British history of almost 140 years ago, Frank concentrated on the present. Carefully turning the mini bus into the tree-lined approach to Pinetrees Park, he scanned the area for any sign of the others. Brian and Trevor, two of the stagehands who, along with their wives, were at that very moment walking from the reception office, called and waved in greeting. In their hands they carried keys, maps and the site information booklet.

'At least they've arrived safely,' Beattie said, glad to stretch her legs. 'What about Felix and Gavin? Any sign of them, Frank?'

Frank shook his head. 'Not arrived yet by the looks of it. You certainly couldn't miss a Bentley amongst that little lot.'

Anna, Fudge and Beattie glanced ahead to a varied assortment of less than luxurious, family-sized motor cars, all parked side by side in the allotted bays.

'Hmm. And from what little I know of Felix, I bet he's made Gavin stop at a hotel for proper coffee and those crescent thingies,' Steve suggested with a grin. 'I can't imagine Felix le Sage stopping off at a roadside café for a mug of tea and a fry up.'

'There was nothing wrong with the one we stopped at,' Fudge reminded him, her thoughts on the hearty breakfast she'd polished off en route.

'I never said there was. I merely said I didn't think it was Felix's cup of tea.'

At the mention of tea, Frank's face brightened. 'Speaking of which, I'm gasping for a cuppa. Driving's thirsty work you know. Can I suggest we check in, collect our keys and then sort out the sleeping arrangements?'

Much to Anna's relief, the sleeping arrangements Frank had mentioned weren't half the problem she had been dreading. As an aside she'd already whispered to Frank, 'I don't mind sharing a room with Fudge, but I couldn't possibly share with Beattie. My lungs would never cope with the smoke.'

Following Brian and Trevor, who already knew the way to the trio of log cabins nestling in the trees, the group set off to examine their accommodation. Beattie, Fudge and Anna were to share a two-bedroom cabin with twin beds and bunks, Erik and Jane agreed to the double bedroom in a cabin they were to share with Frank and Steve — again with bunk beds, plus a small single bedroom, and Brian and Trevor, with their wives Mandy and Julie, opted for the third cabin with one double bedroom, one twin and a boxroom-sized single.

Leaving Brian and Trevor to toss for the double bed, Anna volunteered to return to her own cabin to make tea or coffee for those who required it.

'I wonder who'll win,' Fudge said, passing her a jar of Nescafé.

'I shouldn't think it matters,' Beattie replied. 'All the others have to do is push two single beds together. Take it from me two in a single bed isn't much fun. Well, it isn't unless — '

Sensing Beattie was about to go into lurid details about one of her ex-husbands, Anna swiftly changed the subject: Fudge's cheeks were already a delicate shade of pink.

'Fudge,' she said hurriedly, 'do you think you could find the milk and tea bags?'

Thinking of tea, Beattie was immediately reminded of the nicotine she usually liked to go with it. 'I'll — er — just pop out for a breath of fresh air, then I'll come and give you a hand. Is that OK?'

Anna shook her head in dismay, watching Beattie totter out on to the wooden veranda, the familiar gold packet already open. 'Fresh air? I doubt if Beattie's lungs even know what that is. I do wish she'd give up smoking — or at least cut down.'

'Perhaps she will when the baby is born. Tom and Lucy won't want Beattie smoking near their baby, will they?'

'Probably not,' Anna replied, opening the carton of milk. 'Although, if my memory serves me correctly, Tom has a film assignment coming up. I can't see Beattie wanting to visit Lucy — not while Tom's away.'

Spooning coffee into cups, Anna recalled the numerous photos she'd now seen of Tom. Tall and good-looking, he certainly was a striking young man. Although, on reflection, perhaps not quite as tall or as fair as Bjorn. Tom's tawny-gold hair was long and wavy, whereas Bjorn's was long and straight, like . . . the colour of sun-ripened corn, with the texture of silk, she reminded herself, her unfocused gaze drifting from the window.

It was another hour and a half before Felix's Bentley, driven by Gavin, nosed and purred its way along the twisting woodland road to the cabins.

'Hail fellows, well met,' Felix called jovially, emerging from the car. 'I trust our little troupe has arrived safely and in one piece?'

'We certainly have,' Steve called, sprinting to the car to help Gavin with Felix's luggage. 'Most of us have already unpacked, had our elevenses, walked around the plantation and . . . Blimey!' Steve stopped short, examining the vast quantity of cases and boxes still piled high in the boot.

'Whatever is it, dear boy?'

'This little lot for a start, Felix. Lord knows where you're going to put it. There's not much room in those single bedrooms.'

Felix's bushy grey eyebrows shot skywards. 'Single bedrooms! I can't possibly sleep in a single bed. Just look at the size of me. Can you imagine *me* sleeping in a single bed?'

'Probably not.' Steve shrugged, suppressing a smile, because not only had Felix got the most amazing voice, but also he had the build — or should that be stomach? — to go with it. 'Then neither can I see you in a bunk bed, Felix. It's only bunks and singles left, I'm afraid. Frank and I are in bunk beds. They're not really that bad if you — '

Felix mopped his brow with a red spotted handkerchief. 'Bunk beds. Dear God! It's getting worse. I don't believe what I've just heard. Gavin my boy, what shall we . . . ?'

Hearing the commotion, Beattie emerged from her cabin and called down to the unloading bay. 'You should have got here earlier, Felix, then you could have had first pick. It's the married ones who have the larger double rooms. Fudge, Anna and myself are in this cabin: We're singles and bunk beds. Erik and Jane, Frank and Steve, are across the way and Brian and Mandy, Trevor and Julie are in the cabin right behind us.'

Felix frowned hard and stroked his goatee beard, making a mental note of the various cabins and their occupants. 'No matter. No matter,' he sighed briskly, dismissing his audience with a flourish of spotted silk and tucking the handkerchief back into the top pocket of his blazer, then commanded politely, 'Gavin, dear boy. Put all the luggage back into the boot immediately and drive me to reception.'

'You don't mean you're going home?' Steve gasped. 'You can't come all this way, only to leave the minute you get here?'

Leaving the bewildered Steve to help Gavin

reload the car, Felix eased his bulky frame back into the rear passenger seat and gave a regal wave. Gavin then assumed the role of chauffeur once more and switched on the ignition.

'Of course I'm not going,' Felix boomed, winding down the window. 'I've been looking forward to this trip for weeks. However, as I have absolutely no intention of sleeping in either a single or a bunk bed, I simply intend to see what the management of this quaint establishment has to offer this poor, weary traveller.'

'Poor, weary traveller indeed,' Steve snorted, watching the Bentley disappear from view. 'Poor, you most definitely are not, Felix. And, if travelling like that makes you weary, next time you set off on one of your journeys, I would happily come along for the ride.'

11

Less than twenty minutes later the silver-blue Bently returned. Still with Gavin at the wheel it made no attempt to stop. Instead, it wound its way along the woodland road, bordered on either side by hazel, beech and fir trees.

'I wonder where they're going?' Steve puzzled.

Screwing up her eyes against the early spring sunlight, Beattie peered over the rail to follow the car's progress. 'Hmm, it's definitely not stopping at Brian and Trevor's cabin so what's the betting Felix has put on another star performance. In case you hadn't noticed, Steve, our Felix has a wonderful way with words, aided and abetted by that sonorous voice of his. He's also a complete charmer, in the nicest possible way of course. There's not an ounce of malice in him, unlike some I could mention at the theatre.'

'Now then, Beattie,' Frank scolded. 'No talk of the Alexandra this weekend. We're here to enjoy ourselves. Remember?'

Beattie nodded and lit another cigarette, a thin curl of smoke emitting from her nostrils. 'Sorry. I was forgetting. Anyway, as I was saying, Felix has probably procured the key to the honeymoon suite — or whatever else it's called, when it comes to log cabins in the woods. He was looking very pleased with himself.'

Honeymoon suites as such did not exist at Pinetrees Park, but the manager had recognized Felix immediately. It hadn't taken long therefore to secure the key to the very best cabin available. One with three large bedrooms, two double and one twin, a family-sized kitchen-diner, spacious and comfortable lounge and even a corner bath and shower. Small wonder Felix had looked like the cat that got the cream. It was for this reason he later despatched Gavin to purchase cream of the local, clotted kind and also to a family bakers for home-made scones and pastries.

'Felix has invited you all to tea,' Gavin called, slowing down and lowering the window of the Bentley on his return.

Steve blew out his cheeks. 'Tea? We've only just had lunch.'

'Tea at four, dear boy,' Gavin announced with a wink, 'And don't forget to tell the others. We're in the last cabin at the end of the track by the way. You can't miss it.'

'Can't miss it is right,' Frank said, as the weary group returning from an attempt to walk off their lunch, trudged the shady, leaf-strewn track to the cabin. 'Looks like you were right, Beattie; that must have been one hell of a performance Felix put on. Take a look at the size of that cabin.'

Beattie chuckled and made as if to speak but could only manage a croaky wheeze. Totally unused to walking such long distances, she stopped and turned to look around at the scenery. Concerned, Anna ran back towards her.

'Are you all right, Beattie?'

'Yes,' came the gasped reply. 'I'm OK. I was simply admiring the view. Fudge's Aunt Dolly did us proud by finding this place. As you know, I've never been what you'd call a country girl. The view is truly amazing, isn't it?'

Anna nodded, unconvinced that her companion had stopped merely to admire the scenery. Linking arms, she helped her on her way, only to stop moments later when Beattie paused for breath once more. 'I expect Bjorn must be used to this sort of panorama. My Swedish sailor friend used to say Sweden is full of forests and lakes.'

'It certainly appeared to be, but as I only went for a weekend we didn't venture far. Bjorn's parents suggested going to the family's summer house at Trosa when the weather gets warmer and the days longer. It looked very beautiful from the photos.'

'What do you mean by summer house? A log cabin like these?'

'Hardly a cabin, more like a proper house with a Dutch barn-style roof. It also has its own mooring on the edge of a lake. Bjorn's father has a small motor boat.'

'Really? Sounds an ideal setting for a honeymoon then.'

Ignoring yet another of Beattie's leading questions, Anna quickened her pace with the excuse they didn't want to be late for tea. The last to arrive, they found Felix giving a guided tour of the cabin. Gavin mean-while, busied himself in the kitchen.

'You jammy devils!' Steve teased, watching Gavin closely. 'How on earth did Felix manage it? Here's you with all this space when Frank and I are in bunk beds.'

Gavin looked up from where he was pouring milk into a jug. 'I suppose we do have plenty of space. Felix has the double bedroom he wanted and I'm in the twin. You could share with me of course . . . that's if you wanted to. Would you like me to ask?'

Steve hesitated for a moment and shook his head. 'Better not, eh? Felix doesn't know me like he does you.'

'That wouldn't bother Felix,' Gavin said,

arranging the tea tray. 'Anyway, let me know if you change your mind. In the meantime can you help me find the sugar? It should be over there in that box of groceries we brought with us.'

Moving assorted Fortnum & Mason delicacies to one side, Steve picked up a bag of granulated, only to see Gavin shake his head. 'I thought you asked for sugar?'

'I did, but that's for Felix's breakfast cereal. Sorry, I should have stressed sugar cubes. He prefers those in his tea.'

'What's the difference? Sugar is sugar, isn't it? It all tastes the same — sweet. Or does it taste different from Fortnums?'

'It's the amount that's different.'

'Jesus! You don't mean Felix weighs out his sugar cubes?'

''Course not,' Gavin grinned. 'He simply likes the same amount in each cup.'

Steve shook his head in disbelief. 'So . . . is Felix fussy about everything?'

'Not fussy, simply rather particular. He's always adhered to certain standards and likes everything to be just right.'

Spying two broken sugar lumps, that he assumed wouldn't be just right in meeting Felix's requirements, Steve popped one into his mouth. Crushing the tiny grains of sweetness with his tongue, he was conscious of Gavin watching him intently. 'Want the other one?' he asked, extending his hand in Gavin's direction.

'No thanks. It's bad for the teeth.'

'In that case I'd better have that one as well.' Steve gave a wicked smile, followed by loud, deliberate crunching. 'As you can see . . . I believe in living dangerously.'

For what seemed like minutes but in fact was only seconds, the two young men studied each other before Gavin picked up the tray and murmured softly, 'Best not keep the others waiting for their tea. Don't forget what I said about sharing the room.'

With the rest of the group tucking into freshly baked scones, clotted cream and finest strawberry conserve, Steve regarded Felix from the corner of his eye. Just as Gavin had described, he lowered two sugar cubes into his tea and stirring the cup carefully without grinding the bottom, as Steve's father did much to his mother's annoyance, he lifted the cup to his mouth, the little finger of his right hand delicately crooked.

'You're not eating, dear thing,' Felix called, spying Steve's empty plate. 'Someone please pass the scones. The poor boy looks half starved.'

'It's not because he doesn't eat,' Fudge broke in boldly. 'Mum's always saying he eats like a horse.'

136

'Hence the sugar lumps then?' Gavin whispered as an aside.

Acknowledging this comment with a wry smile, Steve reached for a scone and piling it high with both conserve and cream, tucked in eagerly.

'There's nothing wrong with a healthy appetite,' Felix said, patting his own generous stomach. 'As you know I adore my food and simply abhor diets. Now, my dears, do tell me what you all plan to do for the rest of your stay. Gavin's already suggested — because there's so much of local interest to keep us all amused — that we each do our own thing during the daytime and get together in the evenings. What do you think?'

'Sounds good to me,' Frank replied, accompanied by a buzz of murmured approval from the others.

'And, of course, you are all more than welcome to come back here to my humble abode in the evenings,' Felix continued, indicating the spacious lounge with its comfortable settees and cosy log-effect gas fire. 'Perhaps the girls would like to cook and we boys can offer to clear up after we've eaten?'

'Hang on a minute!' Beattie protested, practically choking on her scone. 'I thought we'd come here for a rest from daily chores.

This particular girl has absolutely no intention of doing any cooking in the evenings *and* I certainly wouldn't expect the others to cook for me, either. Surely, there must be plenty of eating places in the vicinity?'

'Um — quite right. Quite right. I stand corrected and humbly apologize to the fairer sex. I confess I'm still coming to terms with all this women's liberation business, not to mention the burning of — er — brassieres in public places.'

'Don't worry, Felix,' Beattie reassured. 'I promise we girls won't be burning any bras this weekend.'

⋆ ⋆ ⋆

The following morning, Frank joined the assembled members of the Alexandra as they prepared to leave for their assorted activities. He nodded in Brian and Trevor's direction. 'Where's everyone going then, or haven't they decided yet?'

Brian looked up from beneath the bonnet of his car and began wiping the dipstick on an oily rag. 'Felix and Gavin are going into Dorchester to hunt for antiques, and Eric and Jane are planning to go to Tolpuddle and Thomas Hardy's cottage at Higher Bockhampton. As for us, it looks as if Trevor and I

138

have drawn the short straw. Mandy and Julie want to go shopping in Weymouth.'

'There's nothing wrong with Weymouth,' Frank said, 'It's a lovely place.'

'I know it is,' Brian agreed, 'But why is it women complain about shopping when they're at home, yet the minute they're away it's the first thing they want to do?'

'That's cos it's a different kind of shopping,' Mandy enlightened him.

'How can shopping be different?'

Trevor opened his jacket pocket, tapped his wallet and smiled ruefully in Brian's direction. 'Shopping today doesn't mean Tesco's and Sainsbury's, it means clothes, shoes and even more holiday souvenirs.'

Grim faced, Brian was reminded of home as he slammed the bonnet shut. More souvenirs? They already had more than enough of those to start their own holiday shop. Curious to know what the rest of the gang were doing he called across to Frank. 'What about you, Frank, fancy coming with us?'

'No, he doesn't,' Anna said, emerging from her cabin. 'Frank's going for a bracing walk from Lulworth Cove to Durdle Dore, with me, Steve, Fudge and Beattie.'

'Lucky blighters,' Brian hissed.

Already anticipating the retail delights of

Weymouth, Mandy climbed into the car and wound down her window. 'While you're enjoying your walk, Frank, I'll try and find us all something nice to take to Felix's this evening.'

'Then I suggest you start with a stretcher.'

'Why a stretcher?' Mandy puzzled, frowning in her husband's direction. 'I was thinking of some nice clotted cream fudge.'

'Because I reckon poor old Beattie's going to need it. Can you really see her walking from Durdle Dore to Lulworth Cove?'

'That's not very far, Brian.'

'Exactly, and not very far will just about finish Beattie off. Didn't you see her struggling up to Felix's cabin yesterday afternoon? She could barely get her breath. That's why Anna stopped and waited for her.'

'Oh dear. No I didn't. Do you think we should offer to take Beattie along with us instead?'

With a murmured. 'No way!' Brian switched on the ignition and drove off in a cloud of smoke.

An hour and a half later, Frank helped Beattie back into the mini bus.

'I can stay with you if you like, Beattie. Keep you company and — '

'Definitely not,' she wheezed. 'Anna and Fudge have already offered to do that. Like I

140

said, I shall be perfectly happy sitting here with the paper and the crossword.'

'If you're really sure?'

'Positive, thanks, so why not go and finish your walk with Steve and the girls? You never know, Anna might even be able to help you with Madge.'

Frank hesitated, fixing Beattie with an air of bewilderment. 'What do you mean?'

'Isn't it obvious as it's Anna who knows her best? Why not try and work out what Madge intends to do, or should that be what the pair of you intend to do, once the baby's born? Surely you'll want to do something?'

'Christ, Beattie. Of course I do. Believe it or not, I do love Madge.'

Unzipping her anorak, Beattie delved into her pocket. 'So where's the problem?'

'The problem, in case you've forgotten, is Pamela. For a start she's my wife, although in name only. Secondly, she refuses to give me a divorce, and thirdly, she keeps threatening to kill herself every time I say I'm leaving.'

Beattie gave a laconic smile. 'Great. Then dare I suggest you buy her a bottle of paracetamol as a leaving present and go?'

'I couldn't possibly do that. What if she tried to — '

'Take my word for it, Frank. She won't.'

'How can you be so sure?'

'Because I've known lots of Pamelas in my time. Those that scream and shout about it don't kill themselves. It's the quiet ones you have to watch. Those who keep their thoughts to themselves. People like Anna.'

'You're not suggesting Anna would kill herself if Bjorn didn't come back?'

''Course not, stupid. Honestly, you men. I was merely giving you an example of two very different people: Pamela, who threatens and shouts, and Anna, who doesn't.'

Frank fixed Beattie with a vacant stare. Somehow he had the distinct feeling he was getting out of his depth. Sensing his confusion Beattie gave him a gentle shove. 'Go on. Go and enjoy the rest of the walk with the others. Promise me one thing, however, sometime this weekend you will give serious thought to what I've just said.'

Bending down, Frank placed a tartan rug across Beattie's knees before kissing her fondly on the cheek. She looked up, bewildered by his unexpected gesture of affection. 'What was that for?'

'That was for Beattie Norman's words of wisdom. I bet no one would ever dream of giving you a bottle of paracetamol as a leaving present.'

Beattie swallowed hard, watching Frank hurry to where the others were waiting.

'Hmph! My words of wisdom,' she sighed, choking back tears, when he turned to wave at her. 'What a joke. If only Tom had listened to them as carefully as Frank. Now, if Lucy ever threatened to kill herself, I'd offer to buy her a whole bucketful of pills.'

Some time later, still alone within the confines of the mini bus and her conscience getting the better of her, Beattie shook her head sadly and retracted her last statement. Peering into the depths of her handbag, she took out the postcard she'd bought early that morning at reception and began writing. *Dear Tom and Lucy, I hope you're both keeping well . . .*

12

Resplendent in burgundy velvet smoking jacket, Felix greeted everyone warmly on Saturday night. Basking in the luxury of his spacious cabin, they took great pleasure in describing their day's activities and assorted delightful eating places discovered along the way. When Felix extended the same invitation for Sunday evening, Beattie's face registered concern.

'Don't look so alarmed,' Felix reassured, grey eyes twinkling in her direction. 'No one has to cook. I've arranged door-to-door delivery from a local restaurant.'

There was a gentle hum of approving voices before Felix continued, 'However, if you'd care to bring a bottle of something by way of liquid refreshment, as well as your good selves of course, that would indeed be most welcome.'

Stepping forward, Gavin whispered something in Felix's ear. 'What's that, my boy? Oh, yes. I was quite forgetting. Anna dear, you are to bring your guitar. I want you to sing and play for us all.'

Momentarily filled with panic, Anna looked

144

about her. As she'd already explained to Frank, apart from Gavin's party it had been ages since she'd sung in public.

'Don't worry,' Frank said, reaching into his pocket, 'You see, it won't be a solo performance. I remembered to bring my mouth organ and — '

'Fudge'll tell you I'm a dab hand with the comb and paper,' Steve chirped in.

Felix rubbed his together hands with glee. 'Wonderful! Wonderful! We already have a trio and the evening will be simply perfect for our little farewell party.'

★ ★ ★

'Perfect for some but not necessarily for others,' Beattie said, twenty-four hours later, once the remnants of a delicious meal had been cleared away.

Mellowed by good food and wine, an idyllic setting and perfect company, Felix's guests were relaxing on assorted sofas and chairs when Anna looked up, strangely perplexed. 'Sorry, Beattie. I didn't quite catch that. What did you say?'

'I was merely reminded of Felix's remark about this evening being perfect.'

'Are you saying you didn't enjoy dinner? Not even those wonderful canapés, Gavin concocted before we'd even sat down?'

Beattie smiled appreciatively. 'Oh, I enjoyed those all right. I reckon Felix must have brought half of Fortnums with him in that hamper. Actually, it's Fudge I was thinking of. She's really been knocking back the drink; even Steve's had words with her.'

'Yes, I had noticed. But she's still young so probably not used to it, especially the champagne and liqueurs.' Anna cast an anxious eye in Fudge's direction, where Mandy was now passing round a huge box of clotted cream fudge.

'Hmm. Rather you than me, Anna. You're the one sharing a room with her. Not wishing to spoil things, I suggest you find her a bowl or a bucket before you go to bed.'

Preferring not to think of such things, Anna was almost relieved when Felix beckoned and pointed to her guitar. 'Maestro, if you please,' he commanded with a gracious smile.

Accompanied by Frank and Steve, Anna soon forgot all about Fudge. To loud applause, constant boisterous encouragement and much stamping of feet, she happily worked her way through her repertoire of songs, until at length she begged for a break.

'Your turn now,' she said jokingly to Felix, passing him the guitar. 'I'm exhausted and it's getting late — or hadn't you noticed?'

146

Laying down the guitar, Felix looked at his watch. 'So it is, but as this is our last night together, we ought to make the most of it. You can't desert us just yet, Anna.'

'I've sung and played almost everything I know.'

'Not quite,' Gavin corrected, passing her a glass of wine. 'You still haven't played my personal favourite. The one you sang at my party.'

'That's right, you haven't,' Steve repeated. 'You know — the one about moving through the fair, or at least something like that.'

'All right, I give in, but first I need a breath of fresh air. Then, if you don't mind Gavin, I'd rather have coffee, not wine. I'd prefer to go home tomorrow with a clear head.'

'Unlike Fudge,' Beattie said tersely. 'If you ask me she's looking distinctly green about the gills.'

Deciding that Anna was probably right, coffee would be the safer option all round, Gavin set off for the kitchen, closely followed by Steve.

Once outside in the chill of the April night, Anna regretted leaving her sweater behind in the cabin. Shivering, she rubbed vigorously at her bare arms with her hands and gazed about her. Overhead the clear night sky was pierced with stars and apart from the gentle murmur of voices inside the cabin and the solitary banging of a distant car door, everywhere was still and silent. With distorted shadows filling the woods on either side, punctuated here and there by solitary rectangles of light, it was a brief reminder not only of just how far the cabins were scattered at Pinetrees Park but also of the few people still awake. Fond memories of myriad other twinkling lights on the journey from Arlanda to Djursholm, sent Anna's thoughts winging away to Bjorn.

I wonder where you are tonight, my dearest? Certainly not with the army, she thought sadly, because only days before Bjorn had written to say his *repetitions* were now completed. She frowned in the darkness, although Eric had mentioned hearing from Bjorn, she still had the distinct feeling that he was keeping something from her. During dinner, when Beattie had also enquired as to Bjorn's whereabouts, hadn't Eric been extremely cagey about what his cousin was planning to do next? Biting her lip hard, Anna forced all manner of thoughts from her mind. It was utterly unbearable to think of not ever seeing Bjorn again. What if he doesn't come back? she asked herself. What if he's changed his mind about me, or even met up with an old girl-friend? Wouldn't he let me know?

'Anna.' A voice called in the darkness, causing her to start with alarm until she realized it was only Frank. Seconds later the veranda was flooded with light from the open doorway. 'Your audience awaits,' he chuckled. 'They've all had enough of Felix's recitations — wonderful though they are — and I've certainly had enough of trying to teach Steve how to play the mouth organ.'

'What's that?' a cheeky voice called, before reminding Frank to leave the door open, because the room had become incredibly hot and stuffy.

'I suggest you stick to the comb and paper, Steve,' Frank replied. 'You'll never learn how to play until you master the difference between the suck and blow technique.'

Doing her best to ignore the saucy comments from Brian and Trevor concerning Frank's aptly described harmonica technique, Anna sat down on a stool. 'I do hope you're not expecting the complete Anna Mason repertoire again.'

'Not this time,' Gavin reassured, placing the guitar on her lap. 'Like the rest of us, I can see that you're tired. If you'll just sing 'Where Have All the Flowers Gone' and 'She Moved Through The Fair', that will be a perfect ending to our evening.'

Having sung and played the first song, Anna was halfway through the second, when she discerned movement in the open doorway. 'Bjorn!' she gasped, open-mouthed. 'What are you doing here? I thought — '

'I came to join the party. But I think I am a little late,' he replied, studying a row of surprised, smiling faces and numerous empty bottles and glasses. 'First my plane was delayed, then I had difficulty finding a taxi. Trying to locate this cabin also wasn't easy.'

'H-how did you know we were here?'

'Anna!' Beattie scolded. 'I would assume from the state of him, poor Bjorn's not long arrived from Sweden. As he's obviously finished his *repetitions* thingy, or whatever else it is they call it over there, will you please let him come in? Must he spend all night in the doorway while you interrogate him?'

'What? Oh, I'm so sorry.' Feeling a deep flush of colour flood her cheeks, Anna moved quickly towards the door, to where Bjorn put down his travel bag, took her in his arms and kissed her tenderly.

'Bravo my boy! Encore.' Felix beamed, extending a welcoming hand in Bjorn's direction. 'That's what I call a fitting finale to a splendid weekend.'

'Not quite, because I've a horrid feeling . . . ' Beattie cried, grabbing hold of Fudge and rushing her to the door, 'that Fudge is going to be sick!'

An hour later, Anna gave Fudge's blouse a final rinse in the hand basin and watched the water disappear down the plug hole. Wishing it wasn't quite so loud as it gurgled noisily away, she realized it no longer mattered. Fudge was already fast asleep, with a bowl placed strategically by her bedside.

'Poor kid,' Beattie condoled, closing the bedroom door on the sleeping victim. 'She's going to feel absolutely dreadful in the morning.'

'In the morning? It's already morning. Do you realize it's gone half past one?'

'Then no wonder I feel absolutely shattered,' Beattie yawned, before clamping a hand over her gaping mouth. 'Sorry. We don't want to wake her, do we?'

'There's little danger of that. She's dead to the world.'

'Would you mind very much if I turned in, too?'

'Of course not. You go ahead while I hang Fudge's blouse out on the veranda. With luck it should be dry by morning. At least it will smell a great deal fresher.'

'Good idea,' Beattie called softly, heading

for her bedroom. 'And if you don't fancy sleeping in the same room as Fudge, there's always the top bunk in my room.'

Anna gave an involuntary shudder, until that moment she hadn't given much thought to sleep. In truth she fancied neither option. Beattie, she had discovered on Friday night, snored excessively and as for sleeping in a room where someone had been sick . . . Choosing to shut such things from her mind, she wrung the excess water from Fudge's blouse and emerged once more into the welcome chill of the April night. To her surprise she found she was not alone. 'Bjorn! How long have you been out here?'

'About five minutes. I went back to Felix's for a shower, then thought I ought to make sure you were all OK.'

'Everything's under control now, thank you. Although, Fudge was rather ill, poor thing. She and Beattie are now sleeping like babies. As for me, I'm still recovering from the shock of seeing you here.'

'I'm sorry, I should have warned you. It was Eric's idea to surprise you. He told me about this trip and thought it would be nice if we could spend some time together.'

Anna gave a contented sigh when Bjorn drew her into his embrace. 'It's a truly wonderful surprise but didn't Erik tell you that we go home tomorrow — or should I say today? as it's almost two in the morning.'

'Then you must go to bed too, you look exhausted.'

Anna paused, reluctant to go back to the cabin and its sleeping occupants. 'Forgive me, Bjorn, but having had to see to Fudge, I've not given it a thought until now. What about you? Where are you sleeping tonight?'

'There's no need to apologize. You're tired and have had more than enough to think about. Felix has already offered me a bedroom in his cabin. It's extremely comfortable and very grand. It is also much bigger than yours, I think?'

'You think, correctly,' Anna teased. 'There's also quite a story behind Felix and that cabin, but as you also look exhausted, I won't bore you with details now. By the way, how long have you been travelling and when did you leave Stockholm? Oh, and how were the *repetitions* and are your parents well?'

Cupping her face in his hands, Bjorn raised a bemused eyebrow and studied her expectantly. 'So many questions, Anna. Perhaps if you were not quite so tired and we went for a walk . . . I could tell you.'

'Why not?' she sighed, 'It's such a beautiful night.'

As Bjorn talked and Anna listened, neither

of them realized they were walking in the direction of Felix's cabin. When at last Anna discovered where they were, she smiled to herself and murmured quietly, 'Shouldn't it be the other way round? Isn't it usually the gentleman who walks the lady home? It appears I've walked you home instead.'

In the moonlight Bjorn's face broke into a broad grin. 'So you have. Which means we should now turn around so I can walk you back to your cabin . . . or you could perhaps stay here with me instead? There is a double bed.'

Anna halted, aware of her heart pounding in her breast and the butterflies on overtime in her stomach. The last time she'd seen Bjorn she'd known that if their relationship was to continue, it was inevitable they would sleep together. It was after all what she wanted, she'd told herself on more than one occasion. Yet, she also wanted that first time to be special. Somewhere private, where they would be completely alone.

'Anna?' Bjorn questioned softly.

'I was thinking about Felix and Gavin. W-what if they're still awake?'

'I can assure you that they're not. When I left they were both sleeping. What was it you said about Fudge and Beattie, like babies?'

Momentarily glancing down the track in

the direction of her own cabin, Anna turned and followed Bjorn into his, where in the darkness, suppressing giggles and stumbling past assorted obstacles, they eventually found their way in to the bedroom.

'This bedroom's huge, compared to the one I've been sharing with Fudge,' Anna whispered, once Bjorn located the switch to the bedside lamp.

Bjorn however, did not reply. Instead, he was regarding Anna's clothes. Seeing she was wearing a simple cotton skirt, blouse and sweater, he turned and rummaged through his travel bag. 'Here,' he said, holding something in his hand. 'You'd better take this. As you already know, the bathroom is next door.'

Moments later and glad that Bjorn was so tall, Anna pulled the khaki coloured T-shirt over her head and returned to the bedroom where he was waiting. He grinned, seeing the T-shirt reach almost to her knees and holding back the covers, watched her shiver and slip hurriedly in beside him.

'Anna, you're freezing,' he gasped, her icy feet, brushing against his legs.

'I know and I'm sorry, I've always suffered with cold feet. When I was at boarding-school, Granny used to knit me bedsocks to keep my feet warm.'

With the coldness of her feet contrasted by the warmth of his smile, Bjorn turned to switch off the lamp. 'I could offer you a pair of my army socks,' he said huskily, 'but perhaps there are other ways of keeping you warm instead?'

Snuggled against his tightly muscled chest, Anna suppressed a yawn, all that walking and fresh air was suddenly catching up with her. Bjorn, too, felt his eyelids beginning to close and, stroking her hair, was reminded of the previous month's gruelling *repetitions*. Added to which there was also the long day spent travelling. Perhaps making love together for the very first time, wasn't such a good idea after all . . .

13

Despite only a few hours' sleep, Anna woke early. Listening to the dawn chorus she glanced towards the window. Only then did she realize she was in a different cabin. She was also sleeping in a double bed and she wasn't alone! Turning to look at Bjorn, whom she assumed to be still asleep, she resisted the urge to smooth down wayward spikes of blond hair and edged cautiously towards the side of the bed. Convinced no one else was awake, she hoped to get up, dress and return to her cabin, all without being missed.

'Surely you're not leaving me?' came a husky voice by her side.

'You're awake. I — er — thought I ought to get back, before Fudge and Beattie discover I'm not there . . . or people realize that we've spent the night together.'

'Does it matter if they do?'

'No, I suppose not. We've nothing to be ashamed of, have we?'

Bjorn fixed her with one of his lopsided smiles and, reaching for her hand, drew her gently back into bed. 'I don't think you're even capable of doing anything to be ashamed of, Anna. Tell me, how were the feet? Last night all I can remember is offering you a pair of my army socks to keep your feet warm. Then I think we both fell asleep.'

Dismissing thoughts of what might have happened, had they both not been so tired, a less than romantic conversation about cold feet, knitted bedsocks and army life, soon gave way to thoughts of breakfast. Reluctant to leave, Anna nevertheless decided it was probably better to return to her own cabin, if only to check on Fudge.

'I'll be back as soon as I've showered and packed,' she said in a hushed voice, opening the cabin door. 'There should be time for me to show you around Pinetrees Park. Felix has also suggested that we take a look at Salisbury Plain before lunch.'

'Salisbury Plane? What sort of aircraft is that? The Swedish airforce has Saabs.'

A smile played on Anna's lips. 'Actually, it's not that kind of plane. It's the site of Stonehenge, an ancient monument where the Druids met for the summer solstice.'

Left on his own and still half asleep, Bjorn puzzled the mystery of Stonehenge. He was familiar with the summer solstice, they celebrated something similar in Sweden. But what on earth were Druids?

Much to her relief, Anna discovered Beattie

and Fudge were still fast asleep. Beattie was snoring loudly and Fudge had barely moved. With trepidation, Anna peered into the bowl by Fudge's bedside. It remained empty. Thank goodness for that, she thought, tiptoeing to the wardrobe where she retrieved her hold-all and deftly packed everything she no longer needed. Returning from the shower she discovered Fudge, clutching at her head in an attempt to shield her eyes against dazzling, morning sunlight.

'Ugh! I feel awful. What's that bowl doing there?'

'Beattie suggested I left it for you last night, after we brought you back from Felix's and put you to bed. You were sick, remember?'

Fudge shook her head and groaned. 'Was I? Oh dear, how embarrassing. I'm sorry, Anna. I expect it was that enormous box of fudge Mandy bought in Weymouth.'

'Mmm. I expect it was,' Anna said, feigning agreement. 'Clotted cream fudge can be very sickly at times and the meal Felix ordered for us was also extremely rich. Anyway, as I washed your blouse and hung it out on the veranda, it should be dry by now. I'll fetch it for you if you like.'

Seeing Anna return with her blouse, Fudge remarked in all innocence, 'You must have got up really early. You're already packed.

159

Though why have you made your bed? The notice on the door says we're requested to strip the beds before we leave, and to place the linen in the bags provided.'

'So it does,' Anna replied, flustered, reminded of not only where she'd slept but also with whom. 'How silly of me. I'll do it now, yours too if you like. The bathroom is free and as Beattie's still asleep — '

'She isn't anymore,' came a throaty voice. 'Although, if you do want the bathroom first, that's fine by me, Fudge. I can't possibly face the thought of a bathroom mirror until I've had a cigarette and a cup of coffee.'

Seeing Beattie frown in her direction, Anna followed her gaze to the neatly made bed. With a nervous flourish she pulled at sheets and pillowcases, bundled them into a laundry bag and hurried away to the kitchen. 'I'll put the kettle on,' she called.

★   ★   ★

Reaching Salisbury Plain the party split up and set off in small groups, each to examine Stonehenge. Erik, Jane, Bjorn and Anna were the first to reach the double circle of stone where, as if by some unspoken command, all four came to a halt at precisely the same moment. They gazed awe-struck at the towering monument. Waiting for the others to catch them up and reminded of some ancient Viking megaliths she'd once seen in Sweden, Jane took the opportunity to explain to Erik and Bjorn Stonehenge's ancient history and the significance of the Heel Stone, over which the sun rose on midsummer morning.

'We have nothing to compare with this,' Bjorn began. 'Although the Runsten or Viking stones at Rostagen are quite impressive.'

'Ah, but don't forget we Swedes have some really big ones at — '

'What's that, boasting again, Erik?' Brian teased, coming alongside. 'I don't know, you foreigners. You ought to be ashamed of yourselves. Can't think why we ever let you Vikings into the country. When I think of all that R and P.'

'R and B?' Mandy puzzled, with a shrug of her shoulders. 'I thought you told me Erik preferred jazz.'

Brian roared with laughter and patted Mandy playfully on the bottom. 'Mandy, my love, you might never make 'Brain of Britain' but thank God you can always raise a laugh. I meant Rape and Pillage not Rhythm and Blues.'

'An' that's not all she can raise, is it, Brian?' Trevor quipped, recalling Mandy's squeals of ecstasy and delight, echoing

161

through the cabin walls during their three-night stay at Pinetrees Park.

Watching Mandy's face fill with acute embarrassment, Anna breathed a sigh of relief. Thank heavens she and Bjorn hadn't made love, especially if the walls of the cabins were that thin. Anxious for someone to change the subject, she was deeply gratified when Bjorn suggested they take a closer look at the Heel Stone. Leaving the others behind, they stood in silence drinking in the sheer magic and mystery of the ancient stone monoliths, now gloriously silhouetted against the clear April sky.

'What did Brian mean by pillage?' Bjorn remarked at length. 'For it would appear my Viking ancestors have quite a reputation.'

'Um — that's just Trevor's way of saying your ancestors weren't to be trusted.'

'Oh,' Bjorn replied, flatly, unsure as to whether or not Anna was being serious or merely teasing. Slowly, he turned to face her, his face filled with renewed anxiety. 'What about me, Anna. Do you . . . would you trust me?'

'Yes, of course.'

'Enough to spend not only tonight with me . . . but also the rest of your life?'

When Anna made no reply, Bjorn regarded her carefully. 'I know I've mentioned it before, but I want this to be a proper proposal. I'm asking you to be my wife, Anna. If, as Jane says, this is where the sun rises on midsummer morning, what could be a more fitting place? With our ancestors celebrating the beginning of many a new day here, shall we make it the place for our new beginning?'

Through misted eyes, Anna moved forward and placed a finger gently on his lips. 'There's no need to explain further. I understand perfectly. I feel the magic of this place too and my answer is yes.'

Sweeping her into his arms, Bjorn held her close. 'You will marry me? That's wonderful! When? And how shall we celebrate?'

'For the moment by going back,' Anna suggested, breaking away from his embrace. 'I think everyone's waiting for us.'

Once more reminded of the others, Bjorn turned to see Beattie and Fudge waving frantically and pointing in the direction of the mini bus. Frank had just switched on the ignition and the Bentley was already moving slowly away.

'Where's Steve?' Anna called, out of breath. 'We can't leave without him?'

'Travelling in style to the pub with Felix and Gavin,' Beattie said, climbing into the bus ahead of her. 'Felix thought — now that Bjorn's here — we'd all have more room if

163

Steve went with them in the Bentley.'

Anna's brow knitted into a frown. Even with Bjorn as an extra passenger there was still plenty of room on the bus for Steve.

'To be honest,' Beattie hissed in her direction, 'it's probably all for the best, anyway. While you and Bjorn went to that sacrificial stone thingy, Steve gave Fudge a right ticking off about last night.'

'Oh, no! He didn't tell her she was drunk, did he? I purposely let her believe it was the fudge and the rich food that had made her so ill.'

Beattie nodded in confirmation and motioned to Fudge, red-eyed and subdued, staring miserably from the window.

'I'm so sorry about last night,' she said in a small voice, turning to see Anna take a seat. 'I had no idea until Steve told me.'

'Shh, you're not to mention it.'

'But Steve said I was to apologize and — '

'And you have and the matter's closed,' Anna insisted. 'When we stop for lunch, I'll make sure I tell Steve the same. OK?'

Marginally comforted, and deeply grateful for Beattie's company, now that Anna and Bjorn were sitting close together, Fudge blew her nose hard, still dreading the moment when they would stop for lunch.

'There you are, dear things,' Felix

exclaimed, spying Bjorn and Anna emerging from the mini bus. 'Why, when I last saw you, Anna, I thought Bjorn was about to lay you on the altar and offer you up as a sacrifice to the gods, never to be seen again.'

Following Felix into the bar, Bjorn smiled broadly and reached for Anna's hand. 'As you can see, she's still in one piece. Although, you're almost correct about the sacrifice. Anna will be making a sacrifice of sorts. She's giving up the name of Mason to become Mrs Bjorn Carlson.'

'You've asked Anna to marry you?' Fudge cried, momentarily forgetting the previous angry exchange with her brother. 'That's fantastic news, isn't it, everybody?'

Amid the chorus of hearty congratulations, Felix was heard to boom a deeply sonorous '*Bravo!*' before ordering three bottles of mine host's best champagne.

★   ★   ★

Later that night as they lay in bed together at the London flat, Bjorn's gaze lingered on Anna's guitar case, propped against the bedroom wall.

'You never did get to finish the song,' he murmured, lazily fingering a strand of her

165

hair as she lay with her head against his bare chest.

'What song was that?'

'The one you were singing when I arrived last night. You also sang it at Gavin's party. Something about going to the fair, I think. Will you sing it for me now?'

'I-I don't know if I can,' Anna said shyly. 'I'm not used to singing to an audience of one, especially while lying naked in bed.'

Bjorn gave a crooked smile. 'Don't you English have a saying, there's always a first time? Before we make love for the first time, Anna, please finish the song for me.'

'With or without the guitar?'

'Without,' he grinned. 'This bed's not big enough for three.'

'It's not even big enough for two,' Anna said, looking up at him. Then, in a soft, clear voice, she began to sing the familiar haunting melody that ended with the words:

And she moved away from me and then she did say, sure t'will not be long now 'til our wedding day.

When Anna finished singing, Bjorn turned on his side to look at her. Once more entwining his fingers gently in her hair, he drank in the beauty of her smooth, silky skin

166

and the way the golden glints from the nearby candles reflected in her eyes.

'I don't want to make love to you in the dark or by the light of an electric lamp,' he'd explained half an hour earlier, while they'd hunted frantically for matches and candles.

'So . . . ' he coaxed, as his hand slid from her hair to her shoulder and then down to caress her breasts. 'When is our wedding day going to be? Please make it soon, because I love you so much, Anna, I couldn't bear the thought of you ever moving away from me.'

'Don't worry, I won't,' she whispered, giving a tiny sigh when he eased his body carefully to mould against hers. 'Because I shall never, ever, leave you.'

14

Within three months of their first night together, Bjorn and Anna were married, the idyllic setting for the happy occasion being the tiny village church where Anna had been baptized and confirmed, her own parents married and her grandmother a long-standing member of the congregation. It was for these reasons the Reverend Wilkinson agreed to marry them on a Sunday. A day when friends from the Alexandra could also join in with the family celebrations.

Blinking back tears, Beattie and Madge watched Anna's father lead her down the aisle to join Bjorn and Erik, waiting at the altar. Her attention momentarily drawn to an exquisite stained-glass window, Madge nodded approvingly in Anna's direction.

'Felix always said she was an angel. See, she's even got the halo.'

Dabbing at her eyes, Beattie acknowledged Madge's hushed remark and smiled. Sure enough, when a sudden ray of sunlight pierced a delicate amber lozenge of ancient stained glass, Anna's silk-tulle veil and head-dress were bathed in a shimmer of gold.

With the wedding service over and family and guests assembled for numerous photographs, Beattie and Madge hurried to admire Anna's wedding dress and those of the two bridesmaids. The exquisite princess line wedding gown was of ivory silk with a sweeping train, and those of the bridesmaids, Fudge and Jane, the most delicate shade of peach. Reminded of her long-distant hopes for her nephew Tom, at least as far as Anna was concerned, Beattie emitted an anguished sigh and fumbled for her handkerchief.

'A perfect day for a perfect couple eh, Beattie? And it certainly looks as if Kent's answer to David Bailey is doing a pretty thorough job.'

Blowing her nose hard, Beattie felt Steve's comforting arm upon her shoulder.

'Yes,' she sniffed. 'It was such a beautiful service and I'm really happy for them.'

'Blimey! If that's what you're like when you're happy, I hope never to see you when you're sad.'

Several hours later, with the speeches made and the wedding cake cut, Bjorn and Anna said their fond farewells and set off for Heathrow and their honeymoon destination. Waving a tearful goodbye, Beattie found herself once more accompanied by Steve.

'Still happy I see?'

Glad of both Steve's company and his reassuring hug, Beattie managed a smile, dabbed at her eyes and opened her handbag. 'I think I need a smoke and a sit down,' she said, swapping the lace-trimmed handkerchief for the packet of cigarettes. 'My feet are killing me after all that dancing.'

Taking Beattie by the arm, Steve escorted her back to the marquee. 'Quite an occasion, wasn't it? I must say this marquee affair certainly puts the last wedding Fudge and I went to, in the shade.'

'Really? Where was was that?'

'Our local village hall. I expect you know the sort of thing. Curled-up sandwiches, sausages on sticks, people piling their plates sky-high with food they don't want and then drinking themselves into oblivion. I hate it when people behave like that.'

For a moment Beattie seemed almost surprised before recalling Steve's unexpected and, in her opinion, unnecessary outburst when he'd accused Fudge of disgracing herself at Pinetrees Park. In case he, too, had remembered, she diverted his attention elsewhere. 'What do you think of your sister? Doesn't Fudge look pretty today? That pale-peach silk, really compliments her colouring to perfection.'

'Yeah. I guess she does,' Steve replied

proudly. 'I never thought Fudge could look that good. Pity Mum and Dad weren't here — not that they expected an invitation of course — but they'll be dead chuffed when they see the wedding photos. Poor Fudge.'

'Why poor Fudge?'

'Cos she's really going to miss Anna. What with the Alexandra closing and all that. It's almost like the end of an era.'

Beattie murmured resignedly through a wispy pall of smoke. 'Mmm. Though I hate having to say it, I think you're right, Steve. It's amazing how our lives have changed in just a few short months. Who'd have thought, following that incident with Andretti and those never to be forgotten yellow silk dresses, that Madge would have got herself pregnant and Anna and Bjorn would be married.'

'It's not all doom and gloom then,' Steve reflected, looking across the marquee to where his sister was dancing with Julian Player and Frank was passing Madge a glass of orange juice. 'You and Fudge have at least got jobs to go to, Bjorn and Anna are man and wife, and it looks very much as if Madge and Frank are friends again. Gavin was saying the pair of them haven't had a cross word all day.'

Studying the lengthening ash on her

cigarette, Beattie contemplated the jobs she and Fudge had been offered by a well-known firm of theatrical costumiers. She was certainly grateful to Julian Player, who'd put in a good word for them both. Yet, in her heart of hearts, she knew she would never fit in. Working at the Alexandra had been something special. With her thoughts still on hearts, Beattie watched Frank untie a peach-tinted heart-shaped balloon and offer it to Madge. Unable to catch the response, she could only assume that Madge had made some comparison between her own heavily pregnant state and the size of the unwieldy balloon.

As if reading Beattie's mind, Steve broke into her chain of thought. 'When's it due, Madge's baby? Poor thing, she already looks as if she's about to explode. You don't think it's twins do you?'

'Heaven forbid! I hope not. Frank's only just resigned himself to one.'

'And dare I ask about the Prickly Pamela who everyone talks about but I've never yet had the pleasure of meeting? Is she also resigned to it? Will she give Frank a divorce?'

Sensing that Frank and herself were the current topic of conversation, Madge glanced across in Steve's direction. She also registered Beattie's face full of renewed concern and gave an apologetic laugh. 'Don't worry, Beattie, you're not going to witness both a marriage and a birth on the same day, Frank's just about to drive me home.'

'Then you make sure he drives carefully.'

'Oh, he will,' Madge grinned, patting her swollen stomach. 'I've promised Anna faithfully to hang on to this until she returns from their honeymoon. And I don't intend to let her down.'

Having said their goodbyes and helping Madge into his car, Frank's gaze lingered on his heavily pregnant companion, the words *I don't intend to let her down* ringing in his ears. Though he knew in this instant they applied to Anna, Frank was suddenly consumed with guilt. Wasn't that what he'd done to Madge? By not confronting Pamela in a more direct way about a divorce, hadn't he let Madge down?

'Penny for them?' Madge said, Struggling with the clasp of her seat-belt.

'I was simply thinking about Bjorn's parents, that's all,' Frank lied, coming to her aid, releasing an extra length of webbing. 'I'm glad they came over for the wedding, despite the language problems. They seem a very nice couple. Did you know they're spending the rest of their stay in London? Speaking of which, as that's where we're supposed to be heading, we'd better get a move on. The Dartford Tunnel can be hell on a Sunday evening.'

Watching them go, Beattie was suddenly filled with a melancholy sadness. Madge's heavily advanced stage of pregnancy and Anna and Bjorn's wedding had only served to remind her of Tom and Lucy, now the proud parents of a healthy son, Alexander Thomas, born in early April. To Beattie's unashamed relief, young Alexander was the spitting image of his father and in no way bore any resemblance to his pale-faced mother.

'It seems I only gave birth to him,' Lucy had said, watching Beattie gaze adoringly into the cot at the lusty, bawling infant for the very first time. 'As you can see, he's a Hudson through and through, make no mistake.'

Much to Beattie's horror, Tom had patted his exhausted wife on the hand and kissed her fondly. 'Don't worry, Lucy. We'll make sure the next one looks like you.'

'Please God there isn't one,' Beattie muttered, without thinking.

'There isn't one what?' a voice questioned by her side.

'A baby.'

'You mean you don't want Anna and Bjorn to have children? But why?'

Blinking her eyes, Beattie turned to discover Fudge staring back at her in utter disbelief. 'Sorry, Fudge. You'll have to excuse me, I was miles away. Don't get me wrong, I wasn't talking about Anna and Bjorn. I was referring to Tom and Lucy. Call it a lapse of mental capacity if you like. It always happens when I think about Lucy. Perhaps I should be thinking of something nice instead, like how pretty you look or else — '

'Going home?' Fudge offered. 'Felix said to tell you he's ready to leave. He's saying goodbye to Anna and Bjorn's parents at the moment, and Gavin and Steve are waiting by the car. Did I tell you Steve's decided to go to London to look for a job? Gavin says there's heaps of opportunities for a plumber and carpenter these days.'

Bidding farewell to both sets of parents and Anna's grandmother, Beattie pondered the real reason behind Steve's decision to go to London. Ever since Gavin's party, Steve had been invited to all the Ragtime Band's social events, so he must have realized that with the theatre closing there was absolutely no chance of finding work in that direction.

Comfortably installed in the Bentley's rear passenger seat with Felix, Beattie soon perceived there was in fact more to Steve finding a job, than his sister had realized.

Gavin and Steve had already become very close and on more than one occasion, when Beattie saw Felix reach forward and pat Steve on the shoulder with a genial *my dear boy* she also found herself wondering who had paid for the expensive-looking three piece suit, Steve had worn to the wedding. Preferring not to contemplate the eventual consequences, Beattie unfastened the silk-covered buttons on her Chanel-style jacket, leaned back against the luxurious padded leather upholstery and closed her eyes.

★ ★ ★

From the honeymoon suite of Stockholm's Grand Hotel, Anna gazed in wide-eyed wonderment at the city's amazing archipelago.

'Bjorn, tell me again. How many islands are there?'

'Thousands. And I suggest you don't try and count them all tonight, or we shall never get to bed.'

Anna smiled and reached for his hand. 'It's not even dark,' she teased, 'And the sun is still shining.'

'Then I suggest we close the curtains, Mrs Carlson, because my intention is to carry you to bed and just like the song, make mad, passionate love to you.'

'What song is that?'

'To be honest I can't remember.'

'Perhaps it wasn't a song,' Anna giggled, when Bjorn lifted her into his arms. 'Perhaps it was a line from an Ingmar Bergman film or — '

'Film? Song? Does it matter?' Bjorn said, bending to kiss her throat. 'When all that matters is our wedding was just as we hoped and planned. Everyone got on so well together and now we're alone at last. What could be more perfect?'

Hearing muted voices in the corridor outside, Bjorn laid his adored wife gently on the bed and entwined his fingers in her long dark hair. 'Mmm, perhaps not quite alone, but we shall be in a few days' time when we go to the summer house to celebrate Midsummer's Eve. As for perfect,' he said huskily, his voice catching in his throat, while he slipped the oyster silk nightie from Anna's shoulders, 'Having found the perfect wife, I must promise to be the perfect husband. For it's quite obvious if I'm not, Beattie, Madge and Fudge would never forgive me.'

Meeting Bjorn's lingering gaze, Anna reached up to brush her fingers against his cheek. 'You can begin by forgetting about the curtains. When we first made love it was by candlelight, tonight . . . we have the midnight sun.'

'Why, so we do,' Bjorn said softly, dropping the merest slip of lace and silk to the floor.

15

With the telephone wedged firmly against her chin, Anna reached for a notepad and pen, scribbled a hasty message to Bjorn and called down the line to Frank.

'Don't worry. Tell Madge I'm leaving right away. I'll be there as soon as I can.'

Less than an hour later, she pushed her way through the double swing doors of the hospital and headed for the maternity unit.

'You can't go in there! It's not visiting time.'

Looking first at her watch and then at the owner of the harsh voice barring her way, Anna responded meekly, 'I know it's only half past six and visiting doesn't begin until seven, but I was told I could visit my — '

'Then you've been misinformed. It's fathers only in the evenings and family in the afternoons. If you want to see your sister, you'll have to come back tomorrow.'

'Madge isn't my sister,' Anna volunteered, without thinking. 'When Frank telephoned, he told me Sister McPhearson had agreed to — '

At the very mention of Sister McPhearson,

the nurse, whose manner was as starchy as her uniform, moved aside reluctantly. 'Hmph. You'll find her in the office. Make sure you knock first.'

Anna knocked at the open office door with trepidation. 'Um — excuse me. I'm Anna Carlson. I've come to see — '

'Your friend Madge,' Sister McPhearson said brightly, greeting her with a friendly smile. 'I'm so glad Mr Webster was able to contact you. I understand he's working tonight and we all thought Madge might benefit from some company.'

Detecting a slight undercurrent of anxiety in the sister's voice, Anna began to worry. 'Madge is all right, isn't she? Frank didn't mention any complications. He only said that labour was somewhat prolonged and Madge has a little boy with fair hair.'

Sister McPhearson rose from her chair and moved towards the door. 'There's no need to look so alarmed, Mrs Carlson. Mother and baby are both fine. Doctor wants to do some tests that's all. I'm sure Madge will tell you about it. If you'd like to come with me?'

Following closely behind, Anna was surprised to see Sister McPhearson walk the entire length of the ward without pausing. At the far end, she turned into a side corridor and stopped outside a small room.

'Here you are, Madge. Just as he promised, Frank's managed to get hold of Anna for you. I'll tell Nurse Fairbrass to bring in baby, shall I?'

'Nurse Fairbrass,' Madge spat, patting the chair beside her bed. 'Wouldn't I just like to stick something up her — '

'Madge,' Anna scolded, hugging her friend warmly before sitting down.

'Believe me, you'd feel exactly the same way, ducky,' Madge snorted, deeply indignant. 'Especially if you'd had to put up with her like I have. Every time I see her I feel like singing, '*Nurse Fairbrass, Nurse Fairbrass, a real pain in the arse!*' Frank's absolutely terrified of her.'

'You're not, I take it?'

Madge gave a self-satisfied smile. 'You should know me better than that, Anna. I'm perfectly capable of giving as good as I get. Old Fairbrass might terrify the younger mums — but not me.'

'Is that why they've put you in an amenity room? In case you cause a riot?'

'Not exactly,' Madge said, her attention drawn to the sound of a cot being wheeled along the corridor.

'Sister McPhearson said I was to bring baby,' Nurse Fairbrass announced primly, through tight lips. 'I only hope this means the

181

other mothers won't be expecting theirs.'

When Madge made no comment, Nurse Fairbrass fixed Anna with a disapproving eye. 'Visiting ends at eight o'clock sharp!'

Anna waited for the nurse to turn on her heels before moving cautiously towards the cot. 'Hmm, I see what you mean. So, am I allowed to take a peek at your son and heir, or must I ask Nurse F's permission?'

Madge forced a tired smile and shook her head. ' 'Course not. You go ahead. He's still rather pink and wrinkled and looks as if he could do with a good ironing out.'

Peering into the cot at what she could make out of the tiny sleeping bundle, wrapped tightly in a white cotton shawl and blankets, Anna felt tears prick her eyelids.

'Oh, Madge, you clever, clever thing. He's beautiful. Frank said he — '

Seeing Madge's face crumple and fill with tears of her own, Anna continued hurriedly, 'I'm sorry. How tactless of me. I didn't realize mention of Frank would upset you. When he rang and told me about the baby, I assumed everything was still OK with you both.'

Madge reached for a box of tissues. 'It's not Frank,' she sniffed, blowing her nose hard. 'It's the baby. Didn't Frank tell you?'

Anna shook her head. 'Frank said only that you'd had a little boy and you were anxious to see me. The baby . . . he is all right, isn't he?'

Looking in the direction of the sleeping infant, with his button nose and light thatch of fair hair, Anna tried to recall Frank's garbled message when he'd phoned: Madge had had the baby. The labour had been a bit of an ordeal by all accounts and no, he hadn't been there. Fathers weren't allowed and some stuffy nurse had been *so* rude . . .

Dismissing thoughts of Nurse Fairbrass, who presumably had also upset Frank before he'd dashed off to work, Anna reached for her friend's hand. 'Madge?'

Through a stifled sob, Madge replied numbly, 'I told Frank they must have made a mistake about the baby. That's why I wanted you to see him. Anna will know, I said. Like me, you think he's beautiful too — don't you? They've got to be wrong.'

Anna felt her stomach lurch, recalling Sister McPhearson's earlier words of greeting. If there was something seriously wrong with the baby, then why hadn't Frank forewarned her? To think that only a few moments ago she'd breezed into this room as if everything was hunkydory. The worried look on Madge's face now told her otherwise. Certainly, from where she was standing the baby appeared perfectly normal, but, as she reminded herself, despite Madge's faith in her she was no expert. Other than holding Tom and Lucy's baby son when Beattie had persuaded them to call at the theatre one lunchtime, she knew nothing at all about babies. Deeply apprehensive, Anna searched Madge's tear-stained face for explanation.

'They want to do tests,' Madge said at length, shredding the wet, soggy tissue in her hands. 'The doctor thinks it could be Down's Syndrome. It's all my fault, Anna. If only I hadn't been so bloody minded and determined to get myself pregnant. I should have realized this could happen at my age. What am I going to do? How will I cope if it is?'

Anna made as if to speak, but Madge ignored her, shaking her head in desperation. 'There was me thinking I was so bloody clever, especially when the midwife told me it was a boy. Every man wants a son don't they? A special son for Frank, I thought, when in fact all I did was produce a freak. No wonder Frank couldn't wait to get away.'

Swallowing hard, Anna watched unchecked tears pour down Madge's face. She had to think of something constructive to say but all that came out was a feeble, 'That's not true, Madge. Just look at the time.'

'What on earth has time got to do with it?'

'Frank couldn't stay, could he? You know as

well as I do, he has to be at the theatre for tonight's performance. That's why he rang me. As for the baby being a freak, you mustn't talk like that.'

'But what if — ?'

'And what if the doctors are wrong?' Anna said, hoping and praying that they were. She removed the crumpled tissue from Madge's grasp and passed her a new one. 'Perhaps *they* made a mistake? Even if they haven't, you can't blame yourself for this. If I remember correctly there was a programme on Radio 4 only recently. Down's Syndrome is a result of an extra chromosome at fertilization. It can come from either parent. Don't you see?'

Madge blew her nose even louder than before and shook her head. No, she didn't. At that precise moment all she could see was Frank rushing from the hospital, within minutes of the doctor making his diagnosis. 'It couldn't have been Frank's fault,' she said, defensively. 'Don't forget he's got two children already. Both his daughters are OK. You've even seen photos of them, Anna.'

Fresh tears coursed down Madge's cheeks. 'All I wanted was to give him a son,' she sobbed, miserably. 'I'd even resigned myself to the fact that he'll never leave Pamela and I'd put up with seeing him just for the odd weekend. Now all that will have changed. Frank probably wants to forget he ever set eyes on me and all I'll be left with is an idiot son.'

'Madge! Stop it this instant! I absolutely refuse to let you talk like that.'

Startling Madge into silence, Anna rose from her chair and walked swiftly to the cot. Wheeling the crib to Madge's side she commanded angrily. 'Look at him, Madge. Look at your baby. You told me when I first arrived that he was beautiful — and he is.'

'But — '

'No. Let me finish. Even if he does have Down's Syndrome, your baby will not be an idiot. This is the 1970s for God's sake, not Victorian England. There's all sorts of research going on these days. We can read up on the subject and — '

'We?'

'Yes. You and me — and Frank. We can get books from the library. In fact I'll go there first thing in the morning. Between us we'll find out *everything* there is to know. We'll cope. You see if we don't.'

Momentarily comforted by Anna's words, even if she didn't quite believe them, Madge turned to look at her sleeping baby. 'Poor little bastard. What on earth has he done to deserve a mother like me?'

Spying Anna's raised eyebrows, Madge patted the side of the bed, motioning for her to sit down. 'Like it or not,' she sighed, 'He is a little bastard in the true sense of the word. Frank and I aren't married, nor are we likely to be now. Pamela and Peter have made doubly sure of that.'

Only too familiar with the name of Pamela, Anna racked her brains. Frank had never mentioned a Peter in his family. 'Who's Peter, one of Frank's relations?'

Madge shook her head and gave a wan smile. 'No. That's what I intend to call the baby. I can't call him Frank, can I? For a start he doesn't look the least bit like him, even making allowance for Frank's moustache.'

'Then why Peter?'

'Because to me he'll be just like Peter Pan. He'll never grow up . . . never grow old. Isn't that what they say about Down's Syndrome children?'

Watching Madge trail her fingers along the edge of the crib, until she reached in to caress the baby's pink cheek, Anna was reminded of J.M. Barrie's story of Peter Pan, Wendy and the Lost Boys. She bit her lip hard. 'I think Peter's a lovely name and I'm sure you'll be the perfect Mrs Darling. Can I therefore volunteer my services as Wendy?'

Madge looked up, deeply reflective. 'Oh, I

had you in mind as Tinkerbell.'

'Gosh, I'd forgotten about Tinkerbell and her fairy dust. In that case I suggest you look no further than Beattie.'

To Anna's delight, Madge suddenly burst out laughing. 'Beattie, Tinkerbell? Are you serious?'

'Most definitely. It could be just the thing to take her mind off the disappointment of Tom marrying Lucy. And when you think of Beattie's wonderful wardrobe: all those amazing lurex sweaters and sequin dresses, she already comes complete with fairy dust.'

With a loving glance at her baby, Madge was heard to whisper, 'What if they make me send him away? Nurse Fairbrass mentioned something about a special home. They might think I'm not fit to look after him.'

Anna followed Madge's gaze. 'I'm not quite sure who you mean by they but Peter is *your* baby. And, as his mother, it will be you who makes the decisions concerning his future. No one else.'

Madge brightened, clasping Anna's hand for comfort and reassurance. 'Do you really think I'll be able to cope? Because . . . somehow I couldn't bear to think of the poor little beggar being sent away.'

When the bell rang to announce the end of visiting, Madge and Anna looked up to see

188

Sister McPhearson standing in the doorway. Smiling kindly, she held up five fingers and with a quiet rustle of uniform, set off determined to keep the ultra-efficient Nurse Fairbrass well out of their way for a further five minutes.

16

With Madge bemoaning the fact that she'd been kept in hospital for the statutory ten days, Anna helped her pack and gather up her personal belongings.

'Once you're home, you'll feel so much better. At least you can do things your way, when you and Peter are alone.'

Madge winced at mention of the word alone. True, she couldn't wait to leave the hospital. Nevertheless, with that moment drawing ever nearer she found the prospect increasingly daunting. *But you won't be completely alone,* an inner voice reassured. *Don't forget there'll be visits from the district nurse and health visitor, not to mention your friends from the Alexandra. They've all been so thoughtful and kind. You've only got to take a look round this room to see that.*

As if in silent acknowledgement, Madge nodded and blinked back a tear. Yes, everybody had been extremely kind and generous. For the past ten days her room had been filled to overflowing with flowers, and her baby son positively showered with gifts of every description. Dabbing at her eyes, she watched as Anna deftly packed away the delicate silk-trimmed shawl, umpteen soft toys, matinée coats and blankets. Fully aware that all the gifts in the world could never make Peter the normal little boy she'd so desperately longed for, Madge relived the day when her worst fears had been confirmed.

The chromosome tests for Down's Syndrome *had* proved positive. Frank had left the hospital numb with shock and grief and Madge had telephoned Anna with the news, before eventually crying herself to sleep. Even now the memory of Frank's ashen face still haunted Madge, which was why she'd called Anna with her latest request. Despite Frank's offer to fetch her from the hospital, she had been adamant in her refusal.

'If he wants to take you home, why won't you let him?' Anna ventured.

'Because it isn't what Frank wants. He only offered because it's what everyone expects him to do.'

Anna frowned hard, retrieving the borrowed Down's Syndrome library books on the bedside locker. She and Bjorn had had many conversations with Frank since Peter's arrival. They both knew his concern for Madge and the baby were genuine. The problem was how to convince Madge, who at this very moment was studying her watch.

'Are you sure Bjorn said he'd be here at eleven-thirty?'

'Positive,' Anna replied, closing the lid of the suitcase. 'I rang him as soon as you'd been given your marching orders from Sister McPhearson. Don't look so glum. It's only a quarter past and Nurse Fairbrass is still dressing Peter in his going home clothes.'

This time when Nurse Fairbrass's name was mentioned, Madge refrained from her usual snort of disdain. For some reason during the past few days, Nurse Fairbrass had become just about human. 'You know, it's almost as if she's forgiven me for being an irresponsible, unmarried mother,' Madge said, voicing her thoughts.

'I'm sure she didn't really think that,' Anna broke in. 'Look how she reacted when you told that other nurse where to go. The one who suggested, in no uncertain terms, that at your age the best thing you could do was to put Peter in a home.'

Madge grinned wickedly. 'How could I ever forget?'

Hearing voices in the corridor, Madge rose expectantly from her chair. With luck it would be Bjorn and Nurse Fairbrass, who, as Anna had so correctly ascertained, had changed from monster to saviour the moment she discovered Madge had every intention of

192

taking Peter home and caring for him herself. Not only that, the usually thin-lipped and po-faced nurse had also been secretly impressed, seeing Madge study every available book on Down's Syndrome children.

'I want to be prepared for *all* eventualities,' Madge had explained, bombarding the bewildered Nurse Fairbrass with questions. 'I know I'm no spring chicken. I also know it's not going to be easy bringing up a child like Peter on my own. But, as you've probably already gathered, I've always been a fighter and I aim to make this my best battle yet.'

'All ready and waiting then?' Bjorn announced from the doorway, spying the two women standing by the bed. 'So — what happens now, Anna?'

'Madge has to check out, get her pills and post-natal appointment and then we can leave.'

'Fine. Let's get going then, shall we? If I take Madge's suitcase and you take the bag of presents, that leaves her free to hold Peter.'

'I'm afraid it doesn't,' Madge replied.

Bjorn's cornflower blue eyes registered bewilderment. What on earth could have happened in the short space of time since Anna had telephoned? Had something happened to Peter, or had Madge uncharacteristically changed her mind about keeping him? And if so, why hadn't Anna rung back and explained? Now he would have to ring Frank and tell him there'd been a complete change of plan.

'It's all right, darling, there's nothing wrong,' Anna said, kissing him on the cheek. 'It's simply that we must follow the rules. A nurse has to carry Peter from the hospital. Madge has to sit in the car first and then they hand over the baby.'

'Just in case I drop him on the steps,' Madge teased. 'Don't forget I'm still a bit wobbly on my feet. Mind you, since I've had my stitches out, things have certainly improved. I don't mind admitting that for a while I felt like that blooming turkey you had all trussed up on your kitchen table last Christmas. Do you remember, Anna?'

Anna smiled fondly. How could she forget? That was when Madge had first dropped the bombshell that if she couldn't have Frank, she would at least have his baby. Who then would have guessed the course of events since?

'Anna?' Bjorn questioned, following on behind Madge and Nurse Fairbrass. 'Are you sure everything's OK?'

'Yes, I'm fine. It's just that mention of Christmas prompted me to think of Frank. I still think it's a shame that Madge wouldn't agree to him coming to fetch her.'

'But he is,' came the barely audible reply.

'He what?'

'Shh. It's going to be a surprise.'

'Surprise is right!' Anna hissed from the corner of her mouth. 'Have you any idea what Madge will say? She'll go absolutely spare when she sees him.'

'Perhaps, but it's a risk Frank's prepared to take.'

'How did he know? Who told him exactly what time Madge was . . . ?'

There was no need to reply. Bjorn's face said it all. It wasn't necessary for him to tell Anna he'd rung Frank the moment he knew Madge was being discharged.

'Then I only hope you and Frank know what you're doing,' Anna said, emerging through the hospital doors, her gaze flashing swiftly from left to right, looking for any sign of Frank. From the corner of her eye, she discerned someone wearing a familiar navy-blue corduroy jacket and grey flannel trousers, heading in their direction. On hearing Madge gasp, she knew her friend had seen him too.

In icy silence, Madge glared at Frank, who stood fumbling clumsily with his jacket pocket. Nurse Fairbrass meanwhile, oblivious to the situation, walked slowly towards

Bjorn's car and waited for Madge to get in.

'I thought I told you not to come!' Madge snapped icily.

'No, you didn't. You said I didn't have to if I didn't want to.'

'Hmph! You only offered because you felt obliged.'

Frank stepped forward. 'That's not true, Madge, nor is it fair. I honestly wanted to be here today.'

'Why? To ease your conscience, because you feel sorry for us?'

Risking another step forward, Frank placed a firm hand on Madge's arm. 'Madge, please! You know as well as I do that's not the reason. Peter's my son . . . and as his father, I should be here to see him safely home.'

'Really? And exactly whose home are we talking about, Frank, yours or mine?'

'Well — er — we can't really take him to mine, can we, because of Pamela?'

'Exactly, because of Pamela!' Madge crowed, triumphant. 'In which case I suggest you bugger off back to her then and leave me to get on with my life.'

Shaking her arm free from Frank's grasp, Madge stormed towards Bjorn's car. To her surprise, he didn't open the door. In turn she flashed her angry eyes at Anna. 'What is this, a conspiracy?'

'Anna knew absolutely nothing about this until a minute ago,' Bjorn broke in in his usual calm voice. 'And even if she had, I'm sure she would be telling you to hear Frank out. Perhaps you should let him explain.'

'Explain? Explain about what?'

'About Pamela,' Frank replied softly, once more standing by Madge's side, only this time he reached out for her left hand. 'I've told Pamela I'm leaving. I've also told her I want a divorce. Even if it means waiting years, I'll get one, Madge. You can, you know?'

For one horrid moment, Bjorn thought Frank was suddenly going to explain all the intricacies of the current divorce laws. He shook his head in disbelief; now was not the time. Not while Madge had been unexpectedly stunned into silence. With a sigh of relief, Bjorn saw Frank reach once more into his jacket pocket and place a blue velvet box in Madge's palm.

'I want you to have this,' Frank said, his voice choked with emotion. 'I bought it for you last Christmas. I'd even planned to give it to you on Boxing Day. The day you — well, you know — the day you told me you were pregnant.'

'But you said . . . you suggested I had an abortion.'

'I know and I still feel really bad about that, Madge. I confess at the time I was totally unprepared for such a shock announcement. These past ten days have not only made me realize just how much I love you . . . but also how much I want to look after you both. You and *our* son.'

Something in the way Frank said the words 'our son' caused a lump to rise in Madge's throat. 'You know Peter's got Down's Syndrome. You know he'll never be like other boys. He won't be able to — '

'I know,' Frank broke in, gently brushing away the tears rolling down Madge's cheeks. 'That's what makes him extra special. Besides, you're not the only one who has been reading books on the subject. If you want my opinion, which you probably don't, I think I'd make him a pretty good father. So . . . will you let me? Can I take you home?'

Opening the tiny blue box to reveal a sapphire and diamond engagement ring, Madge walked away from Frank's embrace and made immediately for Anna and Bjorn. Anna was devastated, surely after such an impassioned plea, Madge wasn't going to spoil everything?

Large tears brimmed in Madge's eyes 'Anna, would you mind? I-I mean would you and Bjorn be terribly offended if Frank took me home? I know I specifically said I didn't want him to ... but if he's getting a divorce — '

'Madge,' Anna grinned, placing both hands on her friend's shoulders. 'Will you *please* tell Nurse Fairbrass exactly which car you intend to be travelling home in? Because, if you don't hurry up she'll probably turn back into the nurse from hell, Peter will start crying for his next feed and that thunderous looking traffic warden, heading in our direction, is likely to give us both a parking ticket!'

Glancing behind at the fast approaching figure in navy-blue uniform, Madge flung her arms round Anna's neck, kissed the highly relieved Bjorn and, hurrying over to Nurse Fairbrass, pointed her and the now wide awake baby in the direction of Frank's car. Realizing he was missing out on not one but two parking tickets, the traffic warden chewed his pen and shook his head grimly.

'Don't look so sad,' Madge called out. 'You see Frank's just asked me to marry him — and I've said yes.'

With the warden tut-tutting disapproval, Madge could only assume he was thinking the worst. 'And if he is, what does it matter?'

she cooed, smoothing down the blue silk edging of the baby's shawl. 'Nothing matters anymore, Peter. You're no longer a lost boy. Your Daddy is taking us home.'

17

SATIN

The Home Counties late 1970s

Bjorn stirred sleepily, to find Anna peering from the bedroom window. 'What's the verdict on last night's weather bulletin?' he called, from beneath the duvet. 'Are we going to get the sunshine they forecast?'

'It doesn't look very promising at the moment,' Anna said, folding back a corner of the curtain. 'At the moment all I can see are grey skies. You don't think it will rain, do you?'

'Most definitely. Which means we'll have to cancel tonight.'

'Cancel? But what about all the food! I was up half the night cooking and didn't get to bed until one-thirty.'

'Exactly, which is why, like me, you're still half asleep. Come back to bed and forget about the party. We can stay here all weekend. At least we know we won't starve.'

When Anna threw him a puzzled frown, Bjorn continued, 'You can sleep for as long as you like and when you feel hungry, I'll simply pop downstairs and prepare us a tray. I'll even take the phone off the hook.'

'I couldn't possibly do that. What if . . . ' Anna protested, before she realized Bjorn had been merely teasing. 'Oh, you!' she grinned, letting the curtain drop back into place. 'For a moment I thought you were being serious.'

'I was.'

'About cancelling our midsummer party?'

'No. About you coming back to bed.'

Turning from the window Anna moved towards him, her loving gaze quickly taking in his tousled appearance and bare chest. 'Hmm. From where I'm standing it certainly seems a tempting proposition.'

'Then let me make it a *very* tempting proposition, Mrs Carlson,' Bjorn said huskily, lifting back the duvet for Anna to snuggle in beside him. Holding her close with his left arm, while her fingers trailed over his naked torso, he reached out with his right and deftly moved the bedside clock.

'Why did you do that?'

'Because I know what you're like: I don't want you worrying about the time.'

An hour and a half later, when golden shafts of sunlight pierced the chink in the curtains, Anna leapt out of bed and made a grab for her bath-robe. 'Oh no! Look, the sun is shining.'

'What's wrong with that? Isn't that what you wanted, fine weather for the party?'

'Of course it is,' Anna said, struggling with the belt of her robe, all the while attempting to peer at the bedside clock. 'But have you any idea of the time? We shouldn't have — '

'Shouldn't we?' Bjorn questioned, meeting her flustered gaze.

Spying the hurt in his face, Anna bent and kissed him. 'I take that back. You know I didn't mean it. I was simply getting in a dreadful flap, reminded of all the preparation for tonight.'

Propping himself on one elbow, Bjorn smiled and reached for her hand. 'And there was me thinking that all last night's frenetic activity in the kitchen, was preparation for this evening.'

'It was. But I still have to lay the table and you — '

'Have to put the final touches to the midsummer pole,' Bjorn finished for her. 'Don't worry, it's all in hand. There's nothing to worry about. It will be an excellent evening, you'll see. Just remind me again who's coming apart from Julian, Madge, Frank, Beattie and Felix.'

Searching for her mules, Anna reeled off a

list of names. Some from the now defunct Alexandra theatre and others from Bjorn's business contacts, made since opening his furniture studio. 'Oh, and don't forget the locals,' she called. 'At least this year they'll be in on the proceedings. Last year, when we first moved in, they must have wondered what on earth was going on when you erected that gigantic pole in the garden.'

Reaching for his own bath-robe, Bjorn's face broke into a lazy grin. 'Mmm. I guess it was bad enough for them having a foreigner in their midst, let alone one who pursued pagan customs.'

'Is midsummer a pagan custom?'

'Quite possibly. At least it's an acceptable one. Not like those of my ancestors who came to rape and pillage.'

Mention of the words rape and pillage, not only reminded Anna of the trip to Pinetrees Park in Dorset but also of their visit to Stonehenge, where Bjorn had proposed. Calmed by his presence and standing on tiptoe, she reached up and kissed his cheek. 'I'm sorry,' she whispered.

'What for?'

'What I said earlier, about us making love.'

'There's no need to apologize. I quite understand. My mother always got in a panic preparing for midsummer. I know you want everything perfect for Alexandra's Ragtime Band.'

Surprised to see Anna's eyes fill with tears, Bjorn clasped her to him. 'Anna, what's wrong?'

'Nothing,' she sniffed.

'Anna, my darling, it's not like you to shed tears over nothing. What's really troubling you?'

Feeling in her pocket for a tissue, Anna studied her husband closely. A sweep of blond hair fell across his forehead when he looked down at her, and his clear blue eyes searched her face intently.

'I'm just being silly. Mention of the Alexandra always makes me sad. Then . . . I got to thinking how sorry I was that your parents couldn't be here to celebrate midsummer and also — '

'And also?' Bjorn prompted.

'How much I love you . . . and how I wish I could give you a baby.'

Bjorn sat down on the bed and lifted her onto his lap like a child. 'I know it was a very sad day when the Alexandra closed, but at least we've tried to keep in touch with everyone. And most of them are coming tonight, remember? As for my parents, I agree it's a shame they couldn't make it, but we did see them at Easter. Anyway, now that they're so involved with the new timber factory, there'll be so much that needs my father's attention before the autumn.'

'I know,' Anna said weakly, fully aware that Bjorn hadn't mentioned the third thing that was troubling her.

'As for a baby ... ' he said, moments later, reading her mind. 'We've only been married for five years. There's still plenty of time.' With a curious smile, Bjorn turned to where his gaze encompassed the recently crumpled sheets. 'Who's to say we haven't already made one?' he acknowledged, desperate to cheer her. In response to Anna's sorrowful expression, Bjorn placed a tender hand gently across her abdomen. 'All sorts of wonderful things could be happening in there.'

Strangely comforted by the thought that even now she could perhaps be pregnant — it was certainly the right time of the month to conceive — Anna released herself from her husband's embrace. 'And all sorts of things should be happening in the kitchen and garden. Can I remind you, you have your erection to deal with.'

Bjorn looked at the bed in complete disarray and grinned wickedly. 'I thought I already had.'

'I meant the one in the garden. The

midsummer pole we intend to decorate with wild flowers.'

'What a shame. And there was me thinking you wanted to go back to bed.'

★   ★   ★

Several hours later, leaning from the bedroom window, Bjorn secured the Swedish flag onto the flag pole. 'How does it look? Will they be able to see it from the bottom of the drive?'

'If they can't, they'll need their eyes tested,' Anna called from the front garden, watching the flapping pennant of Swedish blue and yellow. 'I only hope the council won't object.'

'Why should they object? What's so wrong with being patriotic? In Sweden nearly every family has a flagpole. On national days they always fly the flag.'

'I know, and as far as I'm concerned, there's nothing at all wrong with being patriotic. I only mentioned it because someone on the parish council said — '

'Who's talking about the parish council?' came a voice.

'Madge!' Anna gasped, looking down the drive. 'Where's Frank and where's Peter? You're not on your own?'

'No, ducky, I'm not. Because we're so early, Frank decided to park in the village. He thought I should come and check with you first.'

'That wasn't necessary. I suggested purposely that you came early in order to get Peter settled, before everyone else arrives.

'I know, but Frank's still a bit wary of interrupting you two love birds. He thought you might have been having an afternoon nap or something.'

Reminded of the *something* that had taken place early that morning, Anna suppressed a smile and shook her head. 'No, there's been far too much to do this afternoon.'

'Well, now that I'm here and once Frank's been told the coast is clear, perhaps I can give you a hand?'

Dispatching Bjorn to fetch Frank and Peter, Madge followed Anna into the coolness of the hallway. 'We picked our wild flowers on the way,' she explained, 'Once we left that awful Ml. Apart from masses of dandelions in the lawn, wild flowers are in short supply in Finchley at the moment. Not having been able to make last year's party, I wasn't sure what you had in mind.'

'Anything wild as long as it's not protected or from a nature reserve,' Anna replied, putting Madge's bunch of dog-daisies and buttercups in a vase. Hearing the sound of

Frank's car in the driveway, she reached for the kettle.

Leaving the kettle to boil, Anna and Madge joined the two men unloading Peter and all his belongings from the car.

'You're sure you didn't mind us bringing him?' Madge asked, lifting the little boy from his car seat.

'Of course not. He's my special godson, aren't you, Peter? I'm also thrilled that you're stopping over with us. We've been looking forward to it for weeks.'

Hearing his name and recognizing Anna, whom he adored, Peter gave a shy smile and reached out to be taken into her arms.

'My goodness! Haven't you grown?' she said, lovingly smoothing down his wispy, fine hair. 'And don't you look smart?'

Pointing first to his blue and yellow T-shirt and then to the flag flying overhead, Peter replied. 'Sweden. Bjorn.'

'That's right,' Bjorn acknowledged. 'And I asked my mother to send you your very own flag, plus a map of Sweden, so you can see all the lakes and trees I was telling you about the last time we saw you.'

More confident than when he'd first arrived, Peter wriggled free of Anna's arms and trotted off with Bjorn and Frank to find his flag. Seeing them disappear into Bjorn's study, Anna turned to face Madge. 'Dare I ask — how is he? What did the doctor say about Peter's heart? Will he need another operation?'

Madge shrugged her shoulders. 'Hopefully not. Although most Down's children are born with heart defects, that last operation to repair Peter's certainly appears to have done the trick. Thank God.'

'Thank God indeed,' Anna murmured to herself. She'd been dreading the reply.

'And you'll be pleased to know his hearing's OK too. We had our appointment at the audiological clinic only a couple of weeks ago.' Madge's face filled with pride. 'In fact everyone at the hospital says they're really pleased with him. He's doing very well.'

'I'm not surprised,' Anna replied, pouring the tea. 'You and Frank have both worked so hard.'

'I like to think we have. Isn't that what any parent would do?'

'Not necessarily,' Anna mused, recalling some far less fortunate children at the other end of the village.

Sipping thoughtfully at her tea, Madge studied the fine Swedish bone china tea cup before placing it carefully in its saucer. 'As you know, Anna, it's not been easy. Especially just after Peter was born, when I was positively bogged down with advice. It was do this, do that, don't do this, don't do that, until I said to Frank I'd had enough. In the end I simply decided to take one day at a time and rely on my own common sense.'

'You've certainly got plenty of that,' Anna replied, full of admiration.

'Hmph! I'm not so sure I'd agree with you there. I didn't possess much while working at the Alexandra. If I possess any now, then Frank and Peter must take all the credit.

Hearing the sound of approaching voices, Anna asked softly, 'I take it Frank's OK too?'

Madge gave a contented sigh and looked to where Bjorn was leading Peter and Frank into the back garden. 'Oh, yes, ducky. Frank's fine. Ever since Pamela finally agreed to a divorce, he's been a completely different person. Can you believe his daughters have been wonderful too? They've been so supportive and guess what? the Prickly Pamela has actually got herself a boyfriend.'

'You're joking!'

'Well, not so much a boyfriend, as I gather he's about sixty, but he's done wonders for Pamela. She's gone all Afro hairstyle and Laura Ashley. Can you imagine — at her age?'

Shaking her head in disbelief, Anna tapped on the kitchen window to remind Bjorn and

Frank about their tea. Moments later, Peter appeared waving his miniature flag. Spying the familiar Peter Rabbit mug and plate that Anna kept especially for him, he sat down beside his mother.

In between drinking his milk and munching his favourite malted biscuits, he told Anna and Bjorn about his swimming classes, showed them his latest tooth and recited a poem about sausages sizzling in a pan.

'And who's my clever sausage?' Madge asked, giving him a hug.

'I am,' came the delighted response, as Peter plonked a milky-wet kiss on her cheek. Once more in the garden, this time watching Frank and Bjorn decorate the midsummer pole with greenery, aided and abetted by a curious and excited little boy, Anna linked her arm in Madge's. 'I'm so happy things turned out for you. It's obvious Frank adores you both.'

Looking in Frank and Peter's direction, Madge swallowed hard. 'I do believe he does. And Lord knows I love them both to bits too. It's just that sometimes I get so terribly maudlin. I start to wonder what would happen to Peter if anything happened to Frank and me, and then worry how Frank would cope if I was to — '

'Madge? You're not ill, are you?'

'I sincerely hope not, but you know what it's like. You see something on TV or a film, like *Love Story* and — '

'Imagine yourself in similar circumstances?'

'Exactly,' Madge replied, deeply reflective. 'Then you become even more paranoid. When you love someone so much *and* you've got a child to worry about.' Madge froze, acutely aware of her last remark and gave a quick sideways glance in the direction of Anna's perfectly flat stomach.

'Oh shit! I'm sorry, Anna. Talk about opening my mouth and putting my foot in it. I take it there's still no sign of a baby?'

'No,' Anna replied hurriedly. 'And Dr Anderson assures me there's nothing wrong, simply that I should stop worrying.'

'What about?'

'All sorts I suppose. Maintaining this huge old house, Bjorn's business, his parents' new factory and of course, why after five years, there's still no sign of a baby.'

'Whew! No wonder you haven't had time to conceive. Anyway, what's with the house and Bjorn's business? And why concern yourself with his parents' new factory?'

Going indoors to finish last minute preparations for the party, Anna described Bjorn's proposed plans to extend his business and their house, Laburnum Lodge. Both projects involved a great deal of money and work.

'I don't doubt for one moment that Bjorn isn't capable of dealing with it all,' Anna said, folding blue and yellow napkins into fans.

'But . . . ?' Madge prompted, sensing an undercurrent of concern.

'My thoughts follow a similar path to your own. What if anything were to happen to Bjorn or the business? I've always preferred to live within my means and thanks to the generosity of both sets of parents when we married, we're certainly not hard up.'

'So where's the problem?'

'For the moment there isn't one. Maybe I'm just being silly. Although, I confess I am deeply concerned that Bjorn's father has taken out such a huge loan for the factory. Not only has he dismissed it as a good long-term investment but also, when we were in Sweden at Easter, I overheard Henrik suggest that Bjorn considers something similar for the new furniture studio.'

Laying down her own pile of napkins, Madge gave Anna's hand a reassuring squeeze.

'Come now, Bjorn's a pretty level-headed sort of guy. He won't take any unnecessary risks. I insist you forget all about his parents' business. Why not let Bjorn concentrate on the house and studio? Then all you have to do is have a baby.'

'If only it could be that simple,' Anna sighed, her hand moving unconsciously to her stomach.

18

With Frank and Madge getting Peter ready for bed, Bjorn watched Anna add the finishing touches to the table decorations.

'What do you think?' she asked, tucking loops of Swedish ribbon into dark green foliage. 'Does it look OK, or have I forgotten anything?'

Bjorn slipped an arm round her waist. 'No, but I have. I've forgotten to tell you how beautiful you look this evening. In fact everything looks beautiful. It couldn't be a more perfect setting for our midsummer celebrations.'

'I only hope our guests agree with you,' she said, lifting her face to be kissed.

'Now then. You two lovebirds!'

Bjorn and Anna drew apart, surprised to see Beattie framed in the doorway.

'Beattie!' Anna called, arms outstretched, hurrying towards her. 'I didn't hear the doorbell.'

'That's because I didn't ring it. Frank saw my taxi pull up as he was coming downstairs. He said to come along in. I hope I wasn't interrupting anything.'

216

'No,' Bjorn replied, giving her a hug. 'Anna and I were simply checking the table decorations.'

'Is that what you call it? Oh well, I suppose it makes a change from come up and see my etchings.'

One by one as the guests arrived, each carrying sprays of wild flowers, they were all ushered into the garden. There, with the decoration of the midsummer pole complete, Anna secured some stray ox-eye daisies and stood back, ready for Bjorn and assorted helpers to pull on the rope and haul it into position. To loud applause and cheers of bravo, they congratulated each other on their handiwork.

'How simply magnificent!' Felix exclaimed, reaching for a glass of chilled white wine. 'And I do like all that blue and gold ribbon amidst the flowers and greenery. Quite a contrast in fact to our dear Queen's Jubilee.'

Madge nodded, recalling the assorted bunting adorning the streets on their journey from Finchley to Laburnam Lodge. 'I don't know about you, Beattie, but seeing London decorated in all that red, white and blue, reminded me of just after the war.'

'Hmm. It certainly brought back lots of memories. Though, I'd far rather you didn't remind me. Don't forget, I must be the oldest person here.'

'Not quite,' Felix corrected. 'As I'm fifty-nine too and with my birthday in August and yours, I believe, in September, that must make me the oldest.'

Leaving Felix and Beattie to discuss birthdays and star signs, Anna hurried away to remove the fine muslin cloths that were covering the food.

'They're a good idea,' Madge said, following on behind.

'Yes. Aren't they? Bjorn's mother gave them to me.'

'I'm more familiar with muslin squares for babies,' Madge continued, helping Anna fold the cloths away. 'Peter dribbled so much as a baby. I found that a muslin square, placed beneath his head, helped keep his sheet and mattress dry.'

'Then I'll have to bear that in mind, won't I?'

Interpreting Anna's remark as *if and when* she became pregnant, Madge gave her a reassuring hug and offered up a silent prayer. 'Right then, ducky. Shall I go and tell the hungry hordes to come and eat?'

When Julian Player began piling his plate with *gravadlax, inlagd gurka*, potato salad and sour cream, Beattie winked knowingly

218

in Anna's direction.

'You do realize Julian's been starving himself all week, knowing that he was coming here this evening. He knows you always put on a good spread.'

'Not only that,' Julian enlightened her, 'I aim to have second helpings as well. You would too, Beattie, especially if you were going where I'm going.'

'Really, Julian? And where's that?'

'Eastern Europe. I've been invited to assist an old friend who's working on a new TV costume drama.'

Felix gave a low whistle and stroked his goatee beard. 'Have you, dear thing? How simply wonderful.'

'It will be if we're on schedule.'

Beattie paused, progressing from the *gurka* to the *gravadlax*. 'From the tone of your voice, Julian, does that mean you're expecting problems?'

'Afraid so. According to Ashley Munroe — he's the director — they're having all sorts of nightmares with the casting and crew at the moment. Progress is so incredibly slow that it wouldn't really surprise me if we end up filming in the depths of a Polish winter.'

'Oh dear. Poor Julian,' Anna comforted, offering him some especially prepared herring. 'Then you had better tuck in. We can't

219

have you going away half starved.'

Examining his heavily laden plate, Julian looked across the table at his host. 'Bjorn, you're a jolly lucky fellow. Not only do you have a beautiful wife, but also she's an extremely good cook and hostess. I don't suppose you'd care to part with her for a bit? You wouldn't let her come with me as my Girl Friday?'

'Certainly not,' came the bemused reply. 'Unless . . . ' Bjorn reflected, turning deeply thoughtful eyes in his wife's direction, 'Anna wants to go back to work. She was saying only this morning how much she misses you all.'

Julian looked up expectantly. 'Is that true, Anna? Are you planning to return to work? If so I'm sure I could put in a good word for you with Ashley. Someone with your experience could be just what he's looking for.'

Anna turned and patted his hand. 'I'm terribly sorry to disappoint you, Julian. For the moment I'm perfectly happy here in Hertfordshire, acting as personal assistant to my husband.'

'Oh, well. You can't blame a fellow for trying,' Julian muttered sadly, taking solace from the mouthwatering selection of *smorgasbord* on his plate.

Much later, waving a final goodbye to most of their guests, Anna gave Bjorn a playful dig in the ribs. 'I've a bone to pick with you, Bjorn Carlson. Missing the theatre is one thing, leaving you and going half way across Europe for months on end is another. Whatever made you suggest such a thing?'

'I only wanted to make sure you weren't bored being at home all day.'

'I'm not at home all day, and I'm certainly not bored. Why only last week — ' Anna got no further, being interrupted by the sound of wheezy coughing coming from upstairs. 'Poor Beattie. Her cough seemed even worse this evening. You didn't mind my suggesting that she stay the night, did you?'

'Of course not. If you hadn't suggested it, I certainly would have. Besides, Madge and Frank will be able to drop her off on their way home tomorrow. Have you noticed how Peter is fascinated by her?'

'Yes, and according to Madge, he's always talking about her cat.'

'That's a good sign,' Bjorn said, turning the key in the lock. 'So let's hope Peter will take Beattie's mind off her nephew.'

'Oh dear. What's happened now? I thought everything was OK now that Beattie's finally resolved to accept Tom's marriage to Lucy, if only for the sake of their little boy. I take it they are still married?'

Bjorn gave a cynical smile. 'So I believe. Nevertheless, something tells me Beattie still wishes that they weren't.'

'Meaning?'

'I'm not sure. Perhaps you'd better ask Madge in the morning. I merely overheard Beattie telling her something about Tom and Lucy, that's all.'

'By that shall I assume you don't want to tell me?'

'No,' Bjorn said, leading her towards the stairs. 'By that I mean I'm simply exhausted and you must be too. Don't forget the amount of time you spent preparing all that wonderful food, which somehow or other, has quite miraculously disappeared without trace.'

'Other than in Julian's stomach or on Felix's beard?'

★ ★ ★

Peering into the moonlit garden from the bedroom window, Anna nestled contentedly against Bjorn's shoulder. 'It *was* a wonderful evening wasn't it?'

'Yes. Simply wonderful, dear thing, as Felix

would say, even without the midnight sun.'

'Ah! But at least we had your magnificent erection,' Anna teased, reminded of the numerous lewd comments from their guests as the evening wore on and more and more bottles of wine were consumed.

'So we did,' Bjorn said sleepily, climbing into bed. 'Unfortunately, unlike this morning Mrs Carlson, I'm far too tired to . . . '

'So am I,' Anna yawned, curling next to him, her eyelids beginning to close.

* * *

With shafts of early morning sunlight dancing on the dew-filled grass, Madge and Anna watched Peter skipping up and down the twisting garden path and round and round the floral pole.

'Just look at him,' Madge said, her voice catching in her throat. 'Running about like that you'd think he was almost normal.'

'He is to me.'

'It's kind of you to say so, Anna. You know as well as I do that isn't quite true.'

'Only yesterday you said he was doing so well.'

'I know and of course I've never kidded myself he'll be any different. Look how short he is for a start.'

'Perhaps, but his posture's already improved since he started swimming lessons and, watching him now, I'd say he'd probably enjoy dancing classes as well.'

Reaching for her cup of tea, Madge studied the flaxen-haired little boy who was weaving his way in and out of the shrubs and flower beds. 'What *is* he doing?' she pondered, when Peter stopped, bent low over a heavily scented bloom and began flapping his arms.

'I'd say pretending to be a butterfly. He's been watching that clouded yellow on the orange blossom for the past five minutes.'

'Why, so he is,' Madge exclaimed, touched by Peter's powers of observation as the butterfly dived and swooped, before settling on delicate, creamy blossoms. 'What a pity Frank's still asleep.'

'Bjorn too,' Anna said, looking at the kitchen clock. 'However, you'll rarely find Bjorn up before eight-thirty on a Sunday.'

Finishing her tea, Madge watched Anna collect assorted cutlery and china for the breakfast table. 'If we're to leave before lunch, perhaps I should go and wake Frank?'

'There's really no need to rush away, unless of course you've got to get back to London. Why not stay and have lunch with us? Also, don't forget Beattie. She's still snoring soundly — at least she was ten minutes ago.'

'Yes, it's a wonder she hasn't woken the entire neighbourhood. It never ceases to amaze me how she makes so much noise. Mind you, all that nicotine in her lungs can't help. I do wish I could persuade her to stop smoking.'

'You and me both. Goodness knows I've tried often enough. Although, I have noticed she never smokes when Peter's about.'

'And if my memory serves me correctly, never when she's with Tom and his little boy,' Madge added as an afterthought.

Anna paused in the process of cutting bread into soldiers for Peter. 'Speaking of Tom, what's happened now? Bjorn's convinced Beattie was upset about something last night.'

'He's right: she is. And if Beattie's upset it can only be related to one of two things: Tom and Lucy, or else Stavros, her landlord, and that damned cat of hers — who, just like her mother, Ariadne, still keeps having kittens. You'd think Beattie would have learned by now. She's even trying to persuade me to have one for Peter?'

'I expect he'd like that,' Anna said, without thinking.

'Huh! I'm sure he would,' Madge snorted, getting up to close the kitchen door, 'But I'd rather not dwell on that now. I'll tell you the latest about Tom and Lucy instead.'

Some time later, reassured that Tom and Lucy were still together and that Tom's career was going from strength to strength, including not only theatre and television but also films, Anna broke in, bewildered, 'So, where's the problem? Why can't Beattie accept the fact that Tom and Lucy appear to be happily married?'

'You mean particularly as she was convinced the marriage wouldn't last?'

'Exactly,' Anna cautioned in a low voice. 'And, as neither of them are involved in extra-marital affairs, at least there's no danger of divorce or messy custody battles over their little boy.'

Checking to see that her own little boy was still playing happily in the garden and that the door to the hallway was still firmly closed, Madge lowered her voice to a whisper. 'I have to confess I used to think Beattie was being paranoid about the whole Tom and Lucy thing. Now, I'm not so sure. By the way, have you ever met Lucy?'

Anna nodded, criss-crossing bread and butter soldiers on the Peter Rabbit plate. 'Only briefly, and that was years ago. Tom and Lucy brought the baby into the Alexandra one lunchtime.'

'And what did you think of him?'

'He was a dear little thing. Just like his daddy, with deep blue eyes and a mass of tawny hair, which pleased Beattie no end.' Anna looked up to find Madge grinning at her. 'What's so funny?'

'Actually, I meant what did you think of Tom?'

'Oh, I see. Well, from what I can remember he was extremely good-looking, although not as handsome as Bjorn, of course. But very stylish and a bit — you know . . . '

'You know,' Madge mimicked. 'What's that supposed to mean?'

'I'm not sure. It's difficult to say. He's obviously very confident.'

'Like big-headed?'

Anna shrugged her shoulders, trying to think back to the last time she'd seen Tom Hudson. 'No, definitely not big-headed. More self-assured really, knowing exactly what he wanted in life, where he was going and, at the same time, equally determined to do his own thing.'

'Not if Lucy has anything to do with it he won't. According to Beattie, Lucy's becoming very possessive. She wants to know where Tom is every minute of the day.'

'Perhaps she doesn't trust him? Perhaps he has been unfaithful?'

'That's where you're wrong, Anna, because

Beattie even confronted Tom about that.' In response to Anna's raised eyebrows, Madge explained, 'Beattie's very old-fashioned on that score. She might have had three husbands but she's never condoned extra-marital affairs. Anyway, Tom denied it emphatically, saying he adored Lucy, which only makes Beattie more convinced that it's Lucy who's got a guilty conscience.'

Curious to know even more, Anna also knew it would have to wait. At that precise moment the back door opened and Peter came bursting through, his thoughts on only one thing — breakfast! Spying his special mug, egg cup and plate of waiting soldiers, he eyed his mother expectantly. 'Is that for my egg?'

'Yes, it is. Anna's just popping it in the pan. But before you sit down, young man, go and wash your hands.'

His hands duly washed, Peter returned to the table and watched fascinated as Madge sliced the top off his egg.

'Pink stuff?' he asked, looking at Anna. 'Pink stuff for Peter's egg.'

In complete bewilderment, Madge looked first at Anna and then at the newly arrived Bjorn, freshly shaved and showered.

'Gosh! You've got a good memory,' Bjorn said, reaching out to sneak one of Peter's soldiers. 'I know what you want. You want some caviar.'

'Caviar? Good Lord! Since when has my son had caviar on his boiled egg?'

'The last time he was here,' Bjorn explained, crossing to the fridge. 'Don't worry, Madge. It's not Beluga Peter's referring to, it's only Kalle's and it comes in a tube. We always bring some back with us from our trips to Sweden.'

'Oh, you mean the pink stuff you spread on that peculiar bread? The bread that looks like huge, cardboard wagon wheels.'

Bjorn roared with laughter, while unscrewing the cap on the blue and yellow tube. 'If my memory serves me correctly, you and Frank were extremely partial to those cardboard wagon wheels. You ate practically a whole packet.'

'A whole packet of what?' Frank quizzed, bleary-eyed, coming into the kitchen.

Before Bjorn had chance to reply, Peter called out gleefully, 'Look, Daddy! Pink worms!'

With a groan, Frank's gaze alighted on the pink swirl of caviar now gracing the golden yolk on Peter's egg. 'Oh, my God! What's that he's eating? Madge, you don't by any chance have — ?'

'It's Swedish caviar,' Anna interrupted.

'However, I shall assume from that look on your face you'd rather have some Alka Seltzer.'

'My apologies, Anna,' Frank said, moments later, passing her an empty glass. 'I appear to have over indulged a little.'

Madge fixed him with a look of sheer incredulity. 'Did you say a *little*?'

'Well, it was partly your fault.'

'My fault,' Madge protested. 'How exactly am I to blame for your excesses of last night?'

'You said yes, when I asked you to marry me.'

'What?' Anna gasped. 'Madge! Why didn't you tell me? To think we've been up for over an hour and you never breathed a word.'

Madge coloured and shifted uneasily. 'To be honest, I didn't know if Frank was being serious. It could have been the drink you see.'

'Oh ye of little faith,' Frank teased, raising her hand to his lips. 'Very well, in case you're still not convinced, and in front of these witnesses here present before me, as they say, I'll ask you again: will you marry me, Madge?'

19

Following an impromptu celebratory lunch for Madge and Frank, Anna placed an impressive-looking basket upon the table.

'I know you all said you couldn't eat another thing, but there's still this wonderful fruit. Felix brought it with him when he arrived yesterday evening.'

'Anna, if I eat anything else I'll burst.'

'Oh, Frank, what a shame. Does that mean I can't even tempt you with these?'

'Hey! Hold on a minute,' Madge cried, when Anna picked up a cluster of shiny black cherries and popped one into Frank's mouth. 'That man's already spoken for. If there's any tempting to do, I'll do it myself.'

'So he is,' Anna teased. 'I'd quite forgotten. I shall have to remember that in future.'

Seemingly oblivious to the good-natured banter taking place at the table, Peter gazed longingly at the cherries, gleaming like jewels in the corner of the basket.

'Peter likes cherries,' came a tiny voice.

'Then you must have some,' Anna replied, scooping a handful of cherries onto his plate. 'Now, I wonder if we can find . . . '

Puzzling as to what Anna was hunting for, Peter soon discovered she'd been searching for four pairs of linked cherries. Fascinated, he watched her loop a pair over her ears like ear-rings and then with a mischievous giggle, he proceeded to do the same.

'Gosh. That brings back memories,' Beattie said, biting into dark juicy flesh. 'I remember doing that years ago, when we used to go cherry-picking in Kent. Very Carmen Miranda, Anna. And once we'd finished eating them all, we used to count the stones.'

Bjorn frowned, looking round the table at the mounting piles of cherry-stones collecting on their plates. 'Why count cherry-stones, Beattie?'

'To see who you were going to marry.'

'Or what material you'd wear when you got married,' Madge added.

Meeting her husband's bewildered gaze, Anna fixed him with a gentle smile. 'I'm afraid that's another of our weird customs, darling.'

'You mean like looking at people's etchings?'

'Not exactly. It's more like this you see,' and separating the cherry-stones into tiny groups Anna began reciting. 'Tinker, tailor, soldier, sailor, rich man, poor man, beggar

232

man, thief and so on. And, as I've already eaten — er — thirteen cherries, that means I'm going to marry . . . a rich man and wear — '

Before Anna had chance to discover what she would be wearing, Beattie was already one step ahead of her. 'Silk, satin, muslin, rag,' she began, repeating the four fabrics, until she eventually concluded with silk.

'I guess that sounds about right,' Madge said, examining her own pile of cherry-stones. 'Bjorn's not short of a bob or two and Anna did wear silk on her wedding day . . . so what about me? Let's see, I've eaten ten cherries, so it looks as if I shall be marrying a tailor and wearing satin.'

Here Madge looked across the table at her fiancé. 'Hmm, since you're not a tailor, Frank, where does that leave you?'

'Isn't it obvious? Wouldn't you say I was tailor made for you? As for you wearing satin. Mmm, I rather like that idea. I find satin extremely sensuous, especially when you wear that — '

'Oi! Hold it right there.' Madge blushed, for once unusually embarrassed. 'I don't want you giving any of our secrets away. Besides, remember Peter's here.'

Hearing his name, Peter looked up. Playing with his own cherry-stones, he hadn't really been listening to the grown-ups' conversation, but there had been one word that sounded vaguely like cats. Did that mean Mummy was going to let him have one of Beattie's kittens after all?

'Peter have a kitten?' he questioned.

'Um — I'm not so sure about that,' Frank began.

'But Mummy said give cats away and Peter wants one.'

All eyes turned in Madge's direction while she puzzled as to how Peter could have become so confused. If, as she suspected, he'd been concentrating so hard on making a cherry-stone pattern on his plate, then he could quite easily have misinterpreted secrets away for cats away, particularly as she'd had a mouthful of fruit at the time.

'Peter have a kitten, Mummy?' a tiny voice pleaded for a second time.

'Oh, all right,' Madge conceded, bowing to pressure from the assembled guests. 'You can have your kitten but you must promise me that you will look after it.'

Peter's round cherubic face and bright button eyes, radiated pure unadulterated joy. 'I promise,' he lisped, displaying a mouth and tongue stained with dark cherry juice. Then, sliding from his chair he ran towards Beattie.

'You shall have first pick of the new litter,'

she said, lifting him on to her lap. 'And, if your mummy and daddy agree, I'll take you shopping for a basket and some food. You'll also have to think of a name.'

To everyone's surprise, remembering the litter of tiny kittens, especially an all black one that he'd seen only last week, Peter announced almost immediately, 'Cherry. Peter call cat Cherry.'

'Why Cherry?' Madge puzzled.

'Because Beattie says I have to pick and Peter pick Cherry!'

Completely taken aback by her son's logic, Madge fought back a tear and looked at Frank. Seeing her reach for her handkerchief, he smiled knowingly and swallowed hard.

An hour later, waving goodbye, Bjorn and Anna returned to the house. 'And a good time was had by all, I think,' Bjorn remarked, remembering the events of the previous evening and more recently the unexpected lunchtime celebrations.

'There I'm inclined to agree with you,' Anna replied. 'I've never seen Madge looking so relaxed and happy. I'm so pleased Frank got his divorce. Isn't it romantic to think that he actually proposed to Madge beneath your midsummer pole, and at midnight by all accounts.'

Bjorn smiled reminded of their earlier

conversation. 'Yes. It might be a pagan custom, Anna, but it's obviously got magical properties too.'

Sighing wistfully, Anna ran her fingers gently across her stomach. 'Then I only hope Madge and Frank didn't use them all,' she whispered, her voice barely audible. Looking to see if Bjorn had overheard, she realized that he hadn't. He was too busy puzzling over Peter's circle of discarded cherry-stones.

'Ah, I see what it is now. At first I thought it was a happy, smiling face but I think it's supposed to be a cat.'

'So it is,' Anna said, peering over her husband's shoulder. 'And look, he's used the cherry stalks as whiskers. Isn't that clever?'

Equally impressed by Peter was Beattie, who sat listening to his animated chatter in the rear passenger seat of Frank's car as they headed back towards London. For the best part of the journey their conversation was mainly about Peter's kitten. How soon could he fetch it? What would she like to eat? And would she be lonely leaving her mother?

'I doubt it,' Beattie informed him, 'Especially, as she's going to such a good home.'

Satisfied with the reply, Peter wriggled against Beattie's side, closed his eyes and fell fast asleep.

Meeting Frank's gaze in the rear-view

mirror, Beattie began sheepishly, 'I hope you two don't feel as if you were bullied into having that kitten.'

'Don't worry,' Frank began, 'We shan't hold it against you Beattie — not this time. Just promise me you won't ask again. One is more than enough. By the way, why didn't you ask Anna and Bjorn if they wanted a kitten? They don't have any pets.'

'Because, just like Madge, I'm hoping Anna and Bjorn will soon be listening to the patter of tiny feet.'

'Anna's pregnant? That's wonderful news! Isn't it Madge?'

'It would be, if it was true,' Madge said sadly. 'I hate to disappoint you both. Anna isn't pregnant. Of course she'd like to be, but she's still finding it difficult to conceive.'

'Not like someone I could mention,' Beattie muttered grimly. 'When Lucy got herself pregnant, it must have been simply by snapping her fingers!'

'That's not quite how I'd put it,' Madge hissed as an aside to Frank.

She almost said something about Lucy simply opening her legs. For fear of offending Beattie, however, and just in case Peter woke up, she kept her thoughts to herself.

Blissfully unaware of Madge's remark, Beattie watched the disappearing countryside from the car window. 'Anyway, I'm sorry I mentioned her. I'd rather not talk about Lucy if you don't mind. It always makes me depressed. Let's talk about something far more exciting. Your wedding for instance. When do you think it will be?'

★ ★ ★

Two months later, Madge and Frank were married in a simple register office ceremony. In keeping with the cherry-stone prediction at midsummer, Madge wore a dark-navy dress and jacket, piped and trimmed in navy-blue satin. Spying the satin revers on Madge's outfit and the matching satin headband on her hat, Beattie gave Anna a nudge.

'Even Frank's following the theme,' she whispered, spying Frank's navy and gold satin brocade waistcoat and matching tie.

'Not to mention Peter,' Anna said, watching the somewhat overawed and bewildered little boy, when Frank slipped the simple gold wedding band on to Madge's finger. Peter, she observed, was wearing long, navy-blue serge trousers, cream shirt and a scaled down version of his father's waistcoat and tie. 'Madge has obviously been very busy. Did you know that it was Peter who insisted he had an identical waistcoat to Frank's. Even Cherry — '

'You're not suggesting the kitten had to have a waistcoat too?'

'No, I'm not,' Anna smiled, hunting for her box of confetti, 'But Peter did insist Madge made Cherry a matching cushion and collar from what remained of the satin brocade.'

Following the happy couple outside to the town hall steps, Anna kissed Madge on both cheeks. 'You look absolutely lovely. I adore the outfit. Very chic and very Jean Muir.'

Madge hesitated. 'You don't think it's too boring, all this navy? Only I'm far too old for the frothy wedding bit and Frank said he thought it looked elegant.' Madge gave a chuckle. 'That's a laugh for a start, isn't it? Me, looking elegant? I've never looked elegant in my life.'

'You do now,' Anna insisted, 'And those cream and yellow freesias in your corsage set the whole thing off to perfection.'

'That was Frank's idea too. The blue and gold. He was inspired by your midsummer party.'

At that very moment when a flash of blue and gold brocade dashed past, Madge reached out for Peter's arm. 'Hey! Not so fast, young man. Where do you think you're going? We're supposed to be having our photos taken.'

Muttering something about Cherry's cushion, Peter ran straight into Beattie's arms.

'My goodness, you do look smart,' she announced, giving him a warm hug. 'And how's Cherry? Anna tells me Mummy made Cherry a very grand cushion for her bed.'

Leaving Peter in animated conversation with Beattie, and the photographer taking pictures of Frank and Bjorn, Madge took Anna to one side. 'Well, any news yet?'

One look at Anna's crestfallen face told Madge that she wasn't going to get the wedding present she'd truly hoped for. 'Oh, Anna. I'm so sorry . . . I thought — '

'So did I,' Anna began, forcing back tears. 'I was so convinced that this time I was pregnant. Obviously, it was just another false alarm. Poor Madge, it looks as if you'll have to wait a little bit longer for your godchild.'

'Never mind, ducky. You know me, I've got heaps of patience. If I can wait all these years for Frank, I can certainly wait a while longer for your baby. Does Bjorn know by the way?'

'Yes. I told him last night, because I had such a dreadful tummy ache and had to go to bed early. He took it very well, of course, although like me, he's bitterly upset. He suggests we try again next month.'

When next month came, there was still no sign of Anna being pregnant. Recognizing the now familiar signals and seeing her emerge red-eyed from the bathroom, Bjorn reached out and took her into his arms.

'It will be all right, you'll see. Maybe we're simply trying too hard, worrying too much about conceiving. Perhaps you should have a break, even go away for a few days?'

'A break — without you? I've never been anywhere without you since we were married. I could never do that.'

Cupping her face in his hands, Bjorn studied her sad, dark eyes and brushed away a solitary escaping tear with his thumb. 'I'm not suggesting you go away for weeks on end — or even abroad — I was merely thinking of perhaps a couple of days with Madge or Beattie. You always say a day trip to London is never long enough to catch up on all their news.'

Anna bit her lip. 'I suppose I could. Beattie did say she'd got some super photos of us all taken at Felix's birthday party. And, with Beattie's sixtieth birthday coming up, I could also take her shopping for a special present. Perhaps you're right, darling. An overnight stay and the chance to catch up with Madge and Beattie actually sounds quite tempting.'

'An overnight stay? Goodness! Once you

three girls get together, you'll need more than an overnight stay. No, if you go, I insist you go for at least two nights or preferably three.'

Looking up into Bjorn's clear blue eyes, radiating his complete and utter love for her, Anna said softly, 'Three whole nights away from you . . . I shall really miss you.'

'Exactly,' Bjorn replied, determined to hide just how much he too was already dreading the prospect. 'However, it does also mean I shall have three whole days to concentrate on my new brochure. When you're not around to tempt me, Mrs Carlson, I can get twice as much work done. Not only that,' he said, forcing a smile, 'just think of the fun we'll have when you get back.'

Leaving Anna to ring Madge and make the arrangements, Bjorn busied himself in his study. If the truth were told, most of the work on his new furniture brochure had already been completed. Still, he reminded himself, it wouldn't hurt to plan even further ahead. There was also that other *very special project*, he'd been planning. Brightening at the prospect, Bjorn returned to the kitchen to find Anna hanging up the phone. 'Yes,' she said, turning to face him. 'Madge says it's OK. In fact she can't wait for me to go.'

20

Beattie dropped the bags of shopping on the hall floor, kicked off her high heels and padded into the kitchen of her London flat. 'I still think it was wildly extravagant,' she called back to Anna.

'Nonsense. I keep telling you, Bjorn and I would far rather you had something you really wanted for your birthday.'

'That's as maybe, but — '

'No buts. I don't want to hear another word. Wear it and enjoy it, OK?'

'Oh, I will,' Beattie replied, filling the kettle while thinking of the beautiful black sweater, decorated with exquisite copper and gold appliqué and beading. 'I'll wear it when Tom takes me to dinner. He always takes me out on my birthday.'

Leaving the kettle to boil, Beattie couldn't resist another peek into the Harvey Nichols carrier bag. First, removing the layers of tissue paper, she then held the sweater at arm's length and draped it against her willowy frame. Turning as she did so, she caught sight of her reflection in the hall mirror. 'What do you think?'

'As I said in the store, extremely glamorous and very you. Not to mention simply ideal for a dinner date with your handsome nephew.' Anna nodded to the latest black and white studio portrait of Tom, gracing Beattie's sideboard. 'Do you know where Tom's taking you?'

Following Anna's gaze, Beattie shook her head. 'No. It's always a surprise and usually somewhere swish.'

And always somewhere without Lucy, Anna wanted to add, but hearing the kettle boil, decided against it. Why upset Beattie by mentioning Tom's wife, especially when they'd had such a wonderful day shopping together?

Conscious of the heavily overweight Ariadne, purring sleepily in her basket, Beattie removed her precious sweater to the safety of her bedroom. This was one garment neither Ariadne, nor her daughter, Persephone, would be sleeping upon. 'Don't forget the Fuller's cake,' she called, closing the bedroom door behind her.

'As if I could,' Anna grinned, holding up a white cardboard box. 'We did say we'd have this with afternoon tea, didn't we?'

Beattie smiled to herself watching Anna slide an iced walnut cake onto Royal Albert china. Fuller's cakes had been one of Anna's weaknesses when they'd worked together at the Alexandra. Until in the end, Fridays had become known as Fuller's cake day. Although today was a Saturday, the ritual remained the same with Anna removing the walnut half carefully from the top of her cake, and placing it to one side.

'You're just like Peter with those Belgian iced buns. Only in his case he always saves the cherry until last.'

Mention of Peter and cherries, reminded Anna that she and Beattie were due to meet up with Frank and Madge later that evening. 'What time are we supposed to be going out?'

'I'm not sure. Madge said she'd ring once they'd confirmed everything with their babysitter and collected Peter from his friend's birthday party. It probably won't be for another couple of hours yet. If you're anything like me, I'd say you could do with forty winks.'

Anna watched Beattie suppress a yawn. 'You have forty winks if you like and I'll clear away the tea things. I might also ring Bjorn, just to see how he's coping without me.'

Hearing the sound of snoring coming from the bedroom, Anna rang Bjorn before curling up on the sofa with a pile of magazines. Most of them, she noticed, gave extensive coverage of Elvis Presley's funeral. Beattie had been a lifelong fan and even this morning had pondered long and hard over yet another LP of his greatest hits. 'Poor man,' she'd sighed, 'I'm sure it would never have happened if his mother was still alive. Boys always need a mother figure and girls their fathers. Don't you agree, Anna?'

Not wishing to draw attention to the fact that she wasn't exactly the right person to ask, Anna had quickly changed the subject. The purpose of her trip to London had been to forget about having children — or in her case not having them. Half an hour later, she blinked and gazed about her. Beattie, she concluded, from the sound of rhythmic snoring, was still sleeping soundly and, spying the pile of magazines scattered at her feet, Anna could only assume that she had nodded off too. Still feeling decidedly dozy, she was startled by the chiming of the doorbell. How long had it been ringing? And was that what had woken her in the first place?

'Woken me but not Beattie,' she murmured. Stretching and struggling to her feet, in a vain attempt to hurry to the door, she discovered her left leg was numb with pins and needles.

'Er — hello!' came a surprised voice from the doorway. 'I'm Tom . . . Beattie's nephew.'

'Yes, I know. We've already met — several

years ago at the Alexandra. I'm Anna Carlson.'

'Of course. I remember now. Lucy and I brought Alexander in when he was a baby. Jesus! That workroom was a dingy place. I don't know how you all stuck it there for so long. I say are you all right?'

'All right?' Anna queried, a pained expression on her face.

'Mmm. You look sort of lopsided. You haven't sprained your back or pulled a muscle while you've been out on a shopping spree with Aunt Bea, have you? Looks like there's enough shopping bags gracing this hallway to — '

'What? Oh, no,' Anna said, looking up at him, stamping her lifeless foot against the floor. 'When Beattie went for a nap, I decided to curl up with some of her magazines. Seems I must have dropped off too. I've now got the most awful pins and needles in my foot, that's all.'

Without further ado, Tom bent down on one knee, lifted Anna's left foot into his palms and began rubbing it, vigorously, back into life. Somewhat startled and embarrassed by his actions, Anna tried desperately to suppress her squeals of pain. To no avail, however, and it was that which roused Beattie from her slumbers. Spying Tom and Anna

together, in such an unexpected, yet somehow delightful way, was a picture she would
cherish for many years to come.

'Tom?' Beattie began, curious, rubbing at
her eyes. 'What on earth are you doing here?'

'At the moment helping Anna get rid of her
pins and needles. Then I thought we could
have a nice cup of tea and — '

'*Tom Hudson*! I recognize that tone in
your voice. Come on, you can't fool me. What
have you done?'

'I give in, Aunt Bea,' Tom said, standing up
to close the front door. 'I should know by
now that I can't keep any secrets from you.
Anyway, it's not what I've done but what I
can't do that's the problem. I'm going to have
to disappoint you, I'm afraid. I won't be able
to take you out for your birthday dinner after
all.'

Beattie's earlier delight at seeing her
nephew faded rapidly, her face filling with
acute disappointment and sadness.

'However, it's not all doom and gloom,'
Tom continued, taking hold of his aunt's arm
and leading her into the sitting-room, 'As I do
have a perfectly genuine reason for letting you
down. When you hear what it is, I'm sure
you'll understand. You see ... I've been
offered a fabulous part in a film, which,
according to my agent, means flying out on

location towards the end of next week.'

'A film? Next week?' Beattie cried, momentarily forgetting her earlier disappointment. 'That's brilliant news, Tom! Isn't that what you'd been hoping for?'

'Well, it is in a way. But as I've already said, it also means having to cancel your birthday dinner.'

'Oh that,' Beattie shrugged, trying to put on a brave face. 'That can wait until you come back.'

'It could — then I thought to myself why don't Lucy and I take you out this evening instead?'

Suddenly reminded of Anna's presence in the kitchen, where she was presumably making a pot of tea, Tom added as an afterthought, 'Anna can come too, of course. By the way, I didn't realize she was staying with you. You never said.'

'I'm not,' Anna explained, coming in with the tea tray. 'I'm staying with Madge and Frank, but as they've taken Peter to a birthday party, Beattie and I decided to do a spot of shopping.'

'Call that a spot of shopping? Not from where I'm standing it's not!'

Over tea, Beattie took great pains to convince Tom that she'd far rather stick to her original plan for Saturday night — a meal with Anna, Madge and Frank was far more preferable to anything that included sitting at a table with Lucy. Besides, she told her nephew, wouldn't it be better to postpone her birthday dinner until he came home? That way he could tell her all about life on location.

'So, if I can't tempt you to join us for dinner this evening,' Tom shrugged, rising from his chair, 'do say you'll come tomorrow.'

'Why? What's happening tomorrow?'

'Lucy's organized a sort of impromptu farewell drinks-party for me, a chance to say goodbye to all our friends. She thought it seemed like a good idea, especially as I could be away from civilization, as we know it, for at least three months.'

'I'm not sure. I probably won't know any of your friends, will I?'

'Aunt Bea!' Tom protested, his arm curled protectively about her shoulders. 'Since when have you had problems mixing with strangers? Come along now. No excuses.'

It was at this point that Tom caught Anna's eye. He smiled slyly in her direction and winked. 'Of course you'll know someone. Anna will be there — won't you, Anna? And Madge and Frank too, if you like? Bring them all along. Peter can play with Alexander, they must be about the same age. In fact, the more the merrier I say.'

★ ★ ★

At twelve o'clock on Sunday lunchtime, Beattie, Anna, Madge, Frank and Peter, all found themselves outside Tom and Lucy's London home.

'OK, troops,' Madge hissed, once the introductions were over and Beattie was busy taking Peter to meet Alexander. 'Just like we agreed last night, if we can all take it in turns to keep Lucy occupied, Beattie should be able to have Tom all to herself for a while.'

Frank frowned, pensive, and rubbed his moustache. 'I don't know, Madge. What is it with you women? Seems like you've all got a personal vendetta against Lucy. She looks quite a sweet little thing to me.'

'Oh, she's sweet enough, Frank, and I do think the word vendetta is a bit strong. Call it women's intuition if you like, but Beattie still believes Lucy got herself pregnant so that Tom would marry her.'

When Frank raised a bemused eyebrow, Madge dug him playfully in the ribs. 'And before you say anything else, Frank Webster, let me remind you, *I* might have got myself pregnant deliberately, but it was never with the intention of getting you to marry me.'

'Now you tell me! And there was me thinking I did the gentlemanly thing by making an honest woman of you.'

Linking her arm in Frank's, Madge kissed his cheek. 'You did,' she cooed, 'And I shall be forever in your debt. So be a dear and charm the pants off Lucy. No, let me rephrase that. Keep Lucy and Tom apart — if you can.'

'I'll do my best. Though Lord knows what I shall say to her. I must be old enough to be her father.'

'Oh, I'm sure you'll think of something,' Madge assured, leaving him to it.

★   ★   ★

Two hours later and satisfied with her plan of attack, Madge patted her husband's cheek appreciatively. 'Good work, Frank. Now that wasn't too difficult, was it?'

'Hmph! It certainly wasn't easy. Lucy might be small, but boy can she knock back the drink. Have you any idea how many glasses — '

'Yes,' Madge interrupted. ' 'Cos everytime I looked up she had one in her hand. Now, while Beattie's still chatting to Tom, I'd better go and find Anna. Any idea where she is?'

Frank nodded in the direction of the hallway. 'Last seen being dragged upstairs by Peter. He and Alexander have been playing with Lego. Peter thought Anna might like to play too.'

'Poor Anna. To think I've been so busy concentrating on Lucy and Beattie, I quite forgot about Anna. Perhaps I should take her a drink?'

Hearing children's excited voices, Madge paused on the threshold of Alexander's bedroom.

'Go on! Go on!' urged Alexander. 'What happened next?'

Oblivious to Madge's presence, Anna picked up the book she'd been reading to the two small boys and continued, 'So the big bad wolf knocked upon the door and said, '*Little pig. Little pig. Let me come in . . . or I'll huff and I'll puff and I'll blow your house in!*' '

When Anna lowered her voice to that of the wolf's, Peter and Alexander's eyes widened in alarm until they suddenly caught sight of Madge.

'Anna tell story of pigs,' Peter announced. 'Mummy sit down and Anna finish story.'

'I don't really know if there's time,' Anna began. 'Perhaps we should be going? Alexander's mummy and daddy probably have a great deal to do.'

'No, they haven't,' Alexander replied, adamant. 'So you must finish the story. *Please*!'

Looking to Madge for guidance, Anna was met with the reply, 'It's OK by me. You carry on. I'll just sit on the bed for a bit and rest my weary feet. Anyway, you're far better at telling stories than — '

'*Yesh, she ish*,' came a slurred voice.

When four pairs of eyes turned towards the open doorway, they saw Lucy emerging from the bathroom. 'Do go on. *Itsh shimply* ages since I've heard the story of the Three Little Pigs. I *never* have time to read to Alexander.'

'Daddy does,' Alexander said, watching his mother slump unceremoniously on to a bean bag.

With a knowing glance in Madge's direction, Anna turned the pages and finished the story as requested. Having eventually dispatched the wolf into a pan of boiling water, and with Peter and Alexander making huffing and puffing noises, Anna closed the book and rose from the bedside chair.

'You know, you're really very good,' Lucy drawled, reaching out for the glass of wine Madge had brought for Anna. 'I bet your *kidsh* just love you reading to them.'

'Um — actually I don't have any.'

Lucy's brows knitted into a frown. For a moment she'd mistaken Anna for someone else, someone with children. Looking blearily from Anna to Madge, she eventually made the connection. 'Oh, *yesh*, you're from the Alexandra, aren't you? I remember Aunt Bea telling me you haven't had much luck getting pregnant. That's a shame, *ishn't* it, 'cos you're obviously a natural with *kidsh*.'

Too hurt and embarrassed to respond, Anna passed the book back to Alexander. 'Please stay and read us another story,' he begged.

'I'm sorry, Alexander, but I think Peter's mummy and daddy are ready to leave, isn't that right, Madge?' Anna replied, fighting back the choking feeling in her throat.

'Yes, it is,' Madge snapped, throwing Lucy a withering look. 'In fact, it's *definitely* time we left. We'd also better go and say our goodbyes to Tom, and wish him *bon voyage*.'

Mention of Tom sent Lucy all dewy-eyed. Taking a deep gulp of wine, she perched the glass precariously on Alexander's toy box and struggled to extricate herself from the deep folds of the bean bag. 'Of course I never had that trouble myself,' she drawled nasally, spying Anna, who was now standing at the top of the stairs. 'The month after I stopped taking the pill, it was bingo!'

As a result of the deeply tactless remark made to Anna, Madge had decided to ignore any further contact with Lucy. Now, however, with her curiosity aroused, she stopped halfway down the stairs. 'Bingo?' she questioned.

'Yesh,' Lucy called down after her, clutching drunkenly on to the banister rail. 'The minute I decided to stop taking the pill, I got pregnant. Like I said, it was bingo! Or should I say it was Alexander?' Suffused with laughter at what she assumed to be a hilarious pronouncement, Lucy sank to a crumpled heap at the top of the stairs, her fine blonde hair falling across her face.

Surprised to find no one else sharing her sense of humour, she pushed her hair back from her eyes and looked about her. At the bottom of the stairs was a sea of unsmiling faces. Tom Hudson's was as black as thunder, whereas Beattie's had gone as white as a sheet.

★ ★ ★

'I knew it! I just knew it! Didn't I tell you?' Beattie announced triumphantly, while waiting for a taxi with Anna and the others.

'And does it make you feel any better?' Madge asked.

'Believe it or not, it does. At least my earlier suspicions have been proved correct. Even Tom knows the truth now.'

'And what do you think will happen?'

'Search me,' Beattie said, as the taxi pulled alongside and her scarlet finger nails made a grab for the door handle. 'That's up to Tom, isn't it? The good thing is that it wasn't me who had to tell him. He heard it for himself — straight from the little bitch's mouth!'

Trying to distance herself from the events of the past ten minutes, Anna sat ashen-faced in the corner of the cab with Peter perched sleepily on her lap.

'Not the best of farewells for Tom, was it?' Frank whispered as an aside, aware of Beattie and Madge still muttering on about Lucy.

'No,' Anna murmured, turning sad and thoughtful eyes in his direction. 'What would you do, Frank?'

'Do?'

'Yes. If you were in Tom's shoes and about to go away on location for three months?'

Frank pursed his lips, thus creating a lopsided George Harrison moustache. 'Hmm. That's a difficult one, Anna. As I recall, I was positively furious when Madge first told she was pregnant. Then again, it was in slightly different circumstances. What puzzles me though, is that Lucy positively adores Tom.'

'And he adores her too.'

'Exactly, which is the point I'm trying to make. Wouldn't Tom have married her anyway — only perhaps not quite so soon?'

'Quite possibly,' Anna agreed. 'But if my memory serves me correctly, Tom actually turned down a pretty lucrative contract about the time Alexander was born. I know Beattie thought it was such a dreadful shame.'

'What did I think was a shame?' Beattie quizzed, pricking up her ears, now that there was a lull in the conversation between herself and Madge.

Frank shifted uneasily on his pull-down seat. 'Er — Anna was merely telling me about the role Tom declined in order to be around when Alexander was born.'

'That's right. He did!' Beattie seethed, reminded of Tom's lost golden opportunity. 'And I only hope this latest episode won't stop him from making the same stupid mistake. Even someone with Tom's good looks and acting ability, doesn't get too many bites of the cherry.'

At the mention of the word *cherry*, Peter sat bolt upright. 'Cherry! Peter left Cherry.'

'Yes, that's right,' Frank acknowledged. 'We're nearly home, Son, and you can see Cherry.'

Madge let out a groan of despair. 'He

doesn't mean the real one, Frank; he means the toy one Anna and Bjorn bought him for his birthday. Now what are we going to do?'

'Well, we certainly can't go back for it, because Tom and Lucy are probably in the middle of a row or something.'

Madge fixed her husband with a cynical smile. 'Hmm, and I hardly think it will be a *something* in our sense of the word, Frank. My money's on them having an almighty row.'

★ ★ ★

'But why are you so angry, Tom?' Lucy began, her speech still slurred, when Alexander was out of earshot and the last of their guests had departed.

'Why am I so angry?' he echoed in disbelief. 'Why the hell do you think? You tricked me, Lucy! You deliberately lied to me. You swore to me you were on the pill and all the time you were deceiving me by — '

'It didn't matter in the end — did it?' she broke in feebly, nervously twisting a pale-golden strand of hair around her finger. 'You love me and we have Alexander and this lovely house.'

'We don't have this lovely house, Lucy, it's rented!'

'OK, so it's only rented, but after you've finished filming, perhaps we can buy a place of our own.'

'We could have bought a place of our own long before now, if I hadn't turned down that other job. Property prices are simply going through the roof at the moment.'

'I know,' Lucy whined, trying desperately to placate him. 'While you're away, what if I start contacting some estate agents? Perhaps we could find somewhere that needs a bit of modernization. That way it shouldn't be too expensive. I'm quite a dab hand with a paintbrush and a roller you know. Then, when you get back . . . '

Reminded of Lucy's recent handiwork in Alexander's bedroom, Tom stopped pacing the floor. 'I don't know, Lucy. At the moment I can't even begin to think about what will happen when I get back.'

Lucy's face filled with alarm. 'Are you saying you don't intend to come back to me? You don't mean you want a . . . divorce?'

Tom shrugged his shoulders and ran his fingers though his hair, all the while watching Lucy's eyes brim with tears. 'No, I wasn't thinking of a divorce. It's simply that at the moment I need to concentrate on the next three months. You know how I felt when I first heard I'd got this job. As well as being elated, I was also upset at leaving you and Alexander for so long. I could be away until Christmas — remember?'

Lucy nodded, mascara-stained tears coursing down her cheeks, leaving Tom trying unsuccessfully to forget the recent unpleasant scene on the stairs. Reluctantly, he drew his wife into his arms. 'No, I don't think I want a divorce, Lucy,' he whispered, his voice full of despair. 'Who knows, perhaps a three-month break will do us both the world of good.'

21

Standing outside Madge and Frank's front door, Anna noticed a car pulling slowly to a halt. Initially, not paying too much attention to the driver, she saw him place a copy of the *A to Z* on his dashboard before turning to retrieve something black and furry from the front passenger seat. Tom Hudson! And in his hands was Peter's favourite cuddly toy.

'Thank goodness, you've got Cherry,' she called, as Tom unfolded his tall muscular frame from the car. 'Everybody will be absolutely delighted to see you. We had the most awful job getting Peter off to sleep last night.'

Grateful that he'd at last found the right address, Tom breathed a huge sigh of relief. He'd been driving round Finchley for the past half an hour trying to locate Madge and Frank's house.

'Where is Peter? Is he here?'

Anna nodded in the direction of the open front door. 'Yes, we've just fetched him from school. Madge is taking him to the loo and Frank's also inside, collecting my bags. My three days are up and, despite all my protestations, they've insisted on taking me to Euston to catch my train.'

'Euston? I'm going in that direction myself. I've an appointment with my agent. We're supposed to be going through the finer points of my contract. I can give you a lift if you like.'

'Isn't it a bit late?'

'Well, I would have been here earlier,' Tom said, looking at his watch, 'if it hadn't been for the fact that I've been driving round for ages looking for this place.'

'Um — I meant isn't it a bit late for going through your contract? I thought that would have been sorted ages ago.'

'Oh, I see,' Tom grinned, showing a row of even white teeth. 'Yes, it would, ordinarily, so I can only assume you must have been out of earshot yesterday, when I was telling everybody how I got this part. The original choice decided to participate in a charity jump and ended up breaking his leg.'

'That's unfortunate.'

'It is for him — but not for me,' Tom announced brightly, holding out the toy kitten in the direction of Peter's eager arms.

'Mummy, Cherry's come back!' Peter called, practically tumbling out of the front door.

'One wandering stray, returned safely to its

owner,' Tom said to Madge and Frank, who had come to investigate why Peter was suddenly full of beans, when last night he'd been totally bereft and inconsolable.

'You needn't have come all this way, Tom,' Madge protested, stepping back to let Frank pass with Anna's luggage. 'In fact, Frank and I were just talking of calling on you instead. We're in the process of taking Anna to catch her train, which is why I can't even invite you in for a quick cuppa, I'm afraid.'

'There's no need,' Tom replied, checking his watch for the second time. 'As I've already explained to Anna, I can take her to Euston. I'm heading in that direction myself. I've an appointment with my agent.'

With yesterday's distressing and embarrassing scenario still looming large in her head, Anna was about to insist that she took a cab, while Tom stayed behind, if only for Madge's quick cuppa, when Frank broke into her chain of thought.

'That's jolly decent of you,' he said, casting an admiring glance in the direction of Tom's car. 'I expect Anna would much prefer to travel to Euston in style, especially as our old rust bucket is playing up at the moment. That's why we took the tube and a cab yesterday. It's always a safer option, isn't it? Especially if you drink the odd glass or two.'

When Madge nudged him pointedly in the ribs, Frank remembered, only too late, Lucy's excesses of the previous day. She'd certainly had more than the odd glass or two. Flustered, he picked up Anna's bags. 'Right then. Where shall I put them, in the boot?'

Saying a tearful and fond farewell to Madge and Frank, Anna felt Peter tugging at her skirt. 'Anna come soon? Anna read Peter more stories?'

'Yes, I'll come soon,' she promised. 'I'll also try and find a story about a little boy called Peter.'

'And Cherry?' Peter asked, holding up the black furry toy, before winding the red satin lead securely around his chubby hand.

'Hmm, I reckon that's going to be a bit more difficult,' Madge was heard to mutter, making sure both her son and his favourite toy stayed within her grasp.

Undeterred, Peter insisted on waving goodbye to Tom and Anna, until the car had completely disappeared from sight, only then did he allow his mother to take him indoors for his tea.

'He's a great little lad, isn't he? Quite a character one way and another,' Tom remarked, with a last glimpse in his rear-view mirror. 'Such a shame about the Down's Syndrome.'

'Yes, it is, but Madge and Frank are wonderful parents. I don't think Peter could wish for any better.'

Pulling up outside Euston, Tom scanned the pavements for traffic wardens. Leaving the engine running, he hurried to open up the boot. 'Are you sure you can manage your bags? I could always park in a side street and help you to your train.'

Anna shook her head; she was already feeling distinctly uncomfortable in Tom's presence. Being caught up in that last set of traffic lights hadn't helped at all. 'It's kind of you to offer but they're not heavy. I'd hate for you to get a parking ticket and be late for your appointment with your agent.'

'Good Lord! Is that the time?' Tom said, checking his watch. 'You're right, Anna, I'd better get a move on. By the way, will Bjorn be there at the other end to meet you? As I recall, Aunt Bea said you lived in the country, miles from anywhere.'

Anna gave a curious smile watching Tom pause with his hand on the driver's door. 'I know Beattie always describes us as living in the sticks, but I can assure you it's really quite civilized. Not only are we near Junction 8 of the M1, we also have a decent bus service and an excellent local taxi driver.'

'The M1, eh? So it can't take that long to

get from London to your part of the world. Maybe I can kill two birds with one stone.' In response to her blank expression, Tom slid into the driver's seat and unwound the window. 'Of course, Lucy hates anything remotely rural but knowing how much Aunt Bea enjoys your company, I was thinking, perhaps I could always bring her to see you and at the same time give Alexander a breath of fresh country air. He's always saying he's never seen a real live cow.'

Unsure as to how she should reply, Anna called a quick 'goodbye and thank you', and hurried away across the concourse. Madge on the other hand, would never have had any problems contemplating Tom's farewell remark.

'*Never seen a cow, ducky? But surely you're married to one!*'

'Mrs Carlson!' Anna scolded under her breath, 'Fancy thinking such a thing. You've obviously been away from your husband for far too long.'

When the train pulled into Watford Junction, Anna's heart lifted. Only another ten minutes down the line and she'd be home. Even after five years of marriage, thinking of Bjorn still caused the familiar stirring in her stomach. Though only away for three days, and in spite of Madge and

Beattie's company, there had been several times during the past seventy-two hours when those three days had seemed like three months.

First applying a fresh coat of lipstick and then running her fingers through her recently highlighted hair, Anna peered from the dust-streaked window of the train looking for familiar landmarks: fields and farms and the Grand Union Canal.

'Anna!' Bjorn called, hurrying towards her and gathering his wife in his arms, kissed her full on the mouth. 'Oh, but I've missed you.'

'You're the one who sent me away,' she teased.

'I know, but only because I thought it would do you good — and did it?'

'Yes, I do believe it did. It was simply lovely to see everyone again. Madge and Frank treated me like some long-lost relation; Beattie and I had the most wonderful shopping experience together and, of course, Peter simply showered me with hugs and kisses.'

'I've got a rival, have I?' Bjorn said, loading Anna's bags into the car.

'Not only one — but two. Alexander also plonked a very wet kiss on both cheeks when I said goodbye. *And* he told me that he loved me.'

'Alexander?'

'Tom and Lucy's son. Beattie's nephew's little boy. He and Peter are about the same age. For some reason we were all invited to Tom's farewell party; he's going away on location for three months, and I ended up reading the boys a story.'

'I see,' Bjorn replied, with a lazy grin. 'Well, as long as it was only Alexander that was doing the kissing and not his superstar dad.'

'Tom's not a superstar. He might have been on television and made the odd film or two but I'd hardly put him in the superstar league.'

'He is now,' Bjorn corrected, helping Anna into the front passenger seat. 'That's if the magazine article in the *Woman's Wotsit* thing you have delivered is correct. There's a picture of Tom Hudson attending some London premiere. I don't think he had a leading role but they are predicting he'll be a heart-throb to watch out for in the eighties. Just you wait and see.'

Watching and waiting for Bjorn to appear in the driver's seat, Anna giggled playfully. 'So that's what you've been up to while I've been away — reading all my women's magazines.'

'For your information Mrs Carlson, I've been extremely busy while you were away. I merely flicked through the magazine while I was waiting for the onions to cook.'

'You hate the smell of onions cooking. Why were you — ?'

Bjorn tapped the side of his nose. 'It's a surprise. You'll have to wait until we're home. And yes, I do hate the smell of onions — and garlic too, come to that. Let's just say it was a labour of love, shall we?'

Leaving Bjorn to put the car away in the garage, Anna crept into the kitchen where a wonderfully pungent smell of anchovies, onions and potatoes filled the air. 'Is that Jansson's Temptation?' she asked, when Bjorn appeared by her side. 'Are your parents here?'

'Yes, to your first question, no, to the second. For your information we're quite alone.'

'But you don't like cooking and how — '

'Did I know what to do?' Bjorn finished for her. 'Easy, I rang my mother. Once she'd recovered from the shock of me even attempting to cook something for your homecoming — let alone Jansson's Temptation — she gave me the recipe and I set off for Waitrose.'

Suitably impressed, Anna's attention was drawn to the rest of Bjorn's culinary efforts: tossed green salad, cheese board and a Norwegian Cream for dessert.

'All Scandinavian,' Bjorn said, pointing to

the cheeses, 'and the Norwegian Cream is in keeping with the theme. 'Also, because it's such a lovely evening, what I believe you call an Indian summer, I thought we could eat on the patio.'

Leaving Bjorn to open the bottle of chilled white wine from the fridge, Anna hurried upstairs for a quick shower. Dressed in a simple cotton frock, she tied her hair loosely at her neck and joined Bjorn in the garden.

'Mmm, heavenly,' she sighed, sipping at her wine. 'London was fun but I'm so pleased to be home. I must be in danger of turning into a country bumpkin.'

'We're hardly miles from anywhere, Anna. I know we can't hear them but the A41 and M1 are both practically on our doorstep.'

'Yes, I know. That's what I told Tom when he dropped me off at Euston.'

Bjorn frowned, topping up her glass. 'You didn't say Tom took you to Euston?'

'You didn't give me chance. You practically ravished me the moment I stepped off the train, or had you forgotten?'

'So I did,' Bjorn mused, emitting his lopsided smile. 'Just think, we'll be the talk of the village next week. You'll never be able to show your face at Young Wives again.'

With baited breath, Bjorn waited for her to sample her first mouthful of Jansson's

Temptation. 'Darling, this is delicious,' she murmured appreciatively.

'You don't think I put in too much cream?'

'No, it's perfect. I'm very proud of you. I must tell your mother when I speak to her. How are they and how's the factory?'

'They're well and everything's fine. In fact Father's already talking of further expansion.'

'Is that wise?'

'You know my father,' Bjorn shrugged. 'Anyway, he says the government are offering all sorts of subsidies with loans at the moment.'

Anna stopped eating. 'That's OK now, but what if the government changes its policy? Even you said it was an awful lot of money to borrow and — '

Bjorn held up his hands in mock alarm. 'No more talk about business and politics, you know how they bore me. Especially on such a lovely evening and particularly when I had other things in mind.'

Recognizing the cheeky twinkle in his eye, Anna fixed him with a knowing smile. 'But there's still the cheese board and the Norwegian Cream.'

'Exactly. So definitely no more talk about money matters. I suggest you try the pudding instead. The eggs are from Ginny's farm. She assured me they were freshly laid and also sends her love.'

'No doubt Ginny's exhausted, this being their busiest time of year,' Anna said, reminded of the recently harvested and ploughed fields she'd seen from the train.

'I don't know about exhausted, she was certainly down in the dumps.'

'Why? Does she think it's going to be a bad harvest?'

'No. It's worse than that. It's the proposed M25. If it does get the go ahead then it looks very much as if one of the access roundabouts could be smack bang in the middle of Ginny's milking sheds.'

Anna looked up, mortified. 'They can't do that, can they? How can you run a dairy herd without milking sheds?'

'I've no idea, but I'm sure Ginny will tell you all about it. She said she'd be in touch next week. They're hoping to organize a petition or something.'

When thoughts of Ginny's farm turned quite naturally to cows, it was inevitable that Anna should remember Tom Hudson's farewell at Euston.

Seeing her lost in thought, Bjorn reached out to cut himself a piece of Jarlsberg cheese. 'Penny for them, or should that be an ore as we've gone all Scandinavian this evening?'

'What? Oh, nothing,' Anna replied, uneasily. Somehow it seemed strangely inappropriate to mention Tom again. Looking up, she watched Bjorn move a distinctive blue and yellow candle to a more sheltered spot on the table. A slight breeze had suddenly caused the wax to drip freely onto the delicate cream lace cloth. It was, she concluded, an ideal opportunity to change the subject.

'Aren't they the candles Julian admired so much at midsummer? Remind me to buy him some next time we go to Sweden.'

'Speaking of Julian,' Bjorn said, rising from his chair. 'I almost forgot, he sent a postcard which arrived just after you left. There's also a letter for you from Fudge. At least I think it's from Fudge, as she has such terrible handwriting.' So saying, Bjorn disappeared into the house to fetch the post that had arrived during Anna's absence.

Studying the date and heading on Julian's large picture postcard of the High Tatras mountains, Anna perceived that he was somewhere along the Czechoslovak/Polish border. 'Doesn't it look impressive?'

Bjorn began clearing away the dishes. 'That's what I thought. A pity the same can't be said about the weather. Poor Julian, I bet he'd give anything to be back in England at the moment.'

Intrigued, Anna read Julian's neatly written account of filming so far.

My dears
If we'd wanted to film The Tempest *while we were in Prague, we couldn't have picked a more perfect spot. On average Prague has nineteen inches of rain a year during May to September. I'm convinced we've had the full nineteen in the past week alone! All exceedingly damp about the gills, we're now heading off to Poland, which I'm told is considerably flatter. Incidentally, Ashley has just informed me the swamps and dunes of the Baltic coast are quite a contrast to the undulating forests in the south, so I'll let you know.*

Anna shook her head in sympathy. 'I see what you mean by poor Julian. It hardly sounds his cup of tea. And what's this PS? His writing's become so small, I can barely read it.'

'Yes, I struggled to decipher that, too. In the end, with the aid of a magnifying glass, I took it to read: *Are you sure you don't want a job, Anna? We could really do with you here. It's one disaster after another!*

With a languid sigh, Anna placed the postcard back on the table, stretched and looked about her. 'No thank you, Julian. At this moment the only job I'm interested in is clearing away the supper things, locking the door for the night and then . . . '

'And then?' Bjorn said huskily, taking one of her hands and holding it against his lips.

'Well, having tried your Jansson's Temptation, Mr Carlson, I thought you might like to try a different variety. I just happened to buy some rather special satin undies when I was in London. I put them on after my shower and wondered if perhaps you'd like to — '

'Really?' Bjorn, said intrigued, pulling her gently to her feet. 'Tell me, what exactly did you have in mind.'

Anna trailed her fingers seductively down the buttons of Bjorn's blue gingham shirt. 'Perhaps a little temptation of the Anna Carlson variety.'

Needing no further encouragement, Bjorn blew out the remains of the candles, lifted Anna into his arms and carried her indoors. Later, sated and content and comforted by her husband's firm embrace, Anna whispered in the darkness, 'You know, I love this old house. It has such an air of peace and tranquillity about it. I'm convinced the previous occupants must have been very happy here. Don't you agree, darling?'

'They might have been happy but they were lousy gardeners. Do you remember the problems we had hacking our way through the brambles when we first arrived? It was like a nightmare out there.'

'Spoilsport,' Anna teased. 'Where's your sense of imagination?'

'Of course, I was forgetting,' Bjorn said, stroking her hair where it now fell about her shoulders. 'Didn't you always say it was like something from a fairy-tale?'

'Oh, yes. Very Sleeping Beauty. I could just imagine the prince hacking his way through all those brambles and roses.' With her thoughts winging away first to her favourite fairy-tale and then to Peter and Alexander and the story of The Three Little Pigs, Anna was unaware that Bjorn had already fallen asleep. 'Yes,' she sighed again, snuggling against him, 'Laburnam Lodge is definitely Sleeping Beauty. Please God, we can stay here for ever.'

22

With the passing of a glorious Indian Summer, Bjorn became increasingly worried about Anna. Despite their long-held hopes and expectations, she was still unable to conceive.

'There's still plenty of time,' he reassured. 'At least the tests have shown there's nothing wrong with either of us. Remember what the specialist said?'

'Then why doesn't it happen?' Anna said miserably. 'As for having plenty of time, I'm already in my thirties and very soon I'll be forty!'

'Early thirties,' Bjorn corrected. 'Which means you've a long way to go before you're forty. Besides, look at that actress.'

'Which actress?'

'The one in your magazine. You read the article. She'd been trying for fourteen years and had quite given up hope of ever having a baby.'

'And from that look on your face, you're telling me we've only been trying for five?'

'Yes, so please don't give up hope, my darling. Not yet.'

'I already have,' Anna sniffed, her face full of despair.

Spying a sudden flash of red and gold in the garden, where a goldfinch hung to a solitary sunflower head, Bjorn reached for Anna's hand. 'Come along,' he said brightly, 'get your jacket, we're going blackberry picking. Ginny said there are loads across the fields.'

'What will we do with them when we — ?'

'Make jam of course,' Bjorn continued, turning to the pine kitchen cupboard. 'Now where on earth do you keep those Tupperware containers. Your Young Wives are forever holding Tupperware parties. You must have something suitable.'

Realizing that Bjorn was only trying to lift her spirits and wouldn't take no for an answer, Anna stepped forward and took out a small plastic basin.

'That's no good. If we're going to make jam, we're going to need one like that on the top shelf.'

'That's enormous! I use that for making bread. We'll be out for ages trying to fill that.'

'Good,' Bjorn announced, reaching high into the cupboard. 'That's what I had in mind and it will be fun — you'll see.'

With Anna hauling out her jacket and wellingtons from the under-stairs cupboard,

Bjorn meanwhile fetched what she referred to as his lumberjack's jacket and boots. 'Very Monty Python,' she giggled, remembering a recent episode that had kept them both in hysterics.

Delighted to see Anna smiling once more, Bjorn led her from the house, along the main road, past Ginny's farm and across the footpath to the fields beyond.

'What did I tell you?' he said, an hour and a half later, spying the contents of their half-filled bowl. 'Aren't you glad you came?'

'Yes, very glad. I'm also extremely sorry.'

'Sorry for what?'

'For being such a picture of abject misery just lately. I know I've been simply awful to live with, day and night, ever since I returned from that three-day break in London.'

Ignoring Anna's squeals of protest, Bjorn swung her into his arms and perched her on top of a five bar gate. 'Day *and* night you say? I'm not so sure about the days, because you've been helping Polly at the playgroup and I haven't seen a great deal of you. As for the nights, I certainly wouldn't describe those as awful. In fact I'd go so far as saying they've been pretty amazing.'

Anna blushed and picking a ripe blackberry from the bowl, threw it at him. 'Bjorn Carlson! What am I going to do with you?'

'Just love me, Anna,' Bjorn said, his voice turning strangely serious. 'Just love me — that's all I ask. For the moment does it really matter if it's only you and me?'

'You mean if we don't have a child? I thought you wanted a baby.'

'I did . . . and I do, but it's not the end of the world if we don't — is it? We have each other. Isn't that all that matters?'

Nodding in reply, Anna held out her hands for Bjorn to lift her down from the gate. How long they remained in each others' arms without speaking, she wasn't sure. She only knew that by the time they reached home, she felt as if an enormous weight had suddenly been lifted from her shoulders.

Later that evening, writing labels for the jars of bramble jelly, Anna looked up deeply pensive. 'Bjorn, I've been thinking.'

'I can see that. You've hardly spoken a word since we returned from our walk. Everything is OK now, isn't it?'

'Yes,' she replied, in all honesty. 'The walk did me the world of good.'

Pulling out a chair, Bjorn sat down and studied her across the table. 'So what's the problem?'

'It's not a problem. I merely wanted to ask your advice. As you know I've been helping out at playgroup on a voluntary basis and

Polly — Mrs Bell — was suggesting that as I'm good with children, perhaps I should consider taking a course. Become properly qualified, join the Pre-School Playgroups Association and things like that.'

Bjorn nodded in understanding. 'Sounds like a jolly good idea to me. I take it you don't intend to set up in opposition to Polly?'

'Gracious no! But she says once I'm qualified, I could step in and take charge on the odd occasion that she isn't there. What do you think?'

'I think it's a fantastic idea. How soon can you enrol?'

'There's a new course beginning in January. Polly's going to drop the prospectus in some time this week.'

'And was that it?' Bjorn ventured, sensing this wasn't all that was bothering Anna, 'Or is there something else?'

'Not really, other than that if things work out well and I enjoy the responsibility, it could take up a lot of my time.'

'It's your time Anna.'

'I know, but at the moment I help you with your books and paperwork from the studio. If I work and study full time, I might not be able to . . . '

'Ah! I see what you're getting at now. In which case don't worry about it. Thanks to your wonderful organizational skills, everything's up to date. The tax man and any outstanding bills have been paid, the new furniture brochures dispatched and next year's exhibition already pencilled in the diary. This means you can concentrate on your course and leave the paperwork to me in future. I'm positive I can manage — and if I can't, surely I only have to ask?'

'Of course. You know you can ask me anything.'

'Great,' Bjorn said, slyly, reaching for a newly filled jar. 'So how about us trying some of this jam?'

Next morning, deftly kneading scone dough on the pine kitchen table, Anna was in the process of reaching for the rolling pin when the telephone rang. 'Bjorn, can you answer that please? My hands are covered in flour.'

Hands poised in mid-air, Anna waited to see if the call was for her. Moments later, hearing Bjorn's voice deep in conversation she assumed it was safe to continue with her baking. It was only when he came into the kitchen some ten minutes later, indicating that she was wanted on the phone, she expressed surprise. 'Who is it?' she asked, dusting off her hands.

'Julian.'

'Julian? I thought he was in Poland.'

'He is,' came the reply.

Concerned by the expense of such a long phone call, Anna hurried from the kitchen, only to return herself after yet another ten-minute interval.

'How was he?' Bjorn began, watching Anna reach for the pastry cutter.

'Very tired, exhausted and cold. They've had all sorts of disasters.'

'Mmm. So I gather,' Bjorn replied, plucking a stray sultana from the table. 'He told me the weather's been dreadful and they've had several problems and accidents.'

Deep in thought and reaching for the baking tray, Anna slid the scones onto its shiny surface and made her way to the oven.

'So . . . what did you tell Julian?' Bjorn continued, acutely aware that Anna was keeping her back towards him purposely.

'What are you implying?'

'I meant, what did you tell him in response to his SOS? He's asked you to go and help with the final stage of filming, hasn't he?'

Spinning round to face Bjorn with a how-did-you-know-that? look upon her face, Anna said quickly, 'I told him no.'

'Why?'

'Isn't it obvious? For a start I wouldn't

want to leave you and then there's all sorts of things like . . . '

'Like what for instance?'

Anna shrugged weakly, not wanting to tell Bjorn that in spite of yesterday's conversation, she still yearned to become pregnant by Christmas.

Insisting that Anna sat down at the table, Bjorn poured two cups of coffee. 'Now, I want you to be perfectly honest and tell me exactly what you thought when Julian first explained why he was ringing.'

'Um — when I first heard about their catalogue of disasters, I thought how awful for them. Then, when he said he'd mentioned my name to Ashley, with a view to my helping out, I confess I was deeply touched. Of course, I told him I couldn't possibly undertake such a task; I don't even know if I'm up to it. And last but not least, I also told him I could never leave you for three weeks.'

'Why ever not?'

'You mean why couldn't I cope with the job, or why couldn't I leave you?'

'Both,' Bjorn replied, refilling their cups.

'To begin with filming is a totally different concept to working in the theatre and secondly, it was bad enough leaving you for three nights, let alone three weeks. Or have you forgotten?'

285

'No. But a few weeks would soon pass. Look how quickly the months have flown since Julian was here for our midsummer party.'

Anna sipped thoughtfully at her coffee. 'You almost sound as if you want me to go.'

'I do,' came the immediate reply. 'For the simple reason I think it will be good for your morale. You're also still a union member so there won't be any problems there.'

'And there was me thinking you loved me,' Anna protested with a grin.

'You know I do.'

'Really? And your way of showing it is to send me away, to work from dawn to dusk in freezing cold conditions, because you think it will do me good?'

'Exactly,' Bjorn reiterated, reminded of yesterday's efforts to turn Anna's attention away from babies. 'Joking apart, going away for a while might take your mind off things. We can't go blackberry picking every day, can we? I know you'll never admit it, but I'm convinced you still miss the buzz of the theatre and working to impossible deadlines for the likes of Gian-Carlo Andretti.'

'Andretti!' Anna cried in disbelief. 'Never in a million years would I ever work again for Andretti!'

'No one's asking you to. This time you'd be

working for Julian and Ashley who, I'm led to understand, happens to be an extremely personable fellow. Just think, in a matter of weeks you'd soon be home again.'

Anna looked up, deeply suspicious. 'Why do I get the distinct feeling you're in collusion with Julian? What were you both talking about before you fetched me to the phone?'

'Well — er — amongst other things, the assorted problems they've had to date,' Bjorn said sheepishly, when Anna fixed him with a look that said she didn't believe a word. 'Plus the fact as filming's nearly over, it seems pointless to recruit a total stranger and — um — also the possibility of you flying out in a couple of days.'

'Bjorn! Are you mad? A couple of days!'

Leaving the table to take the scones from the oven, Anna cried, 'I only wish making a baby was as easy as making jam or scones. I'm hardly likely to become pregnant while I'm hundreds of miles away, am I?'

'Perhaps we're not doing it right,' Bjorn said, desperate to ease the current tension. 'You never know, they might have one of those wise old women or a magic wishing well out there in the woods. Julian did say the scenery is pretty spectacular by all accounts.'

'Yes, and he also said the weather was awful. Which, knowing my luck, would mean

287

that wise old woman would have already flown off on her broomstick to sunnier climes; the wishing well would be frozen over, or else covered in snow, and — '

'Speaking of snow covered, did you realize you're covered in flour?' Bjorn chuckled, dusting flour from the tip of her nose and her cheeks.

'No, at the moment all I know is that thanks to you and Julian, I'm simply covered in confusion!'

By lunchtime, still confused and equally reluctant, Anna rang Julian to announce her decision.

'You mean to say you're coming? Oh, that's wonderful! My dear Anna, I can't begin to thank you enough. Ashley will be simply delighted. The poor man has been tearing his hair out, or at least what's left of it, these past few weeks.'

'Then why not send for reinforcements before now?' Anna questioned. 'I'm sure one of the agencies would have been only too willing to assist.'

'To be perfectly honest we did discuss it at one point. With only a few weeks to go, however, we all decided to pull together, share the workload and hope for the best. Having to rely on total strangers, coming in at this late stage, would only complicate matters further.'

'Julian, I'm not exactly — ' Anna began, before being interrupted for a second time.

'Anna, my dear, I know you, Ashley knows of you and between us we're convinced we can trust you to act as our right-hand man — or woman, that's if you're into this women's lib thing. As far as the costumes go, don't forget they're all made up and the local girl sees to the general run of the mill stuff. From your point of view it's merely a question of checking the costumes and making sure everything's in a reasonable state of repair and ready for a day's shooting.'

Convinced the words *merely a question of checking the costumes* was a gross misrepresentation of what lay in store for her, Anna enquired suspiciously, 'Which reminds me, what did you say happened to the person I'm replacing?'

'She slipped on the ice, fell down and broke her leg.'

Listening to Anna's sharp intake of breath, Julian refrained from adding that the poor woman had been so cold during a long, hard day's filming, that she'd also succumbed to temptation of the local brew. Told that it would warm the Polish equivalent of the cockles of her heart, she'd discovered that not only had her cockles been infinitely warmed but also her coccyx extremely bruised and her

289

leg badly broken, when she'd fallen. Airlifted to safety, she'd sworn (both literally and metaphorically), that she'd never again work in such appalling conditions.

Reminded of this pronouncement, Julian found himself suddenly consumed with guilt. Was it really fair to drag Anna away from Bjorn and her delightfully comfortable home? 'Remember, we're in the midst of an extremely severe Polish winter,' he said hurriedly. 'Bring plenty of warm clothing. You know, woollen tights and sweaters, thermals, winceyette nightdresses and Bjorn's army socks, if he has any.'

'Why should I need Bjorn's army socks? They're far too big for me.'

'Not for you, my dear,' came the reply, through chattering teeth, 'but I could certainly do with a pair to keep my feet warm.'

'Ugh! Winceyette nightdresses,' Anna groaned, returning to Bjorn's side.

'What's winceyette?' he puzzled, spreading butter on to a scone.

'The material they use for making those long granny-type nightdresses. That old-fashioned dress shop and haberdashers, at the far end of the village, stocks them all year round.'

'You mean what Ginny's husband refers to

as her passion killers? Those things with the high button necks and long sleeves? You never wear anything like that for bed. Come to think of it, you never wear very much at all.'

'Thanks to you, this is where I start. First, I'm going upstairs to make sure I no longer look like Fred the Flourgrader, then I'm heading to Doreen's. Fancy coming with me to help me choose? Coward!' Anna called back, when Bjorn shook his head.

★　★　★

Two days later, heading for the long-stay car-park at Heathrow, Anna still couldn't believe she was actually doing this. It all seemed so bizarre. Surely Julian and Ashley could have muddled through with the help of the locals and rest of the crew? Bjorn, however, had been adamant that Julian would settle only for Anna.

'Deep down I think he simply needs someone to hold his hand and nursemaid him during the final weeks. As you've known him so long, it's not a lot to ask, is it?'

'I'll tell you when I get back,' Anna replied tersely, convinced Julian would be more interested in seeing the PG Tips, Kellogg's Cornflakes and Walls pork sausages and bacon, that he'd requested so desperately.

Checking first to see that the precious bag of supplies was still lodged safely on the back seat of the car, Anna cast a sideways glance at Bjorn, already bitterly regretting his wife's imminent departure. 'I can't help thinking what a brilliant idea it was for you to visit your parents while I'm away,' she said, trying to ignore the prospect of what lay ahead in Poland. 'At least you won't have to keep stopping to translate for me every five minutes.'

'Your Swedish is very good.'

'Hardly. Improving maybe, and certainly not as good as your English. Seriously though, with you aiming to visit the factory and take in as many show homes as you can, it will be so much easier without me.'

Having each checked in at their respective airlines, Anna and Bjorn bade a heartbreaking farewell, promising to phone or write whenever possible, before heading in opposite directions for their departure gates.

23

Stamping her feet against the cold night air, Anna watched a well-muffled Julian distribute her luggage into the boot of an ancient Tatra.

'Be careful with that one,' she called, through frosted breath. 'That's your duty free. Whisky and brandy.'

'Anna, you're an angel,' Julian mumbled, from the depths of the boot, making sure the bottles were in an upright position, before opening the passenger door.

'And,' she whispered, checking to see that no one was within ear shot. 'The Walls pork sausages, bacon and PG Tips you requested, are in my flight bag. Are you sure it was OK for me to bring them? Going through immigration and customs I was simply terrified someone was going to stop me and make me open my bags.'

Julian's face, or at least what Anna could see of it, beneath the furry hat and scarf à la Dr Who, was radiant. 'Oh my!' he sighed, deliberately avoiding her question. 'You mean to say tomorrow I can have a proper English breakfast? It will certainly be an improvement on gnat's pee tea and raw eggs.'

'What?'

Realizing now was not the time to describe the current food situation, Julian quickly changed the subject. They were still too close to the airport. Anna could quite easily change her mind about staying and catch the next plane back to England.

'At least I've managed to secure you a fairly decent room at the hotel,' he told her, negotiating an icy bend in the road. 'As long as you don't mind having a shower instead of a bath. *En suites* with baths are few and far between, I'm afraid.'

And I'm afraid I could have done the wrong thing by coming here, Anna thought grimly, once Julian had departed with his duty free and groceries, leaving her to examine her fairly decent room. Looking about its dimly lit interior, she took in the dingy surroundings that were to be her home for at least the next three weeks. A simple wooden-framed double bed, chest of drawers and bentwood chair, were the only items of furniture to grace the room. Hanging at the window were faded maroon chintz curtains and on the floor, an extremely threadbare carpet. She groaned audibly. 'If this is decent, Julian, my heart goes out to anyone less fortunate than myself staying in an indecent room.'

Mention of the word heart, sent Anna's thoughts winging immediately across the Baltic to Bjorn. Unlike Anna, he wouldn't be peering into a fly-blown mirror or looking in disgust at the rust-stained shower tray. Instead, he would be wallowing in the warmth and comfort of his parents' house and tucking in to some wonderful home cooking. 'Oh well,' she grimaced, moving away from the mirror. 'As I'm so desperate to spend a penny, I can't delay trying out this ancient plumbing for any longer.'

Relieved to discover that the chain did at least flush, even if it was under sufferance, Anna washed and dried her hands and prepared to unpack. Wardrobe? she thought at length, there's no wardrobe. Having brought mostly trousers and thick sweaters, she could only conclude the best place for her clothes was the chest of drawers to the right of the windows. As for her winter coat . . . that would simply have to hang on the less than shiny brass hook, screwed into her bedroom door.

That is it could, she thought dejectedly, sitting on the bed, if only the hook had been fixed to the door with the required three screws instead of one. Reaching for her travel bag in order to seek out the obligatory sewing kit and small set of screwdrivers (the latter

295

found in last year's Christmas cracker) Anna gave a rueful smile. If only she'd had the presence of mind to add a selection of screws to her list of travel requisites. Failing the appearance of a hotel concierge, and thinking that perhaps one of the carpenters on set might be able come to her rescue, Anna laid her coat on the bed and walked towards the casement windows. Puzzling as to why there should be two curtains at the windows and a solitary third, in the far corner of the room, she decided to investigate.

From the bedroom window she discerned something that resembled a balcony and impenetrable blackness beyond, while from behind the wraith-like curtain in the corner, she found cobwebs, an assortment of dead flies and beetles, two more brass curtain hooks (seemingly secured to the wall) and a single bent and twisted wire coat hanger. 'Eureka! I think I've found the wardrobe.'

Thankful that at the last minute she'd packed two of her best satin coat hangers, Anna hung up her coat and the one decent dress, Bjorn had insisted she take with her. 'In case Julian and Ashley take you out to dinner,' he'd remarked. Most definitely not necessary, she thought, smoothing out the bottle green, button-through midi dress. Although, if it gets really cold, I suppose it could double up as an extra long cardigan.

If it gets really cold! an inner voice exclaimed. *You've got to be joking! It's already minus goodness knows what outside!*

What was it Julian had let slip on the journey from the airport? Winter had come early this year, hence the catalogue of seemingly endless disasters plaguing both cast and film crew. Acutely aware that the temperature in her room wasn't below freezing, in fact if anything it was a little too warm, Anna thanked heaven for small mercies and prepared for bed. Yawning, she reached for Bjorn's photograph. 'Sleep well, my darling,' she whispered. 'At least you'll be well looked after. Unlike me, you're not facing the prospect of raw eggs for breakfast.'

Very early next morning, Anna descended the stairs to the dining-room. To her relief Julian and Ashley, plus two elderly females, were already seated at a table. Tucked away in a far corner they were poring over the day's script, deep in animated conversation.

'Anna, over here,' Julian beckoned, rising from his chair.

Motioning for Ashley to remain seated, Anna sat down and greeted him across the table.

'I can't begin to tell you how grateful I am,' he began. 'And I'm sure you'll be thinking it's a most peculiar way of doing things. But as I said to Julian, let's just crack on and get this thing finished. Why worry the big boys in London with all our problems?'

'Why indeed?' Anna said, still pondering as to why she'd been singled out for the task in hand, yet at the same time curious as to how Julian had been able to secure all her travel papers and permits. 'Julian did say you've been experiencing quite a few problems,' Anna continued, with a sympathetic smile in Ashley's direction.

'Quite a few is right!' came a clear and precise voice by Anna's elbow. 'Do you know, my dear, if it wasn't for Julian offering to share his sausages and bacon with me, I would have returned to England on the very same plane that brought you out to us.'

Reading Anna's mind as she scanned the table for the aforementioned luxuries, Julian explained. 'They're not here. I took them to my office last night, after I dropped you off. My office being a caravan on set — which luckily, just happens to contain a tiny fridge and camping stove.'

'Hmph! You didn't have to go that far, Julian,' a second female voice retorted. 'My room would have done just as well. It was like an ice box in there last night. I very nearly froze to — '

'Anna,' Ashley interrupted, 'before we go any further, let me introduce you to two old friends who are very dear to my heart. Esme Hamilton and Lavinia Bray.'

'And he means old in every sense of the word, don't you, Ashley?' Esme began, extending a thin wrinkled hand in Anna's direction. 'Very pleased to meet you, my dear. Though, what possessed you to come to this God-forsaken place at this time of year is quite beyond me. You must be mad.'

'We're all mad!' Lavinia broke in tartly. 'When Guy Carstairs broke his leg doing that stupid parachute stunt, we should all have realized this production was jinxed.'

Anna frowned. 'Guy Carstairs — a parachute jump? I thought this film was set during the Napoleonic wars. Surely they didn't have parachutes in the 1800s?'

Emitting a delightful chuckle, Esme explained, 'No dear, you're quite right, of course they didn't. The problem was Guy took part in his parachute jump only days before he was due to fly out on location. I know we theatrical folk say *break a leg*, but Guy, poor love, appears to have taken it quite literally.'

'And we old stalwarts should have taken notice,' Lavinia interjected, shaking her head. 'Mark my words, Esme, I said at the time. It was a bad omen and I was right.'

'Poppycock!' came the acerbic reply. 'Loads of people jump from parachutes without breaking their legs. Knowing Guy, he only broke his because he wasn't pulling the right string, or whatever else it is you do, when you land.'

'Probably not. I expect he was more interested in pulling some young blonde, who was waiting on the airstrip for his autograph.'

With Esme and Lavinia discussing Guy Carstairs, Julian leaned over and whispered in Anna's ear, 'They're really a lovable pair of old pros in the nicest sense of course. Esme's playing the part of the dowager duchess and . . .'

Julian got no further as Lavinia groaned miserably, 'Oh, no! Not raw eggs again.'

'How do they know they're raw?' Anna hissed, studying a bowl of what she took to be hard boiled eggs, now being placed upon the table along with a giant teapot of hot water and some rather bizarre looking tea bags.

'Quite simply because they do the same thing every day. We crack open the shells, only to find raw eggs, which we then have to leave in a cup or a bowl on the table.'

Anna raised her eyebrows in disbelief. 'Haven't you tried explaining that you'd prefer them boiled or perhaps scrambled?'

Julian made an attempt to cover his mouth

with his hand. 'Um — it's not that easy. You see they always pretend they don't understand. When we ask for the eggs to be taken away and cooked properly, we never see them again.'

'Which means they probably end up on someone else's plate for lunch,' Lavinia muttered. 'Of course, we've since discovered why they do it, food being so scarce in this part, not to mention the black market. If only one morning I could have an egg, lightly poached or boiled.'

'But you can.' Filling a large earthenware cup with hot water, Anna ignored the tea bag Esme proffered and reached for an egg instead.

Dumbstruck, four pairs of eyes watched as she deftly cracked open an egg and slid it into her cup. 'Of course it will take a while to set,' she explained. 'So if you could pass me some of that black bread while I'm waiting.'

Julian looked on flabbergasted. 'Where on earth did you get that idea?'

'I would have thought you of all people would have remembered that, Julian. You've obviously forgotten the time we met up with some of the Royal Ballet's Touring Company. They'd experienced similar problems in Russia, until someone came up with the bright idea of dropping the eggs in hot water.

301

While they were eating their cheese and black bread or whatever, the eggs were cooking. I'll admit they weren't exactly hard boiled but they were still edible.'

Nodding in understanding, Julian reached across to fill his own cup with hot water. 'Hmm, I think I'd like mine boiled,' he said, lowering the egg into his cup with a spoon. 'That way I can save it for later to have with my pork sausages.'

'Did someone mention sausages?' came a male voice from behind Anna's chair. 'In which case lead me to them. You sly old fox, Julian! How on earth did you manage to find them?'

'He didn't,' Anna began, turning in her chair. 'I brought them out with me last night. If I'd known you were all so desperate I would have — '

'Anna?'

'Tom! What are you doing here?'

'I was about to ask you the same question,' Tom Hudson replied, unable to believe his eyes.

'Gracious! Don't tell me you two know each other?' Ashley Munroe looked up from where he was prodding gingerly at what he hoped would soon become a lightly-poached egg.

'Anna's a great friend of my Aunt Bea's.

They used to work together at the Alexandra,' Tom explained, peering at the occupants of the table, now concentrating on eggs and egg shells. 'And if it's not daft a question, what exactly are you all doing?'

'Cooking breakfast,' Esme replied, with a chuckle. 'Isn't it fun? Anna, bless her, was telling us how the Royal Ballet had similar problems when they were on tour in Russia. Such a simple idea too. I can't think why we never thought of it before, particularly as hot water is the only regular item on the breakfast menu.'

'Quite possibly because you never recognize the obvious, even when it's staring you in the face,' Tom mused, momentarily reminded of how Lucy used to steer him in the direction of both an expensive jeweller's and an exclusive baby boutique, when he in his ignorance had believed she was taking the pill.

'Tom,' Anna's voice penetrated his chain of thought, 'would you like a poached egg? I think this one's just about done.'

'A poached egg would be greatly appreciated, Anna. But what about yourself? Wouldn't you like it?'

'Not really. I've never been a great fan of eggs for breakfast. I usually only eat the yolk. In the current circumstances, it would seem such a pity to waste the white.' Holding a saucer over the rim of her cup, Anna carefully drained off the now tepid water into a bowl. Next, she slid an almost perfectly formed poached egg onto Tom's plate.

Watching Tom and the others savour their unexpected breakfasts, Julian became aware of movement in the dining-room doorway. There, the young waitress who served them each morning, seemed strangely discon-certed. 'Oh dear,' he remarked, in hushed tone, 'I hope we haven't upset Marysia.'

'Who's Marysia?'

Popping a forkful of poached egg into her mouth, Esme leaned across to Anna with a muffled whisper, 'She's the waitress. Rumour has it her brother's a black market racketeer. We've been offered all sorts of things since we've been staying here.'

'Only at vastly exorbitant prices, don't forget,' Lavinia snorted.

'I don't know,' Tom broke in. 'I didn't think the whisky was too badly priced. It might not be Glenfiddich but at least it keeps out the cold.'

'It's all right if you like whisky,' Lavinia informed him. 'As you know I'm strictly TT, I need something other than alcohol to keep out the cold.'

'You mean like me, Lavinia?' Tom teased,

putting an arm about her shoulders.

'No, I don't! I'm far too old for such things. What I had in mind was a nice old-fashioned winceyette nightdress. Those I have with me are brushed nylon, which are really quite, quite useless.'

Without thinking, Anna blurted out, 'I've got three winceyette nightdresses with me. You can have one if you like.'

To Anna's surprise and dismay, two voices, those of Esme and Lavinia, echoed in unison, 'Oh, yes please!'

Five minutes later, before hurrying off for the day's shooting, Anna searched for her two remaining nightdresses. I suppose their need is greater than mine, she told herself, spying her own nightdress, folded neatly on the bed. At least she still had one and for some inexplicable reason, both heating and plumbing in her room, appeared to be working ultra efficiently for the moment.

24

For what appeared to be three very long and miserable weeks, Anna and the rest of the film crew found themselves at the mercy of the elements. Buffeted by blustering gales, submerged in swirling snowstorms and soaked to the skin by relentless rain, it was only the imminent end to filming that kept them all going.

'OK folks. Cut!' Ashley Munroe called to the sea of expectant faces. 'We'll do the rest tomorrow. Let's call it a day.'

'Day?' Lavinia's voice echoed across the frosty landscape. 'By my reckoning it must be about half past nine and almost my bedtime.'

'At least it's not raining,' Esme replied, flapping her thin arms in an attempt to improve her circulation. 'This dry cold I can just about cope with. It's far preferable to penetrating damp.'

Lavinia snuggled her ample form deep within the folds of her fur-trimmed cloak. 'Mmm, I suppose so and rather Tom than me. Poor fellow looks almost frozen to death out there.'

From where Anna was standing by Julian's

side, she noticed Tom, tired, exhausted and cold, having spent the past hour and a half filming in the dark in his shirt sleeves, reaching out for the welcome protection of his own woollen cloak.

'Thank God for that,' he muttered in Julian's direction. 'If we'd had to do that scene one more time, I think I could quite easily have passed for the corpse. At least he was better dressed than me.'

Delving into his pocket, Julian produced a small hip flask containing the last of his treasured Glenfiddich. 'Here,' he called, tossing it in Tom's direction. 'Be my guest. With only a few more days to go, I think I can spare you a drop or two.'

'How very noble of you,' Tom replied, taking a deep gulp. Then, with the comforting warmth of amber liquid penetrating his throat and stomach, he threw back a corner of his cloak with a flourish, bowed low in Julian's direction and returned the silver hip flask to its owner.

Esme looked on admiringly. 'Oh, if only I was twenty years younger.'

'Don't you mean forty?'

'No. I don't. For your information, Lavinia, I was in my sexual prime when I was in my late forties and early fifties. Why, I remember — '

307

'I think I'd prefer not to know,' Lavinia said, through tight lips as she began to walk away. Reluctant to part with the enveloping warmth of her own cloak, she was nevertheless keen to rid herself of the uncomfortable dress and corset beneath.

Helping her disrobe, Anna caught Esme's eye. Though exactly what Esme was signalling when Lavinia's generous folds of flesh burst free, was quite beyond her comprehension.

'I meant unlaced and straight-laced,' Esme explained to Anna, watching her companion leave the set. 'She's really such a dear, but oh, so po-faced when it comes to sex. You know, years ago when we first met, she was convinced you could get pregnant simply by sitting on a lavatory seat or taking a bath, previously occupied by a man.'

Seeing Anna's mouth gape open in disbelief, Esme continued, 'As you've probably gathered, because of our contrasting sizes, we're frequently called upon for period dramas and the like, especially Dickens, Trollope and Jane Austen. You have to admit she makes a wonderful dowager duchess. Anyway, I digress. Where was I?'

'In the bath?' Anna suggested weakly.

'Oh yes, the bath. Well, I could never work out why, when we were on location together and often sharing the same room, Lavinia always turned up with a tin of Ajax and a bottle of Dettol. The reason, of course, was so that she could disinfect the lavatory seat and scrub the bath clean — just in case. Personally, I blame it on her convent education. She doesn't do it now, of course, and mercifully, has long since progressed beyond babies under the gooseberry bush.'

'How very sad.'

'Yes, isn't it?' Esme replied, misinterpreting Anna's concern. 'I've always maintained you can cope with any adversities and disasters in this life if you're in the arms of an experienced and considerate lover.'

'I beg your pardon!' came a voice from the doorway. 'What is this? Aunt Esme's agony column?'

'Hello, Tom,' Esme called out, completely nonplussed, while freeing herself from her costume. 'I was just explaining a woman's needs to Anna.'

Tom raised a bemused eyebrow. 'According to my Aunt Bea, Anna's the last person who needs advice on a woman's needs. She and Bjorn are very happily married.'

Ignoring Anna's blushes, Esme announced with a knowing smile, 'Anna wasn't the woman in question: I was referring to Lavinia.'

'Why should — ?'

Hurriedly pulling on warm woollen trousers and a thick sweater, Esme reached for her watch. 'Gosh! Is that the time. I really must fly. If I don't hurry up Lavinia will have used all the hot water.'

Stepping forward, Tom shrugged aside his cloak to help Esme on with her shapeless parka. 'You still haven't told me why Lavinia — '

'Let's just say that when Lavinia was a mere slip of a girl, I personally believe she would have benefited from a jolly good tumble in the hay.'

Hearing Esme's tiny footsteps scurry away, Tom roared with laughter and turned to look at Anna. 'Did she really say what I think she said, or am I suffering from near starvation of the food and sleep variety, not to mention acute hypothermia?'

'She did,' Anna said, deeply incredulous. 'And, if you are suffering from near starvation and acute hypothermia, Tom, that makes two of us. One of the few things keeping me going this past week — apart from the fact that we've almost finished filming — is the prospect of a wonderful roast turkey Christmas dinner and falling asleep in front of a blazing yule log fire.'

Tom held up his hands in mock protest. 'Anna, please! You're too cruel. How can you even talk of such things? It's all right for you, you've only been here a few weeks. I've been here for months, don't forget.'

'Sorry, Tom, I confess I had,' Anna said, hanging up Esme's costume. 'Still, it won't be long now before we're all homeward bound.'

'And I'm sorry too,' Tom announced sheepishly, holding out his arm. 'It would appear that last tedious take we did, before we packed up for the night, has played havoc with my shirt. Is there any chance of fixing it before tomorrow morning? Just a quick repair should be all that's needed. We'll be filming inside for the rest of the day, thank God, and I'll be wearing a different costume.'

Seeing Anna nod in reply, Tom peeled off his shirt and passed it over. 'Thanks,' he said hurrying to the door of the trailer. 'Now I suppose I'd better dash. I promised to ring Lucy this evening. It will be just my luck if she's already given up on me and gone to bed.'

'You can't go out like that!' Anna gasped, horrified to see him naked from the waist up. 'You'll catch your death out there.'

'After the freezing cold temperatures of the past few days, I think I already have. Don't worry, my twentieth-century gear is only in the caravan across the way.' When an icy blast blew in from the open doorway, Tom shivered and reached for his discarded cloak. 'On second thoughts,' he said, scooping it into his arms. 'Perhaps I'll just borrow this for a bit. Is that OK?'

'Just so long as you don't lose it. There's no way we can replace that at such short notice.'

'Don't worry, I'm exhausted and certainly haven't planned to go anywhere tonight.'

Neither has anyone else, Anna thought to herself, reminded that unlike previous evenings, male members of cast and crew would not be meeting for their customary nightcap and game of cards. To their continued dismay, entertainment, such that it was, had been in short supply at this particular location. Quite possibly because, as Julian had explained on the night of her arrival, their hotel had once been both a sanatorium and institution.

'Mad house, more like,' Ashley had commented at a later stage, following yet another problematic and harrowing day. 'Most definitely *not* a sanatorium. Aren't they're supposed to be places of rest and healing, renowned for their position and climate?'

'Which certainly isn't here,' Anna said, her voice tinged with a melancholy sadness as her gaze alighted on the depressing exterior of their so-called luxury hotel, fronted by an untidy tangle of overgrown shrubs and weeds.

Approaching the main entrance, Anna observed that most of the bedrooms were in darkness. No doubt Esme and Lavinia were both freshly bathed, sprinkled with Yardley's lavender talcum powder, and already tucked up in bed, wearing her wincyette nightdresses. Deeply envious and faced with yet another solitary night in her cheerless bedroom, Anna climbed wearily up the four flights of stairs.

I suppose it is good exercise, she told herself, willing all sorts of positive thoughts to spring to mind. At least she had her own bathroom and balcony. Unlike Esme and Lavinia, she didn't have to go traipsing halfway along a draughty landing to the loo, in the middle of the night. As for the balcony, Anna gave a wry smile. What Julian had referred to as her balcony was probably only part of an old fire escape, surplus to requirements. With regard to the view from this so-called balcony, to date she'd seen very little of it. She got up in the morning before it was light and returned in the evening, long after the sun had gone down. Such a contrast then to the glorious sunsets she and Bjorn had shared together in Sweden.

Feeling a sudden uncontrollable lump rise in her throat, Anna realized it had been a huge mistake to think of Bjorn so soon before going to bed. It only made her more bereft. And it's far too late to ring him now, she concluded miserably. Pausing for breath as she neared the fourth landing and the murky glow of a solitary light bulb, Anna peered at her watch.

Reminded of Tom's parting words that he was going to ring Lucy, Anna's thoughts progressed quite naturally from Lucy to Beattie. She, no doubt, would already be looking forward to her nephew's return and her belated birthday dinner. Unbeknown to Anna, however, Tom was already up to date with news from home, courtesy of Aunt Bea, when he'd tried telephoning his wife.

'Where's Lucy and what are you doing there, Aunt Bea?' Tom enquired anxious, all manner of possible mishaps racing through his head. 'Lucy's all right isn't she? Alexander's not ill or anything?'

'Don't worry, Tom. They're both OK,' Beattie said quickly, wanting to reassure him that nothing was amiss.

'Then why isn't she there? I made a specific point of telling her I'd ring this evening. I realize I'm a bit later than planned, especially as I was hoping to speak to Alexander before Lucy put him to bed.'

'It wouldn't have made any difference if

you had, Tom. Lucy went out at six o'clock. I gave Alexander his tea and put him to bed at seven-thirty.'

'Six o'clock!' Tom's voice had echoed down the phone. 'But where — ?'

'Out to dinner with friends and then to the theatre.'

Asking Aunt Bea to pass on his profuse apologies to Alexander, Tom hung up the phone. 'Dinner with friends!' he repeated angrily, giving vent to his feelings. 'Christ, Lucy! How could you go out to dinner so early, knowing that I'd arranged to call? As for me, I haven't eaten a thing since midday.'

Dejected, hungry and cold, having only bothered to slip on a T-shirt and jeans before hurrying to the phone booth, Tom draped the loose folds of his cloak about his shoulders and trudged back in the direction of the hotel.

'Tom!' A surprised voice called from the bar of the local café. 'What are you doing? They told me you wouldn't be here tonight. It's a bit late if you've come to join us. The game's just finished and everyone's packing up to go home.'

'Hello, Frederic,' Tom called, spying the hotel waitress's older brother. 'No, I haven't come to join you I'm afraid. I've been trying to ring home. It's far cheaper to use a booth

315

than attempting to ring from the hotel.'

'I take it your dear lady wasn't at home?'

Tom looked up in amazement, surprised that Frederic should have known about Lucy's absence. 'How did you know?'

'From the look on your face, my friend. A man who has just spoken with the love of his life does not have a face as long as a . . . '

'In England we say as long as a wet weekend.'

'Ah, I see,' Frederic said, making a mental note of the phrase. 'Then I think the weekend is very wet indeed.'

'You're right, it is.'

'And have you eaten?'

When Tom shook his head, Frederic placed a friendly arm on his companion's shoulder. 'In that case, come. You eat with us tonight.'

'With you?'

'With my family: my grandparents and my sister Marysia. We cook what you English say *slap-up meal* this evening.'

Puzzling why Frederic and his family should be eating at such a late hour, Tom was told they were expecting a very important visitor and Marysia had also been working late at the hotel. 'And it is *very* special cow,' Frederic beamed, screwing up his face and mooing in response to Tom's bewildered frown.

'You mean beef. Well, I'm not really sure, Frederic. It certainly sounds very tempting but as I have to be up at the crack of sparrow tomorrow morning.'

'Sparrow? What is sparrow?'

When Tom began flapping his arms and whistling like a bird, a startled local leaving the bar, stopped and shook his head. One minute Frederic was mooing like a cow and the next his tawny-haired companion was imitating a bird. Knowing full well that Frederic had dealings with the black market, the old man looked furtively into the shadows before hurrying on his way. He could only assume this was some secret sign or password.

Tired and hungry, and still a trifle irked with Lucy, Tom soon saw the funny side of two grown men imitating wildlife to make themselves understood. Yes, he was exhausted but at the same time he was positively starving and the thought of cow — roast or otherwise — sent his taste buds into overdrive as he walked alongside Frederic in silence.

To date, having dealt only with Marysia's brother at the local café or else behind the ancient boiler-room of the hotel, Tom was pleasantly surprised to be ushered into a small but cosy, timber-framed house. A welcoming fire burned in the grate and an elderly couple sat side by side on a simple wooden trestle.

'Grandmother and Grandfather,' Frederic explained. 'They've lived here for years on this smallholding. Of course they know no English, so don't worry about making conversation.'

When Tom nodded and smiled in the grandparents' direction, he was greeted in turn by warm and toothless grins and a gestured invitation to sit by the fire.

'Yes, do sit,' Frederic instructed. 'Supper will not be long and then you shall have some of my very special brandy.'

An hour and a half later, no longer hungry and completely enveloped by the good nature of his hosts, the comforting warmth of the fire, and more than the odd glass or two of Frederic's special contraband brandy, Tom sank into an armchair and closed his eyes. When he awoke, he was astonished to find himself alone, the room lit only by a single oil-filled lantern and the dying embers of the fire.

'Frederic?' he called into the semi-gloom. Deeply disoriented, Tom looked about him with a start when he heard a quiet rustling. 'Marysia? Where's Frederic and where are your grandparents?'

'Frederic go with friend,' Marysia replied.

'And my grandparents . . . '

Seeing her point to the foot of the wooden stairs, Tom could only assume that everyone had gone to bed. 'I'd better go too,' he said, uncoiling himself from the armchair and making his way to the door. 'Will you please thank your grandparents for the meal and also tell Frederic that I shall see him tomorrow?' Tom groaned, catching sight of an ancient pendulum clock. Not only was it very late — or should that be early? — but also there was the most awful dull, pounding thud at his temples.

'Tom,' Marysia, called after him, 'You forget your — '

'What? Oh yes, my cloak. Thanks Marysia. I'd better not lose that or Anna will be furious. I promised her . . . '

Remembering Anna's first morning at the hotel and the subsequent incident with the eggs, Marysia's earlier dewy-eyed expression changed to one of jealousy and anger. 'Anna, she is your lover?'

'Good Lord, no!'

'Then why you worry about Anna? Why you make promise to her?'

'Because . . . ' Tom shrugged, knowing that with Marysia's tiny smattering of English, it was useless trying to explain the importance of his cloak. So far Frederic had managed to procure all manner of things for them via the black market, but eight yards of finest woollen cloth at this late stage, Tom doubted very much.

Relief flooded Marysia's face and her dark-brown eyes filled with renewed expectation. 'Come,' she said, picking up the lantern and stepping through the doorway in front of him. 'Come with me and I show you cow.'

When the cold night air hit Tom full in the face, he ran his hands across his chin in bewilderment. His head had begun to throb even more. All he wanted to do was get back to the hotel, yet here was Marysia offering to show him . . . a cow? 'I thought we'd already eaten it,' he replied lamely.

Laughing, Marysia tossed back her mane of jet-black hair and took his hand. 'Yes, we eat cow but this is not for eat. This is *special*, my grandfather keep for prize. It is very good, yes? And also good cow house. *Ve-ry* big and *ve-ry* warm.'

'Er — I suppose it is,' Tom said, through a drunken haze, not entirely sure how one mustered up sufficient enthusiasm for such a beast and its dwelling. Although, had Anna been here with him, she might have known. Didn't she live in the country? Reminded once more of Anna's warning with regard to his cloak, Tom turned to lift it free from a fresh pile of cow dung. 'Whoops! Anna's going to be very cross with me if I get this dirty. Right, well thanks again, Marysia, for showing me your ... ' The words *your grandfather's prize cow* died on Tom's lips as it soon became abundantly clear that Marysia's intention was to show him a bovine prize all of her very own!

Slowly, unlacing the peasant blouse of her waitress's uniform, Marysia was moving closer and closer towards him, while he meanwhile made a futile attempt to back away. All to no avail, he soon discovered he was heading in the wrong direction. With his way well and truly barred by a pile of sweetly smelling hay, Tom began to stumble.

'Is good? Is cosy?' Marysia cooed, giving him a gentle shove when he tried to haul himself upright. 'Why you not stay here with Marysia? I not get cross with you like Anna. I will make you happy.'

'Um — what about Frederic? He might — '

'Pah! Frederic, my brother. He not mind if I make you happy. Anyway, he go see Boris.'

'Who's Boris? I thought you said Frederic had gone to bed.'

Ignoring all Tom's protests, Marysia began tugging at his T-shirt, causing a jumble of thoughts to swirl untidily in his aching head. They began with Esme's definition of a woman's needs, visions of Lavinia benefiting from a tumble in the hay, and ended with Aunt Bea telling him about Lucy going out with friends. 'So your friends are more important than me, Lucy,' he spat bitterly. 'To think you couldn't even wait for me.'

Momentarily confused, Marysia gazed down into Tom's troubled face. She wasn't aware of a Lucy staying at the hotel. No matter, at least Tom hadn't mentioned that awful Anna again. 'It is no problem, Tom,' she whispered seductively, her lips dangerously close to his. 'Marysia is your friend. I wait long time for you. Each day I wait and now . . .'

And now Tom thought, brushing straw from his face, here he was on a bed of sweetly smelling hay with Marysia. And she was on top of him, her voluptuous breasts spilling forth from over the top of her blouse, her nipples as pink and inviting as her open mouth. Oh, dear God! he thought, his head thumping and the barn spinning, it was all too much.

'*Marysia!*' came a furious voice from the barn door, followed by an angry salvo of incomprehensible expletives.

'Boris?' Marysia gasped, terror and alarm flooding her face as she hurriedly crammed

322

her exposed flesh back inside her blouse and fled to safety.

Shielding his eyes against the blinding torchlight, flashed on his face, Tom discovered the owner of the angry voice was not Frederic — as he'd suspected — but a complete stranger and a truly gigantic one at that. When shock, coupled with a sudden rush of adrenalin brought Tom to his senses, he leapt to his feet with only one thing uppermost in his mind. Escape! Quickly, remembering the closely fought duels of recent weeks, he made a grab for a nearby pitchfork and his cloak, knocked the torch from his startled assailant's hand and ran far into the night.

25

Restless and unable to sleep, Anna tossed and turned in her bed. When another painfully slow twenty minutes ticked by, she switched on the bedside lamp and flung back the covers. She might just as well get up. Though quite what she'd do at twenty past one in the morning she wasn't sure. Reminded of the British custom of when in doubt, have a cup of tea, Anna began to despair. The supply of tea she'd brought with her was now sadly depleted. Like her nightdresses, the last of her tea bags had disappeared in Esme and Lavinia's direction.

'And coffee's hardly conducive for a good night's sleep,' she murmured, peering into the remains of a jar of Nescafé.

Shivering, Anna moved to the chest of drawers by the window. There she gathered together what she'd considered to be her lifeline of the past few weeks: a china mug and Pifco mini travel boiler, also brought from home. Now all she had to do was fill the mug with water, switch on the plug and wait. It might not make her sleep, she thought, putting a scant spoonful of coffee into the mug of hot water, but following three nights in a row without heating, it might help warm her ice-cold limbs.

Rather than feeling warm, it was the heavy thud of footsteps on metal that made Anna's blood run cold. Someone or something was climbing up the fire escape: the fire escape that came to an abrupt halt on the balcony outside her bedroom window! With trembling hands she placed the mug back on the drawers for fear of scalding herself, then wondered if perhaps she shouldn't pick it up again. Maybe she could use it as a weapon against . . .

Against what? she thought, conscious of footsteps drawing ever nearer and the voodoo drums in her chest, pounding hopelessly out of control against her rib cage. 'Dear Lord,' she pleaded, her voice a mere squeak in her throat, when the drumming was joined by frantic hammering at the window. 'What on earth shall I do?'

'Anna! Anna!' came a frantic cry. 'For God's sake open the window. I know you're awake. I saw your light go on.'

'Anna?' Someone was calling her name. Which meant whoever it was outside the window must also know her. 'Or else it's just a trick,' she whispered terrified, clasping her hand to her throat. Someone who'd been watching her these past few weeks. Perhaps Julian wasn't joking after all when he'd described this place as a mad house. With her imagination running riot, Anna was suddenly brought to her senses by further persistent hammering at the window.

'For Christ's sake, Anna! It's Tom, please hurry up and let me in. If you don't, I think he's going to kill me!'

Tom? Tom Hudson was outside her bedroom window and someone was going to kill him? What was going on? Gingerly, lifting back the curtain and spying Tom's anxious face, Anna began struggling with the ancient casement window catch. 'Tom? What on earth are you doing at this time of — '

'Don't ask, just let me in,' Tom gasped, his fingers prising open the stiff metal frame until it was wide enough for him to enter, 'And switch off that bedside light, before Boris realizes where I am.'

'Who's Boris?' Anna queried, waiting for Tom to secure the window and close the curtains, before she switched off the light and they resumed their conversation in darkness.

'Marysia's boyfriend by all accounts. You know — the hotel waitress. The one with jet-black hair and come hither eyes. Her brother invited me to their place for supper.

They said they were expecting a special guest and — '

'Special guest?' Anna repeated, parrot fashion.

'Yeah, special was right! I suppose I should have realized the connection earlier, had I not had quite so much to drink, especially as Frederic's always talking about Boris. He's the guy who supplies Frederic with all his black market stuff and at the same time fancies himself as Marysia's boyfriend-cum-bodyguard.'

'He's big then, is he?' Anna enquired in hushed tones, trying to work out if the peculiar scuffling noise she could hear, meant Tom was now crawling beneath her bed.

'Big? I'll say he is,' came a muffled voice. 'Think of a cross between Giant Haystacks, Neanderthal man and a sumo wrestler and you're part way there.'

'Tom,' Anna hissed, listening to a commotion in the hotel grounds below, 'I hate to tell you this, but I think Boris is also part way here.'

Tom emerged from beneath the bed, banging his head on the bedsprings as he did so. 'What? You don't mean he's coming up the fire escape?'

Anna listened carefully and peered from the teeniest of chinks in the curtain. 'Wait a minute . . . No, I don't think he is. For a moment he looked as if he was thinking about it, but someone's called him back. Perhaps he's decided not to kill you after all. Anyway, why was he going to kill you? You never said.'

'Quite simply because I haven't had time,' Tom replied hoarsely. 'I've been too busy trying to get my breath back and regain my composure.'

Recognizing the familiar creak of her mattress, Anna guessed Tom was now sitting on the bed. At least his breathing was no longer coming in short, wheezy gasps. 'It's a long story, Anna. Suffice to say in the food and wine department, Frederic's hospitality was second to none. As a consequence, I must have fallen asleep after supper — which was hardly surprising considering how exhausted we all were after today's shoot. Then, I suppose you could say Marysia decided to offer me a little hospitality all of her very own.'

Hearing Anna's stifled gasp in the darkness, Tom responded with a vehement, 'Nothing happened. I swear I never laid a finger on her. One minute I was standing up and the next, she'd pushed me into the hay and was all over me — in every sense of the word. That's when . . . '

'Let me guess,' Anna ventured, faintly amused. 'That's when Big Boris appeared?'

'Not only bloody Big Boris but Frederic, too. Mind you, I think Frederic guessed almost immediately that I was the innocent party. It was while he was remonstrating with Boris, I decided to get the hell out of there and back to the hotel. To my horror, reception was locked and bolted, then I remembered the fire escape. As luck would have it, you just happened to be awake.'

On the point of telling him that he'd practically scared her half to death, and also wanting to know exactly how Tom had known it was her room, Anna heard him yawn sleepily, 'I saw you move the curtain. You bent down to look for something.'

Pondering why Tom was still insisting they kept the light off, Anna explained, 'I wasn't looking for something, I was plugging in my mini-boiler. I was making myself a coffee.'

'You've got coffee! I don't suppose I . . . ?'

Still standing near the window, Anna groped for her mug and held it in Tom's direction. With a grateful moan, he drained the last sustaining drops, rose from the bed and made his way to where she was peering gingerly from a gap in the curtains. 'I think it's quite safe for you to go to your own room now.'

'My own room? I can't do that.'

'Why ever not?'

'Isn't it obvious? I haven't got my key. I never checked in this evening. I went straight from the set to ring Lucy. I always use the phone booth near the bar.'

'What about the night porter?' Anna remonstrated. 'Surely he'll be able to help.'

'Afraid not. Like me he'll be suffering the after effects of Frederic's special brandy. I gather Marysia gave him a bottle before she went off duty tonight.'

Only too aware of Tom's close proximity and dreading what was coming next, Anna tugged at the ample folds of her nightdress. No longer numbed with cold, she found herself flushed with panic. If Tom had no intention of returning to his room, where exactly did he plan to spend the rest of the night?

Almost as if reading her mind, Tom brushed past her in the darkness. 'If I remember correctly, Julian said he'd managed to find you an *en suite* room. I thought,' he continued, groping for the bathroom door and reaching for the light cord, 'I could sleep in the bath. By the way I've hidden my cloak beneath your bed — just in case Boris came looking for me. Anyway, as he appears to have slunk back to his cave, I might be able to get a bit of long overdue shut-eye. Do you think you could possibly spare a pillow and a blanket? Although on second thoughts, keep your blankets and I'll wrap myself up in that cloak.'

'I can certainly spare you a pillow, as I only like one, and you're more than welcome to a blanket, but — '

'But?' Tom said, shifting to face her.

'It's a shower, not a bath and it's also one with a permanent leak.'

Turning a crestfallen face to examine the tiny shower tray, with its dripping shower head and rusting water stain, Tom nodded grimly. 'Mmm. I see what you mean. In that case there's nothing for it, Anna. I'll have to sleep with you.'

'I beg your pardon! Sleep with me?'

'There's no need to look so alarmed,' Tom said, attempting reassurance.

Even more convinced that he was now safe from Boris's clutches, Tom crossed back into the bedroom and switched on the bedside lamp. 'Good. Just like my bed and exactly as I hoped. You've got a bolster too. That means we can do an Aunt Bea.'

Wide eyed, Anna watched him shuffling assorted pillows. 'Er — what's an Aunt Bea?'

'By all accounts, something she had to resort to during the war to maintain her good name. If we place the bolster in the middle of the bed, that means we'll be kept apart. It's simple really. It also means we don't have to divide up the blankets. One blanket each is hardly enough in this cold.'

Reminded of exactly how cold her room had become since the heating had given up three nights ago, Anna pulled at the elasticated and frilled wrists of her nightgown in an effort to cover her icy fingers. 'It's OK,' she lied. 'I no longer feel tired. You can have the bed. I'll have the chair.'

'The chair?' Tom protested, mid-bolster-manoeuvre. 'You can't possibly sleep on that old thing.'

'I don't intend to. Like I said, I don't feel tired. I'll probably sit and read my book instead.'

'Then at least take my cloak,' Tom said, retrieving it from the dust and cobwebs beneath the bed.

Anna shook her head. 'I'd rather not. I dread to think what's lurking in those folds now. Don't worry, I can easily wear my coat. It's been doubling up as a dressing-gown these past few nights anyway.'

When Tom made as if to protest once more, Anna made another attempt at convincing him she wasn't tired.

'Oh, well. If you're really sure? You might not be tired, Anna, as for me, I'm well and truly knackered.'

'You look it,' she said, turning to reach for her coat. 'So sleep well.'

By the time Anna had hung up the satin-covered coat hanger, fastened the buttons on her coat and turned up the deep revers of her collar, Tom had thrown his jeans, T-shirt and socks across the foot of the bed and crawled sleepily beneath the covers, wearing only his boxer shorts. 'I don't believe this is happening to me,' she whispered, making her way to the chair.

'Pardon?' came a drowsy voice.

'Nothing,' she replied, 'I was simply talking to myself.'

'Hmm. This place gets to you like that in the end,' Tom yawned, feeling his eyelids beginning to close.

Quite how long Anna sat listening to Tom's steady breathing, she wasn't sure. It was only when she realized she'd been reading the same page of her novel for the past fifteen minutes, she began to regret telling him that she wasn't tired.

Of course you're tired, an inner voice chastized. *Damned tired in fact! Which is hardly surprising since you were traipsing all over the forest today. So, what are you going to do about it?* I don't know, Anna shrugged sleepily, in silent reply.

When her book eventually fell to the floor with a dull thud, it was Tom who awoke with a start. To his relief, finding not Boris but Anna slumped in the chair, he crept quietly from the bed and began to unbutton her coat.

'Come on, Anna, time for bed,' he urged softly.

'I'm not tired, and I really don't think you and I should be sleeping together.'

'No, 'course you're not tired,' Tom smiled, spying her drooping eyelids. 'As for sleeping together, we're not. Don't forget the bolster's there to protect you.'

'Protect me? You mean from Boris?'

'No, sleepy head, from me,' Tom said lazily, thoughtfully brushing her hair from her face, before draping the deep folds of wincyette about her feet and covering her up with the bedclothes. 'I've already had enough excitement for one night, thank you. And, seeing you dressed like that I wouldn't even have the energy to fight my way through all that fabric. Besides, if it will make you feel any better, I don't fancy you, either. So you see, you're perfectly safe.'

Before falling into a deep and troubled slumber, the words 'I don't fancy you', wove their way intricately into the fabric of Anna's dreams, exactly like the threaded satin ribbon in the broderie Anglaise collar and cuffs of her nightgown.

26

Feeling a man's hand draped across her shoulder, Anna stirred sleepily and turned on her side. For a single, brief, wonderful moment, she thought she was back home in England with Bjorn. The events of last night purely a dream. However, one look at the open bathroom door and its rust-stained shower tray told her otherwise. There was also her coat, folded neatly on the bentwood chair by the bed. This was not a dream, it was a nightmare. She'd woken to find herself sharing a bed with Tom Hudson!

'Oh, no!' she groaned, shaking herself free from Tom's grasp. 'I can't have spent the night in the same bed with him — can I?'

When Tom's hand fell, heavy with sleep, onto the bolster used for dividing the bed in two, Anna felt marginally comforted. How and when, she puzzled, did she get into bed, when one of the last things she remembered was sitting on the chair, wrapped in her coat and reading a book? The same book which was now cover side down on the bedroom floor. Desperate not to wake her uninvited guest, Anna disentangled her feet from the generous folds of winceyette and began edging her way to the side of the bed. If she was to have her customary morning shower, she wanted to take it now. Firstly, before Tom was aware of her being up and about and secondly, before all the hot water disappeared.

Refreshed in body but not in spirit, Anna was in the process of drying herself vigorously with a towel, when she remembered her clean undies. Not having to share a room like Esme and Lavinia, it didn't usually matter if she padded from bathroom to bedroom semi-naked. With Tom still sleeping in the next room, everything was different. At least I hope he's sleeping, she thought, trying to turn the bathroom door handle without emitting its customary squeak. Giving a cautious glimpse in Tom's direction, Anna tiptoed unnoticed across the threadbare carpet to the chest of drawers. Coming to an abrupt halt, she remembered all too soon how the top drawer, containing her under-clothes, also had a horrible habit of sticking. 'Damn!' she hissed, tugging in vain at the round wooden handles.

'What's up, drawer got stuck?' called a drowsy voice from the bed. 'Mine do that all the time. I'll give you a hand if you like?'

Shocked at hearing Tom's voice, Anna

almost let go of her towel. 'No. It's OK, thanks. I'm used to it by now. I'll just give it a hefty tug. It's been doing this every day since I arrived. I was merely trying not to disturb you.'

With a lazy grin, Tom eased himself onto one elbow. 'Don't worry about me, Anna. I'm quite enjoying being disturbed by you, dressed only in a bath towel. It's the best thing that's happened to me in weeks and certainly a vast improvement on what you wore in bed last night. I don't mind admitting that trying to get you into bed was quite a task. I reckon there's as much material in that nightdress of yours as the Egyptians used to wrap around their mummies.'

Feeling herself colour, Anna clutched at her towel and averted her eyes. It was one thing to discover Tom was awake but to hear him talk of putting her to bed. With an almighty heave the drawer gave up its contents, Anna grabbed the first bra and pair of pants she could find from the top drawer, and a clean checked shirt from the next. 'I won't be long,' she called, suffused with embarrassment. 'Five more minutes and the bathroom's all yours. If you want a shower, I suggest you're quick about it. The hot water's usually all gone by half past six.'

Tom grunted and held his head while

making a vague attempt to sit up, completely unaware that Anna's last remark had been made deliberately. She was almost correct with regard to the hotel's hot water supply but she also wanted to get rid of Tom before Esme and Lavinia made their morning pilgrimage to the bathroom at this end of the corridor.

Half dressed in bra, pants and a shirt borrowed from Bjorn that reached almost to her knees, Anna deemed it safe to emerge from the bathroom. There, to her dismay, she discovered Tom still in bed. Propped uncomfortably against the pillows, he looked even worse than he had at half past one in the morning.

'Tom, please! Do come along. It's going to be pretty embarrassing if someone sees you leaving my room. Not only is it getting late but also we're due on set, remember?'

Pushing his thick, tawny hair back from his face, Tom looked up apologetically and made as if to move. 'Sorry, Anna. My wretched head aches so much that I hadn't even considered today's filming. I've been too busy thinking about my narrow escape from Beady-Eyed Boris.'

As if on cue, heavy footsteps echoed in the corridor outside, followed by a resounding hammering on the door. Tom and Anna's eyes locked on each other in alarm.

'It can't be?' Anna gasped.

'I'm afraid it can,' Tom said miserably, flopping back against the pillows.

'What on earth shall we do? If he finds you here in my room — '

'On no account open the door,' came a muffled voice from beneath the bedclothes but all to no avail. Hefty shoulders lunged against the door, causing it to splinter and burst open. 'Where is the English pig?' a deep guttural voice bellowed.

Panic-stricken, seeing her door offer up no resistance to Boris's sturdy frame, Anna could only think of the story she'd told Alexander and Peter at Tom's farewell party. '*Little pig. Little pig. Let me come in*,' the big bad wolf had demanded, before blowing down the house of straw. Only this was no children's story. This was for real. For big bad wolf read Big Bad Boris. To add even further terror to the situation, Boris was also carrying an axe!

'Tom!' Anna screamed, running round to his side of the bed. 'Look out, he's got an axe!'

'What the . . . ?' Tom called, leaping immediately from the bed and positioning himself between Boris and Anna. 'Why, you bastard!'

'No! Is you bastard!' Boris yelled. 'Marysia is my special woman. Last night you . . . '

Indignant with rage and unmindful of the six-foot-four-frame, towering menacingly above him, Tom tossed Anna's coat to the floor before wielding the chair like a lion tamer, confronting a ferocious beast. 'Now, look here!' he commanded angrily. 'I never even touched Marysia. Never laid a finger on her in fact. Frederic invited me to the house for supper — that's all.'

At the mention of Frederic's name, a second pair of footsteps came hurrying along the corridor, swiftly followed by a third. Looking in the direction of the shattered doorway, Anna discerned Frederic and his sister, Marysia.

'Boris. My friend,' Frederic pleaded, in an attempt to placate the giant of a man. 'I'm sure you've made a mistake. Marysia said she was only showing Tom our grandfather's prize cow. Tom had been drinking, don't forget. He fell over in the hay.'

'Bah!' Boris snorted, his nostrils bulging like a raging bull. 'Then why he make with my woman?'

'I did not make with your woman!' Tom replied, putting down the chair. 'I have no need to. Anna will tell you, I already have one of my own.'

Shrugging aside Frederic's arm, Boris stepped further into the room and looked to where Anna was sheltering behind Tom. Pointing the axe directly towards her, he demanded in a gruff voice, 'She is your special woman — yes?'

With no reply forthcoming, Boris screwed up his eyes suspiciously and moved in Tom's direction. 'She *not* your woman, yet you spend night together? You use her like the English pig you are!'

Only too aware of the increasing tension in the room, Anna swallowed hard and slipping her arm through Tom's, found herself stammering in reply, 'Y-yes. I am his woman. His *very* special woman in fact, which is why we spent *all* of last night together.' Nodding towards the bed, where mercifully the crumpled sheets and blankets hid all evidence of the notorious bolster, Anna made sure she clung on grimly to Tom's arm. If she released her grasp now, she was convinced Boris would see just how much her hands were shaking.

With his own free hand, Boris dragged sausage-like fingers through his black wiry beard. Then, casting an admiring glance at Marysia, he fixed Tom with a look of pure disdain. 'She is not what I call *special* woman,' he said, his dark beady eyes sweeping over Anna from the top of her head to her bare legs and feet. 'She is skinny — like chicken!' So saying Boris swung his axe over his shoulder, grabbed Marysia firmly by the hand, nodded for her brother to follow and turning on his heels, strode off in silence down the corridor.

With Anna still clinging on to his arm, Tom slumped heavily onto the bed, taking her with him. 'Jesus! That was a close one. Thanks, Anna. I owe you.'

Numb with shock, Anna sat in silence, her whole body shaking and her heart thumping.

'Hey, it's all right,' Tom assured her, placing his arm about her shoulders and drawing her close. 'He's gone and every-thing's OK. The guy's obviously out of his head. Let's try and forget all about it, shall we?'

'I wish we could,' Anna gulped, from where her face was resting against Tom's bare chest. 'Unfortunately, something's telling me we won't be able to.'

Mildly curious, Tom turned his head to follow the direction of Anna's gaze. To his complete surprise, he saw Esme and Lavinia huddled, open-mouthed, in the doorway.

'Of course they're going to think the worst,' Anna called miserably to Tom, some ten minutes later, pulling on her sweater. 'Put yourself in their shoes. What would you think, if you were Esme and Lavinia and you saw us both half naked and huddled together on a bed? A bed, which I hate to remind you, we'd obviously slept in together.'

'They weren't wearing shoes, they were wearing slippers. Tartan ones with pom-poms on.'

'Don't be so obtuse,' Anna flashed, angrily. 'This is serious, Tom.'

'Sorry. I was just trying to get you to lighten up a little.'

'Lighten up!'

Tom pursed his lips and continued hunting for his socks. 'I hardly think wearing a bra and pants, plus a shirt down to your knees, constitutes half naked. Besides, I wasn't naked. I was wearing — '

'Please don't remind me. The look on Lavinia's face was bad enough. Whatever are we going to do?'

'Do? Nothing of course, other than explain to them all over breakfast exactly what happened last night, and also why we slept together.'

'I'd rather you didn't describe it quite like that. You make it sound as if we . . . well — you know?'

Retrieving his jeans and boots from the floor, Tom gave a wry smile. 'Look,' he grinned, dealing first with the zip of his jeans before struggling into his boots. 'You and I are both fully aware that we didn't — as you politely described it, '*well — you know*', so why get upset about it?'

'I would have thought that was perfectly obvious. Lovable, as they both are, Esme and Lavinia are the most notorious gossips. I'm prepared to bet that by the end of the day everybody in this hotel and practically the entire film crew, will have heard about your little escapade last night.'

'Precisely,' Tom said flatly.

'And what precisely is that supposed to mean?'

'It was *my* little escapade, Anna. Not yours.'

Delayed shock getting the better of her, Anna's tone became derisive. 'Oh yes, so it was. How silly of me to forget. What I can't forget, however, is that it was *my* bed you slept in, not to mention the fact it was you who put me to bed!'

Striding briskly across the room, Tom ignored all Anna's efforts to break free from his grasp as he curled his arms protectively about her shoulders. 'Anna, please believe me when I say I'm truly sorry. Like you, I wish last night had never happened. Regrettably, it did. And if Lucy had been at home, we wouldn't even be in this predicament.'

'What has last night got to do with Lucy?'

'In my opinion, everything,' came the dejected reply. 'If Lucy had been in when I telephoned . . . '

Anna's face softened as she looked up into Tom's deeply troubled eyes. 'She knew you were going to ring. You told me that, when you asked me to repair your shirt.'

'I know, only it would appear something better came up. According to Aunt Bea, who'd apparently been looking after Alexander since six o'clock, Lucy went to the theatre before going on to dinner with friends. Or was it the other way round?'

'And to cheer yourself up, you went for a drink with Frederic?'

'Not initially. I can only assume that when he saw me coming out of the phone booth, looking pretty miserable, he took pity on me. Then, before I knew what was happening he'd invited me back for supper and far more wine and brandy than was good for me. The rest you know.'

'Yes. I suppose I do,' Anna said kindly, her anger dissipating.

Walking towards the dining-room together, Tom gave Anna's hand a brief, reassuring squeeze. 'Thanks for being so understanding. I certainly appreciate it.'

'Let's hope Esme and Lavinia are equally understanding,' she whispered in hushed tones. 'Because, the ever perky Julian and *les girls* are heading in our direction at this very moment.'

Quickly releasing Anna's hand, Tom heard Julian call, 'Sorry, folks. It looks as if we're out of luck. There's no breakfast this morning. By all accounts our delightful Marysia — she of the ample bosom and come to bed eyes — has been whisked away by a madman wielding an axe. There's a story if you like. I wonder what Ashley would make of that? I can see the posters now. *Mad Max and his axe.* What do you think of that, Tom?'

'Not a lot,' came the sardonic reply. 'I'd say Big Bad Boris was far more appropriate.'

When Julian shook his head in bewilderment, as if to say, 'Why Boris?' Tom muttered wearily, 'Don't worry about it now, Julian. I'll tell you later. For the moment can I please suggest that we get this film in the can? The sooner it's finished, the sooner we'll all be able to hop on that plane back to England.'

Not intending for anyone to take him literally, it was Lavinia who later ended up hopping on to the group's homeward-bound plane. Within an hour of leaving the hotel for the day's shooting, she slipped on an icy pavement and ended up in hospital with a broken arm and twisted ankle.

'What the f — !' Ashley proclaimed, when Julian delivered the disastrous news. 'I don't believe what's been happening here. This production's not only jinxed, it's in danger of turning into a Whitehall farce. Now what are we supposed to do? With the final scenes taking place in the ballroom, would someone care to enlighten me? How the devil can the dowager duchess greet her long lost grandson and heir, with her ankle strapped up in bandages and her arm in a bloody great plaster cast and sling?'

There was a deathly silence as everyone shook their heads in despair. At length, Anna ventured meekly. 'Is there any chance we could go back to where we were filming yesterday?'

'Go back?' Julian scowled, his voice breaking through the murmur of disgruntled voices. 'Why the hell should we want to go back?'

'Because the costumes and scenery still haven't been packed away. Therefore, I was — um — wondering . . . if we kept just part of the ballroom scene, perhaps we could have a messenger delivering a letter to the dowager duchess instead? She could then arrange to meet her nephew in a carriage, somewhere in the forest.'

All eyes fixed on Ashley Munroe as he considered Anna's suggestion. 'Hmm, I suppose we could try. That way she wouldn't have to be seen walking. As you say, everything's still in place from yesterday but what about the problem of the plaster cast?'

'I don't think it's a problem.'

'You don't? Well, not wishing to appear facetious, Anna, particularly as you're the only one to come forward with a possible solution, but did they did have plaster casts in the early nineteenth century?'

Ignoring the last part of Julian's statement, Anna declared, 'I could make Lavinia a muff.'

'A muff?' Ashley's eyes widened in curiosity, leaving Julian to break in with an excited cry, 'Of course! A muff would be the perfect solution. You'd never see the plaster cast then. We had some wonderful muffs in the costume department at the Alexandra. Anna, do you remember that gorgeous confection of fur and satin brocade we made for Madame Alicia? So wonderfully exotic and . . . '

'Er — that wasn't quite what I had in mind, Julian, particularly at this late stage of filming. It could also be extremely difficult to get hold of both fur and brocade.'

'Nonsense!' Julian cried, undaunted. 'All we have to do is get Tom to ask that black market friend of his. Didn't someone say he can get hold of anything? Tom . . . ?'

Tom shuffled uneasily in the snow. After the horrors of the previous night and early this morning, the last thing he wanted was further confrontation with Frederic, let alone Boris.

In a daze, and with Julian having brushed aside all his excuses, Tom found himself installed, somewhat reluctantly, in the ancient Tatra that was to take him back to the village. 'I'll see what I can do,' he called as an afterthought, unwinding the front passenger window. 'Although, it might be an idea if Anna came with me. She's the one who knows what's required. If Frederic can oblige in any way, wouldn't it be better to let Anna choose? I wouldn't have a clue.'

Waiting for Ashley's chauffeur Jeremy, to help Anna into the car, Tom turned back to face her. 'That was quite an intelligent suggestion you made about the muff.'

'As it's crucial that I find some fabric suited to the period, I could also say the same about yours,' she offered in reply.

'Ah, well . . . I confess I had an ulterior motive,' Tom said, without thinking, watching Jeremy engage first gear and pull away from the sea of expectant faces. 'You see, we've got to go back to the hotel first and I'll also need the key to your room. I left my cloak in your bedroom last night. Of course, I'd fully intended to collect it after breakfast, but as you know we didn't have any, owing to the fact that Boris stormed in on us both and . . . '

Anna meanwhile, wasn't listening. She was far too preoccupied studying the look of pure shock and surprise, registering on the chauffeur's face in his rear-view mirror.

'Thanks very much, Tom,' she bristled, once they'd been dropped off at the hotel. 'Even if Lavinia and Esme haven't yet managed to tell all and sundry, you can bet your life Jeremy will certainly oblige. Even now I can almost hear the distant jungle drums, banging out the news.'

'I wouldn't have thought it's the right part of the world for jungle drums,' Tom said, in an effort to cheer her. 'It's far too cold.'

Stamping snow from her boots, Anna sniffed the wintry air filled with the pungent smell of woodsmoke. 'Perhaps you're right. Shall I change that to smoke signals instead?'

27

In the process of packing to go home, Anna heard a gentle tapping on her door. Assuming it to be Julian with confirmation of the coach taking them to the airport, she called for him to come in. It was Esme, not Julian who entered the room, holding out the two borrowed night-dresses.

'I thought I'd return these, Anna. It looks as if I've caught you at just the right moment, before you snap the lid shut.'

'That's very kind of you, Esme, but there was really no need. I've already told Lavinia that I didn't want them back. With Bjorn insisting that our house is heated to Swedish standards throughout the winter, and him to snuggle up to at night, I shan't be needing them any more.'

'Lucky you, Anna. My place is like an ice box. I'm very envious on both counts: a warm house and snug in the arms of the one you love. As for myself those days are long since past. In Lavinia's case I doubt they ever existed at all.'

Anna nodded appreciatively. Yes, it was a truly wonderful feeling knowing, that within a few short hours, she would be heading home to Bjorn and the prospect of a quiet Christmas together. 'I'm really sure about the nightdresses, Esme. Bjorn's already described them as looking like Swedish army tents. If I take them back with me, they'll only go to the local charity shop.'

'Will they? Then if you don't mind I'll certainly accept, on behalf of both myself and Lavinia.' Clutching both nightdresses to her tiny frame, Esme grinned cheekily. 'You're quite right about the tent effect. Lavinia didn't have quite as much room to move around in as myself. At least she wasn't bursting at the seams as she does usually.'

Reminded of the problems she'd experienced with some of Lavinia's costumes, Anna remarked, 'The assistant in our village shop did describe them as one size fits all, which sums them up admirably, I suppose.'

Turning to go back to her own room, Esme heard footsteps approaching from the far end of the corridor. 'That will be Julian,' Anna explained, 'he said, he'd let me know the minute the coach was booked. I can't tell you how relieved I was when he confirmed the return flights.'

'Me, too, my dear,' Esme acknowledged, 'particularly after those problems we encountered as a result of Lavinia's injuries. Wasn't it kind of Julian to let her keep the muff?'

Relieved that her suggestion had at least guaranteed the long-awaited end to filming, Anna looked up, fully expecting to see Julian.

'Hello, girls,' came a familiar voice, 'I'm glad I've managed to catch you both.'

Anna frowned. 'Tom, where have you been? Ashley's been looking for you everywhere.'

'Doing some special last-minute shopping and having a final, farewell drink with Frederic.'

Reminded of the last time Tom and Frederic had been drinking together, Anna threw him a withering look.

'It's OK,' Tom assured. 'Don't look so alarmed. I'm as sober as a judge *and* I've brought you girls something nice.' Peering into the carrier bag he was holding, Tom produced two hand-rolled, pure silk scarves. 'Here you are,' he said, extending both in Esme's direction. 'I'll let you have first pick.'

Touched by Tom's generosity, Esme studied the intricate, paisley patterns. 'How very kind, Tom. But I think Anna should have first pick. Especially as she's been so generous as to give me this wonderful nightdress.'

'Oh, the other scarf isn't for Anna: it's for Lavinia. I've got Anna something else. Something *really* special.'

'Ooh!' Esme, enquired, curious. 'And am I

allowed to ask what it is?'

Tom fixed her with a cheeky smile and shook his head. ''Fraid not, Esme, but you can have a quick peep if you like.'

Even more curious than before, Esme stepped forward and peered inquisitively into the depths of the carrier bag. Chuckling like a schoolgirl sneaking off to the bike sheds for a crafty cigarette, she held both scarves and nightdresses against her chest and hurried to the door. 'You are a naughty boy, Tom. Whatever will Bjorn say? I can't wait to tell Lavinia.'

Emitting a long drawn-out sigh of exasperation, Anna slumped wearily against her suitcase. 'Thanks, Tom. That's all I need. As if it wasn't bad enough before.'

'You worry too much,' Tom scolded. 'You know perfectly well I've already explained to Esme and the others about that little incident with Boris. I'm convinced they've all forgotten about it by now.'

Anna motioned to the carrier bag. 'So why that?'

'You haven't even seen what it is yet.'

'I'm not sure that I want to.'

Tom looked mildly hurt. 'Why not? It's only a peace offering, to make up for all the trouble I caused. Like the scarves for Lavinia and Esme, it's merely a simple souvenir of the time we all spent together.'

'You honestly think we need souvenirs of our time here?'

'Come to think of it, perhaps not,' Tom replied, strangely pensive, laying the bag on the bed before heading for the door. 'Oh, well. At least I tried. If you don't want them, you can always give them away.'

'Them?' Anna puzzled, when Tom closed the door behind him. What on earth were *them*? With curiosity eventually getting the better of her, Anna reached warily into the depths of the bag, her hand resting immediately on smooth and sensuous satin. It certainly wasn't a scarf, there was far too much fabric for that. And it also wasn't underwear. Highly relieved that Tom hadn't caused her even further embarrassment by buying her underwear, Anna drew luxurious folds of jet-black satin on to her lap. There she discovered the *them* Tom had been referring to. A pair of exquisitely cut, and obviously very expensive, black satin pyjamas. 'Oh, my goodness!' she gasped, taken aback, 'And how very appropriate. Black satin from the black market!'

Moments later, when the third visitor knocked on Anna's door, she was relieved to discover that at long last it was Julian.

'Just to let you know the coach is booked

for . . . I say! Is that black satin? Now, where did you get — ?'

Feeling herself colour, Anna made a hurried attempt at putting the pyjamas back into the carrier bag. 'It's only a pair of pyjamas,' she said, desperately trying to sound nonchalant. 'It was Tom's idea of a peace offering for — um — the other night?'

'I see. Well, as it's only Tom we're talking about and he's a happily married man, I'd say that was just about acceptable in the circumstances. If it was anybody else, however, I'd have my doubts. What do you think Bjorn will say when you pull those out of your suitcase?'

'Oh Lord! I hadn't even thought that far ahead. Tom's only just left.'

Julian nodded. 'Yes, I know. He passed me on the stairs. Personally, I thought he was looking pretty downcast.'

'Then it's probably my fault. I told him off for buying the pyjamas.'

Giving Anna a fatherly pat on the shoulder, Julian announced. 'Or else simply the strain of endless weeks away from his family?'

'I hope you're right. Maybe I was over-reacting. What do you think, Julian?'

'I think you should simply forget about the unfortunate goings-on of the other night and accept Tom's gift gracefully. I have to say

— from what little I saw of those pyjamas, before you whisked them away — they did look rather lovely.'

'They are,' Anna acknowledged.

★   ★   ★

Several hours later, with a small crowd gathered together in the hotel lobby, Ashley clapped his hands loudly. 'OK, folks. Let's have a quick roll call before we bid farewell to this delightful place and head for the coach. Is everybody here? Or would it be better to say, who isn't?'

From the back of the group, Jeremy mentioned the names of a few stragglers who were at that very moment ambling along the corridor, completely unconcerned about the time.

'And don't forget Tom,' Lavinia's voice broke in. 'He's not here yet.'

'He was ten minutes ago,' Esme replied, lovingly fingering her new silk scarf. 'I wonder where he can be?'

'Probably hiding under Anna's bed,' Jeremy quipped. 'Perhaps you'd better go and look for him, Anna?'

'Actually, he's gone to make a phone call,' she said, her face flushing scarlet. 'He told me he wouldn't be long.'

When Jeremy and some of the crew began nudging and winking Monty Python style, Anna became even more embarrassed.

'Just ignore them, my dear,' came a voice by her side. 'They're only ignorant pigs, with one-track minds.'

'Ignore them, Esme? How I wish I could. Somehow, I don't think it's going to be that easy. Not only have we got that nightmare journey to the airport to contend with but also the long flight home.'

Nodding astutely, Esme looked behind her. 'In which case as soon as Tom arrives, I'll have a discreet word with him, explain what's happened and also suggest that as far as possible he doesn't sit near you on the plane — or speak to you, unless it's absolutely necessary. How does that sound? Would it make you feel any better?'

'Very much so. And Esme . . . '

'Yes, dear?'

'If you do have a chance to speak to Tom, without Jeremy eaves-dropping in on the conversation, can you please thank him on my behalf for the pyjamas? Tell him that I think they're really beautiful and that I didn't mean to appear so ungrateful.'

'Of course, Anna. I understand. I'm sure Tom will too. These past few weeks have taken such an enormous toll on us all.'

★ ★ ★

Waiting in the crowded baggage reclaim at Heathrow, Anna looked up to find Tom coming towards her. Filled with renewed panic, she scanned the crowds for Jeremy. Comforted by the fact that Jeremy was too busy fumbling in his bags of duty free to notice, she then realized that although Tom was heading in her direction, it wasn't with the intention of speaking to her.

'Got it!' he called, heaving a bulging suitcase from the conveyor belt. 'One more to go and then I'm on my way.' Conscious of the sparrowlike Esme, attempting to reach one of her own suitcases, Tom nudged her gently to one side. 'Here, let me. In fact while I'm here, I might just as well help all of you ladies. Who's waiting for what?'

'A nice young man like you for a start,' Esme replied, her eyes twinkling brightly.

'Sorry, Esme. I'm already spoken for. Lucy will no doubt have me under lock and key the minute I set foot in the door.'

'You mean she's not coming to meet you?'

Tom shrugged his shoulders. 'I doubt it. Let's just say the last time Lucy and I spoke on the phone, we had words in more ways than one. All my fault, I suppose. I was still angry with her about going out on the night

360

I'd arranged to phone home.'

'Oh dear. How sad,' Esme remarked. 'Well, whatever you do, you must make it up to each other as soon as you can. I'm sure you're both familiar with the saying 'never let the sun go down on your wrath.' It was an old favourite of my mother's and well worth bearing in mind.'

'I will. Thanks, Esme,' Tom said, stretching forward to retrieve Lavinia's two large travel bags. 'So — what's left? Only yours, I believe, Anna?'

Motioning to her own suitcase, now trundling along the conveyor belt, Anna explained, 'It's just the one. This time I'm not carrying sausages, bacon, and tea bags.'

'Mmm, just the one,' Tom repeated, as an aside. 'That's what I should have said, the night I went drinking with Frederic.'

'Tom. Look . . . I'm truly sorry about — '

'There's no need, Anna. Esme's already explained. Let's call a truce, shall we?'

Nodding her head in reply, Anna felt Tom's fingers brush gently against hers as he handed over her suitcase. 'Truce,' she whispered, the word barely audible.

'Daddy!' A child's voice cried out excitedly, seeing Tom emerge through Arrivals. 'Alexander? What are you doing here, and where's — ?'

'Mummy's over there,' Alexander said, wriggling free from Tom's arms. 'She said you'd be surprised to see us. Are you?'

'Yes. Yes I am,' Tom gulped, spying Lucy hovering in the back-ground.

For a brief moment, as Tom pushed his luggage trolley through the crowds with Alexander chattering merrily away by his side, it was as if he and Lucy were the only couple at the airport. 'Lucy, darling,' he said huskily, his voice catching in his throat.

'Tom!' she called, rushing into his arms, her eyes filling with tears. 'I'm so glad you're home and I'm so sorry I wasn't in when you — '

'Shh, not now,' he murmured, holding her close. 'Let's just get home, shall we? A certain young man's been telling me it will soon be Christmas. I can't tell you how much I've been looking forward to it.'

At the mention of Christmas, Alexander studied his father's bulging suitcases and assorted bags. 'Did Father Christmas give you a present for me when you were away? I've been very good, haven't I, Mummy?'

Released from Tom's embrace, Lucy dabbed at her eyes. 'Yes, Alexander. You've been very good. Exceptionally good in fact.'

'Then I'm pleased to hear it,' Tom said,

'and what about Mummy? Has she been good too?'

Cocking his head to one side, Alexander thought long and hard for a moment. 'Oh, yes,' he said, matter of factly. 'She's been 'ceptionally good too.'

'Apart from the night I wasn't in — when Daddy rang,' Lucy confessed, linking her arm in Tom's.

Walking across the concourse to the main exit, Tom said as an aside, 'By the way, not that it really matters now, who did you go out with that night? You never said.'

'You never gave me the chance. If you really want to know, it was just a few of the girls I used to work with.'

Mention of 'the girls' reminded Tom he'd been so surprised and delighted to see both his wife and son, that he'd quite forgotten to say goodbye to his own girls and the rest of the crew. 'Hang on to this for a moment,' he called, passing the trolley in Lucy's direction. 'I'd better just go and say goodbye and wish them all a Happy Christmas.'

Shaking Julian and Ashley by the hand, Tom proceeded to kiss Esme and Lavinia on both cheeks, before hugging them warmly and searching the noisy bustling throng for Anna. 'She's over there,' Esme, whispered, reading his mind.

Following Esme's gaze, Tom caught sight of Anna, locked in Bjorn's embrace.

Blinking back tears of joy, Anna acknowledged Tom's mouthed goodbye, waved and murmured something to her husband. For a brief moment, Bjorn appeared to hesitate before acknowledging Tom's gesture of farewell with a knowing smile. 'Have a good Christmas,' he called out.

'You too,' Tom replied, hurrying away to rejoin Lucy and the very impatient Alexander. 'I'm sure we shall,' Bjorn said, once more enfolding Anna in his arms. 'This Christmas is going to be perfect. Simply perfect.'

28

Pleased to see Alexander deeply engrossed with his toy Vignale-styled Tatra 613, Lucy reached for Tom's hand. 'Come along,' she urged, taking him by the arm. 'I've got something to show you.'

Intrigued, Tom followed Lucy upstairs to their bedroom. 'There!' she announced triumphantly, opening the bedroom door. 'What do you think of that?'

'Ve-ry nice,' he enthused, spying the newly decorated walls. 'I like the colour.'

Lucy clasped her hands about his neck. 'What about the bed? Do you like that too?'

Peering over her shoulder, Tom spied the recently purchased sheets and pillowcases. He smiled appreciatively. 'Mmm. New bed linen?'

'Hardly linen,' Lucy corrected, slowly and deliberately unbuttoning his shirt. 'That my darling, is satin. Exceedingly sexy, black satin.'

Tom eased himself free from his shirt. 'How do you know it's sexy? Have you already tried it out?'

'Definitely not!' Lucy cried in mock

indignation, when Tom nuzzled against her throat and began running his fingers down her body to encircle her breasts. 'I've been saving those sheets expressly for your return. They're a sort of welcome home present. I saw them in a magazine and thought you might like to try them.'

'I think I might like that, very much,' Tom replied, deftly unzipping Lucy's dress and letting it fall the floor.

Convinced Tom was going to finish undressing her, sweep her into his arms and carry her to the bed, Lucy registered complete bewilderment when he didn't. At Heathrow, Tom had made it quite clear that he was no longer angry with her. Why then, had he paused with his fingers hooked so tantalizingly in her bra straps?

Panic coursed through Lucy's veins. Tom's farewell party! That never-to-be-forgotten afternoon when she'd announced to the world, or at least a houseful of guests, that she'd deliberately got herself pregnant. 'Tom . . . what's wrong. Is it because of Alexander?'

Tom nodded and refastened Lucy's bra. 'Great minds think alike, eh? Here we both are, desperate to hop into that oh-so-inviting bed, while at any moment our son and heir could come bursting through that door.'

Hardly able to believe her ears, Lucy fixed

Tom with a coquettish smile and reached for the zip on his trousers. 'Yes,' she lied, 'that's exactly what I was thinking. Then I remembered the present you brought him. There's no need to worry about Alexander. With that new car of his he'll play happily for ages. You know, there were times when you were away, I hardly knew he was around. He'd play for hours on his own, either with his toys or else reading a book. He's been really keen on books since Anna was here and read the boys that story. Do you remember?'

Only too late, Lucy realized she'd mentioned the very day that she'd been trying so hard to avoid. Chewing nervously at her lip, she waited for Tom's reaction.

'How could I forget?' Tom said, recalling the unpleasant scene that had brought their party to such an abrupt halt.

Much to Lucy's surprise, Tom quickly took off his socks and shook himself free from his trousers. 'Er — Lucy . . . as you've mentioned Anna, I think there's something you should know?'

'As long as you're not going to tell me you slept with her,' Lucy teased.

'Well . . . ' Tom began after a pregnant pause.

With Lucy's face initially registering abject horror and disbelief, Tom explained the whole embarrassing scenario: beginning first with Marysia, Frederic and the cow, and ending with Anna, Boris and the black satin pyjamas.

'Poor Anna and poor you,' Lucy said, pulling back the covers on the bed. 'The trouble with you, Tom Hudson, is that just like me, women find you utterly irresistible.'

'Anna obviously didn't.'

'Then more fool her,' Lucy said, dropping her bra and panties to the floor. She gasped sliding in between the slippery coldness of the sheets. 'Ooh! These sheets strike cold when you first get into them. I thought they'd be warm, somehow.'

'They soon will be — that's if you're really sure about Alexander leaving us in peace for a little while.'

'Little while? I shall expect more than a little while, Tom Hudson! You've been away for months, don't forget.'

'As if I could,' Tom murmured huskily, his mouth closing on hers.

★ ★ ★

Opening the lid of her suitcase, Anna began unpacking assorted piles of practical and unfeminine clothes. 'That's the last I ever want to see of these,' she grimaced. 'I'm convinced they smell musty. Once they've been washed and ironed, they're all going to the charity shop.'

'Was it really that bad?' Bjorn questioned, from where he was sitting on the bed, concerned to see her looking so unusually thin and drawn.

'Oh, I don't know. It depends what you mean by really bad. Since we've been married I've got used to my creature comforts: plenty of hot water, decent food and comfortable surroundings. Whereas, had I still been working at the Alexandra, I probably would have coped with conditions like that for months on end, instead of giving up like a wimp after only a few weeks.'

'Did you give up? From what Julian said at the airport, he thought you'd coped admirably in the circumstances.'

Still kneeling on the floor, Anna rested her hands upon her lap and gave a wistful smile. 'Let's just say towards the end, I almost gave up. It was only the prospect of coming home to you that kept me going.'

'You missed me then?'

'Missed you?' Anna cried. 'Oh, Bjorn! I don't think you'll ever know how much.'

'That's a relief. Because, I don't mind admitting that when I discovered Tom Hudson was out there too, I thought I might have lost you.'

'Why should you lose me?'

'On account of that magazine article we read ages ago. What was it they said about Tom? Heart throb of the future?'

'Oh that. Rest assured, there's only one heart throb in my life and he's sitting right here.'

Looking up from the pile of musty clothing, Anna continued with a grin, 'And, in case you need reminding, just think back to how glamorous Lucy was looking at the airport. Unlike myself, who must have looked like Nanouk of the North — or something that had just escaped — when I trudged wearily through Arrivals.'

'Hmm. Julian did mention you'd been staying in what had once been an institution,' Bjorn reflected. 'It did sound pretty grim from your description.'

'It was,' came the reply, when Anna absentmindedly, removed the satin pyjamas from her suitcase.

Bjorn raised his eyebrows, spying black satin amongst the piles of thick shirts, thermal underwear and sweaters. 'They're not institution clothes! Where did they come from?'

Shifting uncomfortably on her knees, Anna realized this was the moment she'd been dreading. She'd known all along she'd have to tell Bjorn about the incident at the hotel. The problem was when? Telling him in the car on the way home from the airport hadn't seemed appropriate. Even now, it didn't feel quite the right moment. What she'd been hoping for was to tell Bjorn once she'd had a bath, washed away the unfortunate experience from her mind and eventually slipped into something a great deal more feminine.

'Bjorn . . . ' she faltered, her fingers lingering nervously on the black satin jacket with its self-covered buttons, 'there's something I have to tell you. Something you need to know. The pyjamas . . . they were — '

'A present from Tom,' Bjorn finished for her.

'H-how did you know?'

'Tom rang me.'

'He rang you? How? I mean . . . when did he ring you?'

'This morning, presumably before you left for the airport. He was on the phone for ages.'

Anna took a deep breath, hardly daring to contemplate the all important question. 'And — er — what did he say?'

Extending both hands in Anna's direction, Bjorn pulled her gently to her feet. 'Well, first he told me about someone called Frederic — who I understand dealt in black market

371

goods — and then he mentioned a certain buxom waitress called Marie.'

'Marysia,' Anna corrected.

Bjorn nodded in acknowledgement, his brow furrowed as if trying to remember what else Tom had told him. 'If my memory serves me correctly, there was also some rather lethal contraband brandy, a prize cow in a barn, a giant of a man called Boris, with a bloody great axe — Tom's words, not mine. And last but not least, there was you.'

When Anna made as if to speak, Bjorn placed a finger across her lips. 'My poor, poor darling. What a truly horrendous tale. Although, to be perfectly honest, if it hadn't been you in that bed with Tom, I think I'd find the whole thing highly amusing and entertaining.'

'Except that it wasn't,' Anna said miserably, pushing Bjorn's hand away from her lips. 'As you've so kindly reminded me, it was your wife in that bed with Tom Hudson. To think I actually slept with him!'

Bjorn shook his head. 'My turn to correct you, I think. You *didn't* sleep with Tom Hudson, Anna. You merely shared a bed with him. A bed that was divided down the middle with an enormous bolster.'

'He actually told you about the bolster?'

'Not only the bolster, but also the fact that

he'd had far too much to drink and you — stubborn thing that you are — wearing some monstrosity of a nightdress and your coat, insisted on reading in a chair until you fell asleep. Whereupon, Tom had to put you to bed.'

Anna blushed, looking in the direction of her one remaining nightdress. 'Monstrosity of a nightdress? Is that really how he described it?'

'Afraid so. And to add insult to injury, I gather in his inebriated state, he also said you were perfectly safe because he didn't fancy you at all.'

'Hmph! And to think the next morning, I even tried to protect him from the barking mad Boris, who was threatening to kill him!'

Drawing Anna on to his lap, Bjorn stoked her hair. 'Don't look quite so affronted. From my own point of view, I'm jolly glad he didn't fancy you, or else I wouldn't be sitting here feeling quite so kindly disposed towards him. I reckon telephoning me as he did, also took considerable courage on Tom's part.'

'I suppose so,' Anna conceded. 'It could also explain why he went missing before we left for the airport.'

'Exactly. And now that that's been sorted and is out of the way, will you please stop looking so worried.'

'I wasn't aware that I was.'

'Believe me, you've had a haunted look on your face ever since I met you at Heathrow. Perhaps I should have told you about Tom's phone call then? Only you looked so exhausted, I thought the best thing to do was get you home. That was me being selfish, I'm afraid. I couldn't wait to have you all to myself.'

'And you have,' Anna said, curling herself in Bjorn's lap. 'So what do you want to do now?'

'I would have thought that was perfectly obvious, but knowing you as I do, I expect you'd prefer a long, relaxing bath, first.'

Savouring the lopsided smile that she loved so much, Anna traced her fingers along Bjorn's rugged jawline. 'Oh, I don't know, I don't want you dropping off to sleep while I'm in the bath, do I? I was thinking perhaps a quick shower would be better, and I could slip into something a little more comfortable than what I'm wearing at the moment.'

'Like clean sheets for instance?'

Sliding from his lap, Anna looked at the bed with its delicate floral duvet, valance and matching pillowcases. 'Hmm. Although, that's not quite what I had in mind when I said something comfortable. Nevertheless, I do think slipping into clean sheets would be pure, unadulterated bliss.'

Ten minutes later, towelling herself dry, Anna heard Bjorn call out, 'I've put most of the clothes in the laundry basket as you suggested, but wasn't sure what to do with these.'

Padding barefoot into the bedroom, Anna discovered Bjorn, holding up the black satin pyjamas.

'I didn't know if you wanted them left out — to wear later on — or if you wanted me to put them in your lingerie drawer.'

'Neither,' she said, taking the pyjamas from his grasp. 'Even though I never tried them on, I can tell, simply by looking at them, the jacket sleeves and trousers are way too long. Perhaps Tom should have taken them home for Lucy instead.'

Bjorn gave a curious smile, watching Anna fold the pyjamas and push them hurriedly to the back of her wardrobe. 'Perhaps, but it wouldn't surprise me if Lucy was just like you. I don't suppose she wears anything in bed either.'

'I do . . . sometimes,' Anna protested, reminding him of her honeymoon lingerie.

'And there's also that monstrosity of a nightdress?' Bjorn teased.

'I've already told you: I won't be wearing anything like that ever again.'

'Lucky me, cos I'd say that sounds extremely promising.'

'Does it?' Anna replied in mock surprise, letting her bath towel slip to the floor.

★   ★   ★

For the umpteenth time on Christmas Eve, Alexander made sure his stocking was in exactly the right place for Father Christmas. Tired, yet still very excited, he snuggled down beneath his bedclothes.

'Night night, Daddy,' he called to Tom.

'Good night, Alexander. Sleep tight. I hope Father Christmas brings you everything you wanted.'

'I hope so too, Daddy. Do you really think he will?'

'All quiet in the land of nod?' Lucy enquired, moments later.

'Sort of,' Tom replied with a lazy smile.

'What's so funny?'

'Something Alexander said, once I'd finished reading him his bedtime story.'

'Really, and what was that?'

'Something else he wanted for Christmas.'

Lucy looked up, aghast. 'Surely not! We've been through his list umpteen times already. When Beattie and I took him to Hamley's and Selfridges, to see Father Christmas, we made sure we'd checked everything. Oh Lord! I hope he's not going to be too disappointed if I've forgotten anything. If I have, he'll only go and tell your Aunt Bea, when we see her on Boxing Day and I'm bound to get the blame.'

'Hold on a minute,' Tom said kindly, offering her a glass of wine. 'Don't start getting in a panic over Aunt Bea, especially as the two of you seem to be the best of friends these days. At least something good came out of me being away.'

Lucy sipped thoughtfully at her wine. 'Go on then, you'd better tell me. What is it Alexander wants — that I appear to have forgotten?'

'Nothing.'

'But you said . . . '

'I know. However, it's not something you can buy; it's something that we have to do.'

Kicking off her shoes and curling up on the sofa, Lucy groaned wearily. 'Then you'll have to do it yourself, Tom Hudson. Having spent all afternoon cooking and preparing veg-etables for tomorrow's Christmas lunch, I'm absolutely exhausted.'

'Really? That's a shame. Because it definitely needs the two of us. Alexander's put in a request for a baby brother or sister and I thought . . . particularly as you happened to remark only the other day, how lonely he is sometimes.'

Lucy's eyes widened in surprise as she regarded Tom over the rim of her glass. 'Are you suggesting what I think you're suggesting?'

'Well . . . I did sort of explain to Alexander that Father Christmas might not be able to make it this Christmas.'

Passing Tom her glass, Lucy's eyes sparkled with expectation and her lips parted seductively. 'Did you indeed? So . . . where do you suggest we start practising? Upstairs in the bedroom or down here in front of this wonderful fire?'

Placing both glasses on the coffee table, Tom kicked off his own shoes. 'Hmm. Decisions, decisions. Let's see, perhaps in front of the fire might be the perfect place to begin?'

★   ★   ★

Hurrying in from the cold with a huge basket of logs, Bjorn rubbed his hands with satisfaction. 'Right, that's it for the evening. The studio's all locked up, supper is ready, the wine nicely chilled and we've enough logs in that basket to keep us going for hours. Tell me, did you eventually decide what it's to be?'

Anna blinked and looked up from where she was preparing a last minute list of people to ring on Christmas Day. 'Sorry darling. You've lost me, I'm afraid. What do you mean?'

'The Swedish way, or the English way,' he said, kissing the tip of her nose. 'It's your decision.'

Standing up to peer at the clock, hidden by numerous Christmas cards, Anna laid down her pen. 'I wasn't aware that we'd categorized it like that before. It's only half past seven.'

'Anna Carlson!' Bjorn said, tapping her playfully on the bottom. Did you know that since you returned from Poland you have had a one-track mind? For your information, I was referring to our Christmas presents. I merely wanted to know if you wanted to open them on Christmas Eve — as we do in Sweden — or else wait for tomorrow morning and open them English style, by the Christmas tree? Anyway, while you're making up your mind, I'll just pop upstairs to the spare room and get the box of presents I brought back with me from Sweden.'

When mention of Poland and presents, sent myriad thoughts swirling like snowflakes in Anna's head, she gave an involuntary shudder. The last present she'd received had been that infamous pair of black satin pyjamas. Why, oh why, couldn't Tom have given her a paisley silk scarf, instead as he had to Esme and Lavinia? At least that was something she could have worn without feeling guilty. Not that she'd ever wear those pyjamas, now banished to the back of the wardrobe. As for feeling guilty, Anna reminded herself, conscious of Bjorn coming back into the room, there was absolutely no reason to feel guilty. She'd done nothing wrong, had she?

Seeing Anna shake her head, and misinterpreting her gesture as meaning she'd rather wait until tomorrow to open their presents, Bjorn placed his parents' gifts by the tree. 'The English way it is,' he smiled, reaching out for her hand.

Moments later, guiding her to beneath a sprig of mistletoe, Bjorn held Anna close and whispered in her ear. 'Happy Christmas, darling. I hope Father Christmas brings you everything you wanted.'

'I didn't want anything, other than to spend Christmas alone with you,' Anna replied. 'Wasn't that what you wanted too?'

'Most definitely,' Bjorn said, cupping her face in his hands. 'I merely wanted to make doubly sure that you didn't mind it being just the two of us.'

'Just the two of us,' Anna repeated, keeping

her innermost thoughts to herself. Yes, Bjorn was quite correct, that was what she'd wanted this Christmas. But this time next year it wasn't presents she expected Bjorn to collect from the spare room. In fact if all her prayers were answered they'd no longer have a spare room: they'd have a nursery.

We do hope that you have enjoyed reading this large print book.

Did you know that all of our titles are available for purchase?

We publish a wide range of high quality large print books including:
Romances, Mysteries, Classics
General Fiction
Non Fiction and Westerns

Special interest titles available in large print are:
The Little Oxford Dictionary
Music Book
Song Book
Hymn Book
Service Book

Also available from us courtesy of Oxford University Press:
Young Readers' Dictionary
(large print edition)
Young Readers' Thesaurus
(large print edition)

For further information or a free brochure, please contact us at:
Ulverscroft Large Print Books Ltd.,
The Green, Bradgate Road, Anstey,
Leicester, LE7 7FU, England.
Tel: (00 44) **0116 236 4325**
Fax: (00 44) **0116 234 0205**

Other titles published by
The House of Ulverscroft:

SUNFLOWER MORNING

Danielle Shaw

Catherine Wickham arrives at Whycham Hall, delighted to help her aunt who is housekeeper there. However, she discovers that the new owner, property developer Roderick Marchant, intends to alter the Whycham Estate beyond all recognition. Then when she learns that she is a descendant of the original owners of Whycham Hall, Catherine resolves to halt Rod's plans. But she must face Rod's determined girlfriend Francesca . . .
Forced to spend time in Rod's company, Catherine has two choices: leave Whycham le Cley forever, or hide her love for Rod as she fights to save her beloved village from property developers.

CINNABAR SUMMER

Danielle Shaw

Rosemary Fielding is delighted when impresario Oliver Duncan suggests turning her novel into a mini-series. However, less delightful is the prospect of meeting Oliver's leading man, the actor Stephen Walker. His rudeness and arrogance cause Rosemary to retaliate, so in an effort to settle their differences, author and actor spend a weekend together in the Norfolk countryside. Rosemary likens their blossoming relationship to the scarlet and black cinnabar moths that abound. But the colours of the cinnabar also herald danger. Increasingly concerned by a predator close to home, are the couple destined to share only one summer together?